BOOK OF BRAVERY

A NOVEL 2,000 PLUS YEARS IN THE MAKING

JAMES BURKE

GOOD EMPIRE

J.R.R. Tolkien

'Not all those who wander are lost'

This novel is dedicated to my wife, Teresa, our son Cameron and my parents, Terry and Kate.

CHAPTER I

Your Narrator

Beyond my comprehension, I have been dedicated by others to tell this tale. My grammar is woefully lacking, so forgive me in advance. For example, I sometimes have a habit of jumping from past to present tense; a product of the fact that I do not value time so much, but I know you mortals are obsessed by it, so I will do my best to oblige as such.

By way of introduction, I was made to create, to create that which destroys. Throughout history, there have been many of us who have contributed to this necessity, and I have been but one component.

There is no sentiment amongst those of us who have this purpose. Situated between Heaven and Earth, there is naught but our commitment to what we need to do. And that commitment, dear reader, is war.

For centuries, I have molded men into armies, and the army of the Romans was by far my greatest triumph. I cared for it, nurtured it. I whispered into the ears of its leaders, men such as Regillensis, Scipio, Julius Caesar, and Pompey.

They were efficient. They were brutal. They were merciless.

I advised them how to smash the likes of the Sabines, the Samnites, the Carthaginians, the Greeks, the Gauls, and many, many others. Even themselves.

But today, I will see them cast aside by the Parthians, a people who, at their peak, formed an empire wedged between the Romans and the Han Chinese.

From what I saw, they proved to be very worthy adversaries for the Romans. On an arid, dusty plain, in a place that you now understand to be a part of southeast Turkey, they served up another lesson in humility to me and my Romans. Here, seven legions were obliterated by a smaller number of Parthian warriors. Yet I could only observe. There was no meddling allowed during the Battle of Carrhae.

So be what it may, I could only watch as my Romans were harried by the Parthian's mounted archers and then smashed by their heavy cavalry called cataphracts. They were slowly bled and then bludgeoned to death. Seven eagle standards were lost.

Oddly, you may think, this is not by far the day's true significance. The importance is that among all those who fought and died below me is one who would, one day, shine like the sun. The substance of which I shall reveal in the pages ahead.

But it was here, in the year 53 B.C., where this tale begins.

The Fray

The remaining 12,000 or so Romans formed a large defensive square. Thousands of mounted Parthian archers galloped around them, sending great amounts of swirling dust into the air. With their high-power composite bows, the Parthians had, for hours, let loose volley after volley of arrows into the Roman ranks. Despite the legionaries locking shields, arrows found targets. An exposed neck, foot, or face. Those who remained unscathed hoped in vain that their enemy's supply of arrows would run out.

Amongst them all, I watched a fresh-faced centurion try to inspire any of his men capable of fighting. He was in his 20s. A fine example of a mortal. Tall. Broad-shouldered. Sandy hair. Bright blue eyes that contrasted starkly with the red crest that traversed his bronze helmet. In all, his features were typical of his people who lived near the source of the Tiber River. His name was Quintus Aemilianus, the third son of a large landholder.

I observed his mind and found that despite his outer bravado, he was pessimistic about his chances of living beyond the day. It was a rational assessment given the circumstances. He had accepted his fate, but as a proud Roman, he would go on fighting until the end. Death was preferable to slavery.

The slain, Quintus believed, would step from this brutal world to the next, where a ferryman would take them across the River Styx. Each of them would provide an account of their life to the three judges — Minos, Rhadamanthus, and Aeacus — who would decide if they were to go to the bliss of the Elysian Fields or to the torment of Tartarus. In the afterlife, they shall drink from the river of forgetfulness, so the memory of their earthly existence would be washed away.

I wanted to mutter in his ears. Advise him. But that was something — as I mentioned — I'm not allowed to do. I could only watch as he stumbled over a dead body and then regain his feet. After straightening his helmet, he glanced sideways at what was meant to be the hollow of the defensive square, which was instead full of the lifeless and dying. He again indignantly swore under his breath.

I understood how their situation angered him. It surely was avoidable. It was a debacle. They were drawn into the desert like fools. All this for an old politician's pride and glory. Their leader, Marcus Licinius Crassus, Rome's richest man, may have once had the good fortune of beating the slave rebel Spartacus but he'll gain no triumph from this business, nor will those who have followed him in his vain attempt to conquer the East. Quintus had already contemplated that Crassus may be dead. Crassus' son, a cavalryman, certainly was. The young man had led a contingent of Roman cavalry into a trap, and now his decapitated head was a trophy stuck on the end of a Parthian lance.

But none of that mattered now to those still alive as the enemy made their next move.

'Parthian heavy cavalry!' someone yelled as the attacking arrows abated.

Quintus stood to his full six feet, and over the shoulders of his half-crouching men, he saw a near endless line of approaching cataphracts riding knee to knee.

Again, they come. This will be their third charge, he thought.

So heavily armored these riders were they needed no shield. Even the horses were protected by head-to-knees armor. Each rider carried a lance called a kontos that was pointed with a three-foot-long spearhead.

'Men prepare!' Quintus shouted. 'Prepare for heavy cavalry!'

The soldiers began to do as ordered. Discipline is a beautiful thing.

He next called to his optio, his second in charge. 'Catulus, loosen the formation but maintain a fighting line. Get the wounded to the rear.'

Quintus made his way up front and passed through the front line of legionaries. After walking ten paces, he stopped and turned to face his men.

'Soldiers of the first cohort, there is no option but to stand your ground and fight!' he yelled. 'We never give up, so rise! We do not fear death, so stand by your brother and meet your fate, whatever that may be!'

There was a pause as he breathed deep to again fuel his voice.

'You will not fail, nor be found wanting. The first cohort does not lie down. Courage is your finest possession. You will fight your way back to Rome, one dead Parthian at a time!'

His legionaries responded by beating their weapons on their shields and roaring in rage, no matter how futile it may have appeared.

Quintus turned to look at the approaching cavalry. There were thousands of them.

He joined the frontline of his men.

'Don't let yourselves down boys!' he yelled.

The rumble of the galloping horses increased.

'Ready yourselves. Show these Parthians who you are.'

He drew his double-edged gladius.

'And let the Gods look down upon you with admiration.'

Not far from the Roman lines, the pace of the cataphracts refused to slacken. The riders urged on their mounts and steadied their heavy lances.

Quintus fixed his gaze on one Parthian, a mail-clad rider with an iron mask, who seemingly was galloping straight towards him.

'Send them to Hell!' Quintus yelled.

The charging Parthians were by now only 40 feet from the first line of Romans. Only seconds away, and they'd be upon them.

Quintus steadied his shield and tightened the grip on his gladius.

He had time for one more shout. 'Nunquam cede!' Never give up.

Legionaries hurled their pilum javelins at the attacking cavalry, but nothing stopped them. They tore into the legion's lines. It was mayhem. Men, animals, and steel clashed.

An armored horse and its rider smashed into Quintus, hurling him onto the ground. He quickly regained his senses and picked himself up. He threw his shield aside and joined two of his soldiers dragging a Parthian from his mount. With a sword thrust, the Parthian was dispatched. A split second later, another cataphract barged Quintus back into the spoilt dirt.

Mars, give me strength, he thought as he impacted the ground.

He rolled onto his side and used his elbow to lift himself up, but a hoof from a frenzied horse whacked him on the side of the head, just above the right ear. His plumed bronze helmet went flying. The blunt trauma knocked him unconscious.

Sent East

I must now talk with some broad but short strokes to push this tale along. Some 20,000 Romans perished at the Battle of Carrhae, a loss that halted Rome's eastward expansion. It was a humiliating defeat, one that was not avenged in a timely manner as Rome itself was soon plunged into a civil war between Crassus' rivals Julius Caesar and Pompey, the results of which would see Rome move from republic to empire.

In the centuries to come, there'd be more bouts between Romans and Parthians, but for Quintus, his trials and tribulations were more immediate. Post-battle, I watched as he woke from his concussion to find himself a prisoner. He and 8,000 of his fellow legionaries were then force marched eastward, where they would become slaves.

There have been a few theories about what occurred next. I have to say the ancient historian Plinius was pretty accurate on what happened to these men, that being they were taken to the Parthian's eastern borders where they were either sold off as slaves or used as slave soldiers against barbarian tribes.

As for Quintus, he and 20 or so other men were eventually sold to the Xiongnu people, who were ancestors of the Mongols. They were meant to be put to work in the mines, but they ended up being used to defend a fortress against an invading Han Chinese army. There they put up a good fight, but a handful of men can only do so much against many.

A Horrible Predicament

Dunhuang was a Han garrison town situated by a desert oasis in what is today far-west China. At the center of the town was the residence of Meng Rang, the Han governor for the western regions. While I look down upon his residence, I see a short, pudgy middle-aged eunuch, wearing a Zhan Chi Fu Tou spread-wing head cover, walk out into a courtyard. As far as character goes, the eunuch's greatest failing was his total cult-like dedication to his master — Governor Meng, a man both feared and loathed across the lands he controlled.

Meng's mercenary bodyguards were held in the same regard. The worst of them was the chief bodyguard, a tall brute named Yongan who came from lands further northeast. Dressed in a dark robe, he now followed the eunuch walking towards a half-naked Caucasian strung up on a wooden frame in the courtyard. The semiconscious Caucasian's feet were four inches off the ground.

Yes, it was Quintus.

The eunuch and Yongan stopped in front of the near-dead Roman, who didn't register their presence. The eunuch prodded the prisoner with a stick.

'Wake up, barbarian. Will you cede to Governor Meng's demands?'

Quintus didn't respond.

The eunuch prodded again, and Quintus' eyes squinted open.

'Will you train his army?' the eunuch asked, this time more forcibly.

Quintus tried responding but could only speak weakly in Latin, saying something about the eunuch's headwear.

'What?' exclaimed the eunuch. 'Speak Han!'

Quintus summed up his remaining strength and spat at the eunuch's feet.

'There is your answer,' said Yongan, who then grabbed the eunuch's stick and whacked Quintus repeatedly and relentlessly with it.

The eunuch didn't have the stomach to watch. Instead, he walked back to where he had just come from.

Yongan finished thrashing Quintus, who had lapsed back into semi-consciousness. *This foreigner will soon be food for vultures,* Yongan thought as he walked off in the same direction as the eunuch.

Meng the Merciless

Inside Governor Meng's residence, two men dueled with swords. One was Meng himself. He was in his early 40s and dressed in black silk. A wispy goatee beard. Skin so pale it was near translucent. Yes, he is even wicked to look at. He was also masterful with a two-handed sword, much more than his opponent — a boyish soldier with protruding ears.

Meng's top military officer, General Lu, observed the sword fight from the side, as did several court eunuchs and bodyguards. But let's be clear, this was not training or a playful bout, this was a one-sided fight to the death that would not last long.

The boyish soldier tripped and fell to the floor. He tried to scramble away, but no mercy was shown. With several strikes from his sword, Meng slew him.

General Lu did his best to hide his displeasure. Meng shot him a glance.

'I hope the rest of your new conscripts show more potential general,' Meng said. 'Big-eared fools don't make good soldiers.'

The general could only nod. Inside he burned with indignation. The corpse at Meng's feet a month ago was a lazy goat herder. The lad never stood a chance, especially with only a dull blade to defend himself with.

The general regretted not plotting to get rid of Meng earlier. Local forces would have supported a move against the tyrant as early as a year ago. Indeed, even among the region's population, there'd been a feeling of disgust towards the governor and his bodyguards since the spring.

For General Lu, the turning point was upon learning the campaign against the Xiongnu was conducted through a false edict, meaning it did not have the emperor's consent. Meng now had to be removed. There was no other course, and the general soon had to make a move. Much evil had already been committed that couldn't be undone, and General Lu himself was implicated in much of it. He could only try and make amends with himself and the Heavens.

The stick-prodding eunuch entered from the courtyard and shuffled towards Meng, who was washing his hands from a large bowl held by a bodyguard. After stopping at a respectable distance, the eunuch knelt.

'Speak,' Meng ordered.

'Lord, the barbarian continues to refuse your mercy,' the eunuch replied.

'I thought as much. Maybe you didn't ask him in the correct manner,' Meng said tersely.

After drying his hands, Meng dropped the towel to the ground and walked to a window where he pushed the shutters open so he could clearly see Quintus outside.

This barbarian, this man, had led a small band of well-disciplined slave soldiers the likes of which he had not seen before. With their long shields and short swords, they proved effectively deadly in close combat before they were ordered to surrender by their Xiongnu overlords.

Despite the pleasure it gave him at the time, Meng now regretted executing the barbarian's men so hastily. Dead men cannot pass on knowledge and now their obstinate leader dangled at death's door.

Besides, there was gossip among the population concerning the foreigner that perturbed him.

'Barbarian, some say you're a man of myth, but you are but an ant. I see nothing,' Meng said quietly to himself.

He turned to his general.

'I've heard there are fantastical rumors being spread about this barbarian; rumors that he will save us all from some great catastrophe. This should cease general. Anyone talking such gibberish should be harshly punished,' Meng said.

General Lu nodded shallowly.

'If the barbarian remains alive in the morning, I want him executed for all to see,' Meng said as he turned away from the window. 'This is a bore; you all bore me.'

And with that, he exited the room with his bodyguards following. It was time for him to eat and to discuss matters on further taxing trade along the silk route, of which much of the proceeds would end up in his pockets.

Meanwhile, out in the dusty courtyard, Quintus was suspended between life and death. As for the outcome of it all, the Roman was unyielding. His father and then the legion educated him long ago to never leave room for despair or fear of death. The only thing he now had remaining in this world was his honor, and neither fool nor monster would steal that from him. No matter the pain. Besides, he had nothing else to take. He would bravely endure, as any self-respecting Roman should.

Deliverance

It was nighttime. A cold wind blew off the singing sand dunes bordering much of the town. A pair of shivering sentries on a wall's parapet huddled around a copper fire bowl. In whispered tones, they spoke about the near-dead foreigner hanging from the frame below them.

Lost in conversation, they failed to notice three figures,

dressed in drab garbs, nimbly making their way across the gabled rooftops of the governor's residence. The three figures climbed off the roof like cats onto the courtyard's wall. One of them carried a composite bow and a quiver full of bamboo arrows.

As clouds moved across the half-moon, two of them slipped into the courtyard unseen. It was the archer who stayed on the wall. He crouched, drew an arrow from his quiver, and covered his companions as they stealthily made their way toward Quintus.

After the two reached the Roman, one took his weight while the other cut through the ropes until he was free. The larger man carried Quintus in what you would today call a fireman's lift, but the heavier movement of their return attracted the notice of the sentries. Having intuited that the sentries had spotted them, the two rescuers froze midway across the yard.

Their supporting archer drew back his bowstring and prepared to let the arrow fly. He aimed at one of the sentries, the one who was retrieving his spear. A beat later, and the arrow would have flown, but the other sentry — the elder of the two — did the unexpected. He placed his hand on the younger soldier's shoulder and held him back.

'Put that away,' the elder said, referring to the spear the young man held and subsequently lowered. The older soldier then gestured peacefully to the intruders below. 'Be quick, get him out of here,' he said loud enough to be heard.

The two rescuers nodded in gratitude.

The archer dropped his aim as his companions hurried away with their prize. After scaling the wall, it wasn't long before they were out of sight, making their way out of the town.

The sentries on the parapet knew that Meng would execute them for what they allowed to happen, so it wasn't long before they abandoned their post. Within a few hours, they gathered supplies and their families and fled into the desert. A week later, they could return. Meng had by then been overthrown by an uprising orchestrated by General Lu.

CHAPTER II

The Cave

Quintus woke to find himself laying on a blanket spread on a solid-rock floor. Yes, he was tender and sore, but he was more clear-headed and rested than he ought to have been. He was somewhat confused by his new circumstances, but he was glad to be both alive and not being tortured.

A series of vague recollections began flickering through his mind. Did he travel for days, or was it more like weeks? Either way, I can tell you that Quintus was unconscious for much of his journey.

Nevertheless, he could recall bits and pieces of a bumpy ox-drawn cart and a smoother passage by riverboat. His most vivid recollection was a group of silent men carrying him in a sling suspended from bamboo poles up a steep mountain; presumably, he thought to here, this cave.

As he gradually regained his senses, the Roman moved to more immediate matters. He found himself wearing unfamiliar clothes; a loose gray-green silk tunic and black pants.

Quintus propped himself up on a shaky elbow and then sat himself up. He began massaging his aching wrists while looking around. To his right, he saw daylight coming through a doorway-sized opening. Its light allowed him to see the murals across the cave's uneven walls. Among them was a painted figure of a deity wearing a colorful robe. The deity sat in the lotus position. Its calm eyes seemed to be looking right at him.

After it was apparent there was no threat inside the chamber, his attention was taken by a whimsical tune that floated in on a breeze through the opening. Someone outside the cave was playing a string instrument.

Under a Plum Tree

After exiting the cave, Quintus quickly ignored the music; the view that greeted him took his full attention. In fact, what he saw nearly took his breath away. It consisted of a broad lush valley and a series of majestic mountain ranges as far as the eye could see. It was even more beautiful than the northern Apennines of his youth.

Taking in the sight, he continued walking out onto an open terrace that was cut into the bare rock of a mountainside. The terrace's surface was flat cobblestone and, to put it in modern terms, it was about the size of a tennis court. It was there that he also saw the source of the music.

In the middle of the terrace, an elderly Taoist ascetic played a two-string fiddle called an erhu. The Taoist was sitting on a rock under the shade of a 12-foot-high non-flowering plum tree that grew defiantly out of the cobblestones.

His name is Tai.

The old man was dressed in a ragged Hanfu robe narrowly cuffed and knee-high in length. A long fine grey beard framed his mouth while his hair was tightened into a bun at the peak of his head.

After a moment of Quintus watching him, Tai ceased playing the erhu and put it aside. He looked at his visitor and then stood and offered a welcoming toothy smile. Quintus couldn't help but be impressed that such a timeworn fellow could have such a full mouth of well-ordered white teeth.

'Welcome to White Dragon Mountain,' Tai said in accented Latin.

A mountain hermit in China talking Latin was the last thing Quintus was expecting.

'I hope you're feeling better,' Tai added.

'I am, thank you, but you speak Latin,' Quintus said, obviously baffled by the unexpected.

'Oh, Latin it's an easy language to master,' the old man said with a smile.

'Who taught you?' asked Quintus, frowning in disbelief.

Tai laughed.

'Too many questions already. You must be thirsty,' Tai said as he turned and walked to a small spring fountain fashioned from the cliffside. Once he reached it, he took a bronze cup out from a small hole in the cliff and began filling it with water.

'This spring water has healing properties, just as the music from my erhu does,' Tai said. 'I've played music for three days and three nights for you. If I didn't, you probably would have long left this world.'

Tai finished filling the cup with water and gave it to Quintus.

'Just go ahead and drink, you've recovered from an ordeal that would've crushed most men, but you still need to regain your strength and my music can only do so much,' Tai said. 'The more spring water you drink, the faster your strength will return; besides, my arms are tired of playing so much erhu!' he quipped with a smile before he sat on a nearby boulder that was shiny and smooth like it had been sat on a million times before.

Tai gestured for Quintus to also take a seat on the other rock that was under the plum tree some 12 feet away.

'Please sit and drink, drink, drink, drink!'

Quintus studied the water in the cup.

'Don't worry, Quintus, the water is fine,' Tai said.

Quintus sat on the rock, but he didn't drink; instead, he looked over the view.

'Where's the desert?' he asked.

'Ha, ha, ha, you have well and truly left that behind. You are very far south and east of where you were. It took you some 12 or so days to get here.'

'And how did I get here?'

'A band of men loyal to General Lu rescued you. The general is a virtuous man who follows the will of Heaven, but it took him some time to wake up to that,' Tai said.

Quintus nodded, acknowledging Tai's explanation, and then he finally took a sip of water.

'It's sweet,' he remarked.

'That it is.'

Tai smiled upon seeing Quintus sip again.

'You can drink it and not need a jot of food,' the old man added.

Quintus then took a gulp of the water.

'Feel free to have more from the spring whenever you want.'

'Thank you, I will.'

For the next several minutes, they sat in silence until Tai again spoke.

'I understand you were a slave soldier captured by Governor Meng.'

'Yes, that Meng was a monster.'

'Yes, he certainly is. He has the habit of casting great darkness wherever he goes, but he is the emperor's cousin,' Tai said. 'Long ago, he turned his back on the wisdom of Confucius and only sought to cultivate cruelty.'

Tai paused briefly before delivering his next words carefully.

'In fact, he rose from the seventh level of Hell to subvert the ruling dynasty. But he has been, thankfully, unsuccessful.'

'He rose from Hell?'

'Yes, or as you Romans like to call it, Tartarus. But all his malicious endeavors have come to naught,' Tai answered. 'General Lu has now restored the emperor's power fully to the western region. Meng and a handful of his followers managed to flee, and they are now nothing more than common bandits with a price on their heads.'

Tai paused talking, and Quintus took a bigger gulp of water. Moments later, a sensation of warmth filled the

Roman's abdomen. It spread through his torso. Soon his whole body tingled with vitality. The energy carried with it a sense of benevolence and clarity. He took another gulp, and the warmth spread further.

'Drink as much as you can. It'll help you recover quicker,' Tai said with a knowing smile. 'The men who rescued you brought some supplies for you to eat, some dried fish, and more. I'll get it for you, and you can have some of that as well, but you don't need it really, the water is enough.'

Tai stood to go find the supplies leaving Quintus alone to reflect on the water's already astonishing effects.

The Prophecy

Quintus ate what Tai offered him and drank more of the water. As the day progressed, he was feeling comfortable and clear-headed, in fact, more than he had been in a long time.

Despite Quintus having many more questions to ask the old man, there had been a couple of hours of silence between them both. They just sat there on their respective rocks, looking over the valley. Eventually, it was Quintus who broke the silence.

'How long have you been on this mountain?' he asked.

'A very long time, but I have never grown tired of the view,' Tai replied with a smile. 'My teacher brought me here to learn the Way during the previous dynasty. He succeeded in his practice and ascended.'

'What do you mean by ascended?'

'He reached spiritual perfection, but that's not

important now, that was some 300 years ago. Since then, I've been waiting for a man from the West to come so I can teach him, train him,' Tai said. 'A man who prophesy said would walk the earth 20 lifetimes for the sake of mankind. A man able to stop humanity from falling into the abyss.'

Tai stood from his rock and walked to the ledge in a bid to give Quintus time to think over what was just said.

Understandably, Quintus wasn't sure how to respond. *Surely, he isn't referring to me,* he thought.

Now near the ledge, the Taoist hoped he hadn't divulged too much too soon. Not many mortals are prepared for such revelations, no matter how they are told. He turned to look at Quintus.

'Nonetheless, prophecies can be mistaken. It certainly wouldn't be the first or last time,' Tai said, changing tact somewhat. 'In the end, it is up to you.'

'I'm pretty certain you've got the wrong person,' Quintus said.

'No, I haven't.'

'I'm not trying to be rude, but it's the silliest thing I've heard all day.'

Tai smiled and nearly laughed.

'My learning Latin wasn't for nothing,' he said.

'Yes, you speaking Latin is certainly odd.'

'Indeed, it must seem so.'

'I'm grateful for the help, flattered by the offer, but I have only one aim, and that's getting back to the West.'

'A worthy goal but goals change. You're free to leave whenever you like, Quintus, or you can stay, and I will teach you what you need to know.'

Quintus wanted to wind the conversation back.

'Firstly, how is it you know my name? I never told you,' he said.

It was now time for Tai to be more convincing.

'I've known you for some time, Quintus. Ever since you were this high,' a smiling Tai said while indicating with his right hand the height of a 5-year-old child.

'I'm not restricted to this physical body. I'm able to cross the boundaries of this material world. The worldly challenges that distance provides don't occur in other planes of reality,' Tai explained while noting the continuing look of disbelief in Quintus' eyes.

'You may find this hard to imagine, but there was more than one occasion that I saw you and your family on your farm. In fact, when you attended Latin lessons, so did I, that's an answer to your earlier question. You weren't, by the way, a very attentive student.'

And that was just the beginning. Tai went back and sat on the rock, and for over an hour, he spoke more about Quintus' youth and described his parents and siblings. Their daily lives, including aspects of several adventures Quintus had with his two elder brothers. All of it accurate and detailed.

'But I only witnessed the period from your birth through till the age of 12,' Tai explained. He had zero interest in watching anyone go through adolescence.

When Tai thought he'd said enough, he stood from the rock and dusted off his pants.

'I haven't talked so much for centuries. I'm going for a short walk around the mountain. One last thing, if you do stay to learn the Way, there is much for you to learn, but for the sake of practicality, you first must master the abilities to do without food, water, and sleep.'

'I didn't know such things were possible,' Quintus remarked.

'It's possible, but you might die in the process,' Tai said, jesting.

'I'll be back before sundown, and I'll play some more erhu. Drink some more water while I'm gone.'

Quintus watched Tai walk off. He was now convinced the old man was no charlatan. In fact, he now believed that the old man was the most incredible individual he had ever met and that they indeed had a bond, given what he was just told. It was as if he was talking with one of his family, relieving days of yesteryear.

It may have all sounded fantastical, but the only rational explanation was, when weighed up, that this Taoist was telling the truth. He believed such things were possible, but like most, his comprehension was lacking, at least initially. He asked himself how would he respond to what Tai was suggesting and was his fate to remain on this mountain to be trained by him in foreign ways. It would take careful consideration.

The Decision

From his core to his surface Quintus still required healing. After that first day of waking in the cave, he slept intermittently for a full week while Tai played the erhu. When he wasn't sleeping, he drank plenty of spring water. After seven days of this, he was fully restored, at least physically. He even regained weight and was as heavy as he was prior to being captured by the Parthians eight years earlier. But it was his spirit that would take more time to heal. Fortunately, if there was a place to do that, it was White Dragon Mountain.

Due to his open nature, it wasn't long before Quintus was relaxed with Tai, who he came to further appreciate as a humble man of extraordinary talents that were quite simply otherworldly. The old man spent much of his time in meditation and exercising. When he wasn't doing that, he was playing music, writing poetry, and painting pictures of a six-legged dragon or of the surrounding landscape. Quintus observed that Tai neither slept nor ate. He didn't even need to drink from the mountain spring.

When they spoke, both men appreciated what each other had to say, which was mostly about things related to philosophy and the values of their separate worlds. Quintus discussed Stoicism and other aspects of Greco-Roman culture. Meanwhile, Tai introduced Quintus to Taoism, Confucianism, and facets of a newer dharma called Buddhism.

Tai explained how villagers in the valley had for generations kept his presence on the mountain a well-guarded secret. Before Quintus was brought up the mountain by his rescuers, the last person the villagers allowed to visit was an evangelizing Buddhist monk who stayed for five years, during which he taught Tai many things. From that, Tai embraced the concept of reincarnation, which he now accepted as a truth, resolving a gap his earlier master acknowledged he was unable to fill. His master, and indeed Tai, understood there are many, many mysteries that were beyond them and that they only had a slight insight into Heaven's secrets.

Quintus asked more about the prophecy supposedly involving him but there wasn't too much to tell. Summed up at its barest yet most accurate form the prophecy indicated that a man from the West would learn the Tao, would then wander the world for some 20 lifetimes, and then return to White Dragon Mountain for a final battle against evil so to save humanity. Like many end-of-time prophesies, it was lite on detail. It was essentially a matter of faith.

The challenge for Tai was that he had to tailor what he knew and pass it on to Quintus, who, by his tenth day on the mountain, agreed to become a disciple of the Way, taking the first step in fulfilling the prophecy.

On day one of his training, the old Taoist simply explained to Quintus some of the things to be taught, with the first being several meditation techniques. Next, would be Tao Yin exercises which are soft gracious moves not dissimilar to what modern people would call Tai Chi. Together the meditation and Tao Yin exercises would allow Quintus to maintain his health and a youthful appearance as long as he did them. The desired outcome was that he'd be able to live for however long his foretold undertaking might take.

Tai would also pass on methods to Quintus on how to control pain levels and repair his body quickly. Just as his master already knew, he'd also learn how to survive just on fresh air with no need for food, water, or even sleep

Added to the list of things to learn were levitation abilities and some techniques that may or may not open his celestial eye (AKA third eye, the mind's eye, or the inner eye).

For self-defense, Tai would teach Quintus shouboa

weaponless martial arts, while during periods of downtime, he'd pass on his painting and music knowledge.

Quite a list.

This should take 100 years or so to learn.

Training Day 2

A cool breeze blew upon the side of White Dragon Mountain, where the Taoist's sanctuary was. The sun had not long been up when Quintus walked across the terrace with his master toward where the plum tree stood. To their left, a kaleidoscope of white butterflies hovered just over the cliff's ledge; their fragile wings highlighted by sunlight.

It was Quintus' second day of training, and everything appeared fresh and hopeful. Every cell in his rejuvenated body was awake and ready to learn, so he listened carefully as his teacher spoke.

'The tree flowers during the winter, the harshest time of the year. That's why the plum blossom embodies determination and hope. It also reminds us how temporary life can be, even for the likes of us,' Tai told Quintus.

'While meditating, the blossoms' scent can be a slight distraction, but it's beautiful nonetheless,' Tai said.

The old man then described to his student the benefits of what they would soon begin to practice under the tree's shade.

'Meditation toughens the mind, which may be necessary, or you may go crazy on this mountain with only me as company,' he jested.

Quintus grinned, acknowledging Tai's quirky self-deprecating brand of humor.

They reached the plum tree, and Tai sat on the cobble-stone under it. He gestured for Quintus to do likewise. Tai quickly folded his legs into a double lotus position which Quintus tried copying after sitting.

'The key to mediation is nothingness. The goal is to strengthen your mind, so you can be your own master and conquer yourself. Mind you, it sounds easier than it actually is,' Tai said.

'I can appreciate that already,' Quintus quipped as he struggled to twist his legs into full lotus.

'In time, you shall perfect, and along the way, as your mind expands, you may even see things you never thought were possible,' Tai said.

'Such as?"

'You may see the White Dragon, but then again, you may not.'

'Is he the dragon you like to paint?'

'Indeed, and he is choosy, so he may prefer not to reveal himself to you,' Tai said.

The old man went on to describe the mystical creature.

'The dragon is similar in size to a horse but longer. He has six legs with eagle talons for feet. From head to toe, he is covered in fur while its head is your typical looking dragon type with long whiskers and a soft-orange colored mane. My paintings don't do him justice.'

'Does the White Dragon have a purpose?'

'To defend this mountain, of course, that is what the Gods have asked of it.'

'Defend it from what?'

'Evil, and I'm not talking about the idea of evil but

the reality of it. Before I was here, in fact before I was even born, my master and the White Dragon fought an 11-headed Red Dragon on this mountain that was let loose from the depths of Hell. Together they chased it back into its lair, minus four of its ugly heads.'

As he listened, Quintus continued struggling to get his legs into position. Tai offered an encouraging smile.

'One leg up is fine; just do a half lotus,' he said.

Quintus did as he was advised while Tai offered further instruction.

'As I mentioned, the real benefit of meditation is bolstering the mind,' he said. 'You'll need strength of both heart and mind when you leave the mountain and return to the West. I, your teacher, will watch over you as best I can, but even I'm limited.'

Tai then softened his tone.

'You must be able to endure the unendurable. You must never give up,' he said.

Quintus picked up on Tai's change of voice and the implied seriousness of it all. It helped him focus on what the old man had to say next.

'Many centuries from now, at a precise moment, you shall return to White Dragon Mountain. The fate of humanity depends on it, at least at a particular point in time when everything will appear as if it is falling apart.'

Quintus felt somewhat uncomfortable with the weight of the old man's expectations.

Despite having his eyes shut, Tai picked up on Quintus' unease.

'Again, I have said too much; now close your eyes and try clearing your mind,' Tai said.

Quintus closed his eyes. He contemplated what Tai had told him until his mind was overrun by terrifying memories of his recent past.

Tortured at the hands of Meng's minions.

Years as a slave soldier.

The Battle of Carrhae.

If he were a modern man, he'd be diagnosed with severe post-traumatic stress disorder. After 20 agitated minutes, he opened his eyes and appealed to his master, who was meditating calmly opposite him.

'I can't do it, teacher, my mind, it's just...' Quintus said, not finishing his sentence.

Tai stayed still, kept meditating but offered advice.

'It's good that you see how busy your mind is, but don't give in to it, Quintus. To begin, maybe focus your thoughts on the mountain — its form, the surroundings, the breeze, the sounds,' Tai advised.

Quintus resumed his meditation and did as Tai recommended. He visualized himself above the mountain and over the valley both day and night. He pictured the sun and the moon blessing it and the visiting winds and waters that had kept it company for all time.

For 15 minutes, he thought in this more positive manner until being disrupted by a suspicious noise that triggered both eyes open.

The first thing he saw was Tai catching an arrow bolt shot from a repeating crossbow used by a black-clad assassin crouched near the terrace ledge. As Quintus scrambled to get up, Tai managed to catch the assassin's next bolt. By the time the Roman was on his feet, he counted five more black-dressed attackers clambering onto the terrace behind the crossbowman.

He then watched in amazement as Tai performed a fly-float kick that knocked the crossbow out of the first assassin's hands. His master followed through with a series of precise jabs that targeted several of the attacker's acupuncture points. The now paralyzed crossbowman promptly toppled over like a cardboard cutout.

'Quintus. My stick!' Tai yelled, referring to a pole near Quintus resting against the plum tree. Quintus grabbed it and threw it to his master. Using it, Tai quickly engaged the next two assassins. It wasn't long till one of them was paralyzed by some well-placed pole prods while the other attacker double-backed to join the other assassins, who were now more cautious.

Meanwhile, Quintus took custody of the paralyzed bowman's sword. As he gauged its weight, he recognized among the attackers the large frame of Yongan, Meng's main bodyguard. He then likewise noted the last assassin who clambered onto the terrace was Meng himself. The former governor looked thinner and more haggard than Quintus recalled. Life on the run had taken its toll.

Tai looked to Quintus.

'Quintus, you must not kill,' he said.

The Roman was caught off guard by the order.

'What, why?'

There was no chance for a reply as Meng's shrill voice filled the air.

'Old man, you have chosen a barbarian as your student. You have disgraced the Han race!'

Tai swiftly responded.

'You are a no-good bandit trespassing on White Dragon Mountain!'

Then the moment exploded. Meng screamed and charged with his three remaining minions trailing.

'Quintus, leave this to me!' Tai yelled as he went to fight Meng's assassins.

But Quintus' legionnaire fighting instincts kicked in, and a deeply suppressed rage likewise emerged. Disregarding his master's order, he quickly met an attacker armed with a spear who he outmaneuvered and shoved to the ground. With one sword blow, he killed the fallen man.

'Quintus! Try not to kill!' yelled Tai as he jabbed another attacker into a state of paralysis.

There was, in Quintus' mind, no time to consider Tai's words. *Hesitation will only result in defeat*, he thought. Moreover, today he had the chance for revenge.

As Tai began to fight Meng, he saw, out of the corner of his eye, Quintus facing Yongan, who came in swinging with a battle-ax. The Roman fended off the attack and then went on the offensive.

'Quintus! Do not kill him!' Tai again shouted.

Tai could only watch as his instructions went unheeded — Quintus managed to push Yongan towards the cliff's edge.

'Quintus, don't do it!' Tai yelled.

But his student pushed Meng's chief minion over the edge.

As Yongan plummeted to his death, Quintus turned to see Tai fighting Meng who was by now the last unwelcome visitor fighting. Quintus picked up a discarded assassin's spear and threw it at Meng.

It was a deadly throw. Meng shrieked in agony as he was hit by the spear in the chest. He collapsed to the ground, and several seconds later, he gave up the ghost.

After Quintus was satisfied that Meng was indeed lifeless, he picked up Yongan's battle-ax from the ground and approached one of the three paralyzed attackers.

'No, you truly must stop Quintus. I cannot allow anymore killing,' Tai said, in-between catching his breath.

Quintus stopped in his tracks, but his stance suggested it was only momentary.

'They're assassins,' Quintus said in a state of barely controlled fury. He then pointed at Meng's body.

'And that filth massacred my men after they surrendered,' he said.

Tai put aside his fighting stick, steadied his breathing, and looked calmly at his student.

'Yes, there's evil in the world, Quintus, and a virtuous man cannot stand idly by; however, you must consider what I'm about to say,' Tai said. 'These three men you've just killed, in their future lives, they will seek you out for retribution. It doesn't just end here today.'

Tai's warnings appeared to fall on deaf ears. Quintus, with ax in hand, stepped forward towards the nearest paralyzed assassin.

'If you are my student Quintus, please do not do this.

Nothing good can come from it. You cannot let rage take over your senses.'

Quintus again halted as a war waged inside him on what he should do. He closed his eyes and sought to clear his thoughts for half a minute which gave him just enough time to quash his anger. It wasn't long until he threw the ax aside and took a seat on the broad rock that looked like it had been sat on a million times.

'Okay teacher,' he said to Tai. 'They get to live.'

Tai looked at his student with a great deal of compassion.

'Be assured, Quintus, I will teach you how to fight and defeat evil and you will be able to do it without killing or causing unnecessary harm,' Tai said while sitting on the rock under the plum tree. 'The three dead, they'll be reborn one day and blindly will seek you out for payback. That is how reincarnation works, in part at least, so we must now take it into account. Perhaps there is something I can do to soften what will come.'

Both men sat there silently for some time; contemplating what transpired until Tai described what they needed to do next with the assassins, both the living and the dead.

'We will burn the deceased, and for those paralyzed, a few taps with my stick on the correct acupuncture points and they will regain their senses,' he said.

'Then we shall tie their hands and walk them down to deliver them to the villagers, who will hand them over to the local powers. It might take us four days to do it, but it's an agreeable walk,' he said. 'So, that is that. Your second day of training, Quintus, has been rather eventful. I just certainly hope they're all not like this,' he added, laughing.

To Hell and Back

When Quintus took up the Way, both Heaven and Hell overlooked his past transgressions, but any committed, while he was Tai's disciple would be much harder to remedy since the standards set for him were now much higher.

Following the fight with Meng and his minions, Tai knew he had to risk everything to try and resolve what he feared might come. He did not share his concerns with Quintus. It would have still been too much, too early for the Roman to comprehend.

Due to Tai still being human, he had no means to visit Heaven, but there was a way he could get to Hell to plead a case and survive. Centuries earlier, his master gave him 10 years' worth of lessons on how to get to Hell and back if needed. Tai's master had already been there done that when he and the White Dragon fought the Red Dragon. In short, it was a bold, ballsy method, and it worked.

Tai left the earthly realm and rode the White Dragon straight into a stiflingly hot cavernous room, a gloomy place of immense despair. Within its shadows, he saw the silhouettes of the 13 Demon Kings of the Pit seated on thrones fashioned from a dark grey stone wall. While he couldn't make out their features, he noted their unclothed boney humanoid figures were twice his height despite each of them being bent and stooped in some way.

'Who are you?' the demon kings shrieked in surprised unison.

Before Tai could respond, they again spoke.

'No, we know you. Get out. You are not allowed here. Only the condemned are permitted here!' they screamed.

Tai and the White Dragon didn't' budge.

'Yes, I'm aware of that, and I don't anticipate being here for long. However, I also know you demons can only command the damned in this vile place,' Tai said, acting as if he had the upper hand. 'So, save yourselves the effort and quit your screaming.'

Tai's bravado was, in one way, no act. His master long ago advised him to take charge if he ever had to go to Hell and deal with the demons. You see, these creatures have no authority over anyone not marked as one of theirs, which of course, Tai was not. Not only that, but his supernormal abilities were also magnified in this realm.

There was no hometown advantage for the 13.

The demon kings knew this, and they began shifting nervously on their thrones. Undeniably, Tai's presence had now upset them to the point of near panic. Even their boss, Satan, couldn't help them, at least on such short notice.

'We despise you. Even more than your master,' they yelled at Tai.

'I certainly take that as a compliment,' Tai calmly replied.

'Be quiet. Get off that creature and kneel,' they bellowed hatefully.

'I'm not here to pay homage or beg,' Tai said.

'Why are you here then?'

'I'm here to issue a warning.'

'You? Warn us? We don't take direction from the likes of you. We have taken precautions since your master's last unwelcome visit,' they said, bluffing. The demons had no backup plan. At one stage, they argued about making one, but out of a combination of arrogance and laziness, nothing ever eventuated.

Nonetheless, the memories of Tai's master and the White Dragon entering their realm and wounding their red dragon were traumatic. He had been the only full human being to enter their territory until Tai's current visit.

'Your master was trespassing. Don't make the same mistake,' they yelled.

'You sent your dragon to attack my master, breaking the laws of Heaven,' Tai said. 'Your beast is not permitted in the human world.'

'Yes, our dragon entered your realm, but it was a long time ago. Get over it, you fool.'

'If need be, I will finish what my master started and destroy you all, plus your pet dragon, but that's not what I came here for,' Tai warned.

'One thing is for certain, your insolence is tiring,' they replied.

'Nevertheless, you have been warned. Ignore it at your own peril,' he said.

'Just tell us why you are here.'

'I have a new student learning the Way,' Tai said. 'He slew three assassins who were attempting to kill him.'

'If what you utter is accurate, he is not coming here. Self-defense is no wrongdoing, you fool!' they yelled.

'But the three he killed will one day seek him out when they reincarnate on Earth.'

'That is how it goes.'

'They're now here in Hell.'

'Suffering as they must, like other sinners.'

'I want to see them.'

The demons moaned.

'Why such fuss over a student?'

'That is what a master of the Way does,' he answered.

'Cast him aside,' they yelled.

'Never!'

'Well, we cannot order these three to do what you want. Free will is even a principle here.'

'So, will you give me your consent and let me see them?' Tai asked.

'If we grant you this favor, we want something in return.'

'Such as?'

'Leave us. Promise that you'll never come back.'

After a beat, Tai nodded, and the demons collectively agreed.

'You can see them. It is seldom we allow such things,' they said. 'So, we will watch your student ever more closely to see if he is worthy of such mercy. If he is not, we will have our way. We will drag him down. Do you understand?'

Tai again nodded.

The 13 demons drew straws to see who would escort Tai to the third ring of the seventh circle of Hell, where Meng and his two henchmen were suffering in a torture pit.

There the souls of Yongan and the other thug killed by Quintus gave Tai pitiable reassurances that they'd seek no retribution upon reincarnation. But dealing with Meng's soul was another thing. It remained full of spite and malice.

'You think you can bargain with me, old man?' Meng's

soul screamed. 'You think you can bargain with the demon kings? They say one thing, do another. They're the kings of lies. You're a fool. I will seek out your disciple and have my vengeance upon him and on you!'

Tai realized there was no point in reasoning with a madman, even a dead one, so he left Meng's soul and returned to the earthly realm, fearing what his student may one day have to face.

Back on White Dragon Mountain, Tai began taking the necessary precautions. Before the incident with the assassins, he calculated it would only take a hundred or so years for Quintus to learn everything he needed to know. After that, the Roman would have been free to return to the West and deal with what would come when the time presented itself. But given his visit to Hell, Tai had Quintus train for some 400 years to ensure he was well prepared to face any type of challenge, earthly or otherwise. Or at least so he thought.

Sealing the Cave

Just before Quintus was due to leave the mountain sanctuary, he built a rock wall at the entrance of the cave while Tai remained inside. As instructed, Quintus then sealed the one-foot-thick wall with sticky rice and limestone plaster to hide it from the outside world.

The last glimpse he had of Tai was him sitting in meditation on a broad flat rock inside the cave. The only thing that would enter the cave from here on would be fresh air via a shaft opening, which could also serve as a last-resort escape route. The shaft went 500 feet up and some 1,000 feet down inside the mountain.

After sealing the cave, Quintus grabbed what he was taking on his journey, which, given he didn't need to eat, sleep or drink, wasn't much.

His last act on White Dragon Mountain was to trim his long beard and tie his long hair into a bun. Despite being on the mountain for hundreds of years, he retained the looks of a man in his mid-30s. He hadn't aged in appearances like Tai had, who mastered longevity later in his practice.

Once he was ready, Quintus went to the terrace's ledge and promptly jumped over it, and made a controlled free fall for some 700 feet until he landed just above the tree line. His well-honed levitation capabilities ensured a landing as soft as a kiss.

Earlier, Tai told Quintus that he would always watch over him as he ventured westwards, and his student had no doubt this would occur. From within the now pitch-black cave, Tai watched, via his mind's eye, as his student made his way through the valley and beyond.

The year was 367 AD.

CHAPTER III

Rise and Fall of Empires

Quintus didn't wander aimlessly after he returned to the West. For most parts, he was quite industrious. The idea of doing nothing as he waited for events to unfold was not appealing.

After leaving the mountain, it took him a year to return to the Roman Empire, which by then had taken up Christianity — a faith he came to appreciate for its demand for human decency.

He found this new religion exalted kindness and mercy as opposed to the old Roman pagan rituals accepted by the culture of his youth. After hundreds of years on the mountain learning the Way, his own beliefs in deities naturally moved on from what he was born into. Now he understood that gods and enlightened beings were unseen and unknown but at the same time were righteous and compassionate — qualities they wished humankind was more attuned with.

In that new Roman Empire, Quintus established a life of sorts in the ancient metropolis of Aleppo in what is today Syria. He stayed there for a decade before moving on. In his next location, he altered his identity by changing his surname only. To retain some sense of self, he retained his first name. It was a pattern repeated over and over every ten years or so to avoid undue attention.

It was in Aleppo that his career in construction began. It was a decision that proved fruitful. From there, he worked his way up in the building trade around various parts of the eastern Mediterranean, and after a hundred years or so, he became a fine builder as well as an accomplished architect.

In the years that followed, buildings accompanied him throughout history. They easily outlived people and outlasted empires. Their durability comforted him in an ever-changing world. Through late antiquity, he went on to build some of the grandest structures of the period, the third Hagia Sophia in Constantinople being a notable example.

Much of Quintus' time was spent within the boundaries of the Eastern Roman Empire, which eventually became known as the Byzantine Empire. Among his favorite cities that he lived and worked in were Jerusalem, Barca, Germa in Galatia, Mokissos, and Mystras in the southeast of the Peloponnese.

From the seventh century onwards, the Byzantine Empire's borders gradually contracted due to invading Islamic armies and infighting. Eventually, the last vestiges of what was the Roman Empire succumbed to the Ottoman Turks in 1453, but by then, Quintus was already long gone. Two hundred years earlier, he left Constantinople and traveled through Eastern and Central Europe to assist with the rebuilding of what the Mongol invasions had destroyed. Given the amount of destruction and slaughtering done, he was busy for some time.

A century later, just after the worst of the Black Death cut Europe's population by half, Quintus headed towards the Italian peninsula. It was overdue that he returned to the land of his birth, although the attachment he once had about returning was no more. For just over a hundred years, from Rome to Bologna, he built hundreds of castles, places of worship, and homes. He similarly influenced dozens of Italian architects who went on to design some of the definitive structures of what would be known as the Renaissance period.

Around 1460, Quintus ventured back north, this time through the Old Swiss Confederacy and then the German states. He kept heading up into the unions of Denmark, Sweden, and Norway avoiding trouble while doing good deeds, his Tao Yin exercises and meditation, as he went. He then did a U-turn and arrived in what is now the Netherlands in the uneventful summer of 1472.

A year later, Quintus was in France, where he spent some 20 years before he moved to Spain, arriving just as Christopher Columbus stumbled upon the New World.

After some time there and in Portugal, he sailed across to England, where he once again applied his building skills which attracted the attention of a certain King Henry VIII, who had him work on construction projects at King's College Chapel and Westminster Abbey. Quintus spoke with the Tudor king only on one occasion during some renovations, sometime before the monarch's 40th birthday when he was still thin and respected. As they talked, Quintus noted the king's mood was off, something one of the monarch's counselors attributed to an old jousting injury.

Four years later, with the king's mood worsening, that same counselor lost his head for treason, as would many others, queens included, in due course. By then, Quintus had traveled north to the Scottish Highlands, where he lived for several decades as a challenge, before migrating to Ireland, which he called home for more than a century. During this period, he repaired old-Norman castles for Irish nobles and taught construction techniques to common folk. He also built several churches and cathedrals for the faithful until 1649, when Cromwell's invading forces put an end to that. Eight years earlier, ethnic and sectarian violence were omens of things to come. He had hoped it wouldn't get any worse, but it did.

However, I can tell you nothing is by chance. All his building — especially places of worship — and his many acts of selfless charity, unmentioned here, had upset the 13 Demon Kings of the Pit, who were good to their word in watching him. The shadowy demons couldn't tolerate so much goodness coming from a single individual, and one who was near immortal. Feeling unbound by heavenly rules and any past assurances they made with Tai, they maliciously set a path for Meng and his two henchmen to return to the human realm. *This one called Quintus, favored by above high, needed to be sternly tested,* they thought.

The Island, the Gibbet

The wooden gallows-type structure built on a small rocky island was the only unnatural feature on the lake in Ireland's Wexford county. It was a gibbet built by English parliamentarian soldiers from Cromwell's New Model Army, an outfit I must say that I had no hand in creating.

On a summer's day in 1652, such men rowed out in boats to hoist a man-sized iron cage onto the gibbet. Inside the cage was Quintus. Apart from a loincloth, he was naked. Filthy and disheveled, he held no malice towards those who had beaten and mistreated him or who were about to hang him out in the elements.

As they hoisted him up onto the gibbet, most of the red-coated soldiers turned their eyes away. Some were even fearful that their God would strike them down for what they were doing. Many of them witnessed how Quintus' bruises and cuts healed fully within a day or, in some cases, just hours. They had to come to appreciate why the Irish referred to him as a living saint.

Despite this, all 13 men on the rocky island that day were more afraid of their commander than heavenly retribution. Their leader, Colonel Alcott Entwistle, watched them intently. Entwistle had a reputation even before coming to Ireland. But he didn't, at least at first glance, appear nefarious. He was tall and thin with clipped, dainty features.

The colonel earned his early infamy by burning at the stake a dozen elderly women accused of witchery in East Anglia. Rumor had it he did so to cover up his own occult activities.

Yes, I can confirm Entwistle dabbled in the dark satanic arts, as did his two provost guards who were always by his side.

But it was his more recent acts in Ireland that shocked most of his soldiers. He'd made it his goal in life to reduce the Irish population in the county by half, and his preferred ways of doing this was either through inducing mass famine or hangings.

Now, as he stood overseeing Quintus' punishment on the island, he and his two provost guards took pleasure in yelling at a couple of soldiers arriving in the final rowboat.

'Hurry up, get those rotting things up here!' Entwistle yelled.

'You're late!' a provost guard bellowed.

The soldiers alighted from the boat, dragging with them a large wicker basket.

'Give them a hand,' Entwistle ordered his provost guards.

Dread washed over Quintus as the men brought the wicker basket to below his cage. They upended the basket and from it spilled a dozen decapitated heads onto the stony ground.

Quintus closed his eyes and bit his lip in anguish, which caused Entwistle to chuckle.

'I guess you now wish you didn't hand yourself into me don't you saint? You should have run and gone into hiding, but too late now,' Entwistle said. 'Now I've made any mention of your name punishable by death, so you've only got yourself to blame,' he said. 'And the rule of law needs to be enforced. You may notice numerous familiar faces among this bunch, even that Englishman, the Royalist

Edward Hyde is under there somewhere. Was he a friend of yours? I was told he was.'

Quintus didn't reply, nor did he look at the heads eight feet below him. He could only think the worst and presume they were folk from the county who had wanted to hide him from the likes of Entwistle.

'The Irish simpletons say you're blessed with everlasting life. How can one fight against such extreme beliefs?' Entwistle chuckled. 'But I must admit, I'm intrigued how you even survived in this wretched backwater. The papists would typically burn someone like you, insisting you were in league with the devil,' he said. 'Therefore, it's up to me to do what they failed to do.'

Entwistle paused, waiting for some reaction from Quintus, which was not forthcoming, so he resumed speaking and raised his voice by a decibel or two.

'All this talk of everlasting life does fascinate me, though. We should wager on who will die first out of the two of us,' he taunted. 'I'll even gamble a farthing on it.'

Again, Quintus did not react.

That frustrated the colonel, who ordered his provost guards and the other soldiers back to the boats, leaving just himself in front of Quintus. He stared hatefully at the caged man.

'Listen to me, saint, and listen intently. If you escape from this island, I will kill every living being in a ten-mile radius. Every child, every swallow, every lamb. Even the butterflies won't be safe,' Entwistle said.

Each of his words carried a malevolence that was centuries old.

Entwistle turned and made his way to the boats. Just before getting into one of them, he took a final look at Quintus and chuckled again. It wasn't long before the colonel, and his soldiers rowed away.

Quintus wouldn't have any more visitors step foot on that small rocky outcrop for another 12 years.

When Endurance is Everything

With no water, a normal person perishes in three days. Deprived of food it takes a human around three weeks to die. Given Quintus' abilities, he would not have to contend with such scenarios while locked in the cage. Physically and mentally, he was equipped to cope with such an ordeal, at least for a decade or so.

Due to his training, his body could continuously repair itself from any abuse suffered in the cage. But that doesn't mean he didn't feel the pain and discomfort of his predicament. He tolerated and endured it.

But I don't think I can do justice describing to you what Quintus went through. I'd say most of you would not make it past 48 hours in a similar situation before your mind unraveled.

In contrast, after his own 48 hours in the cage, Quintus managed to get himself into a steady frame of mind. He put aside the grief for those who Entwistle had murdered and whose heads were below him like rubble. Quintus looked at his situation for what he understood it to be. Meng had finally come back for revenge in the form of another megalomaniac, that being Entwistle. It was no surprise. Entwistle even looked like Meng, just a Caucasian version.

To keep his mind clear, Quintus recalled his time on the mountain. From the Tao Yin exercises to talks on philosophy, he recollected them all in accurate detail. If any moments in the cage kept his mind strong, it was when he thought of his teacher and his own responsibility to mankind at the end of time.

He reminded himself repeatedly what Tai had told him: 'You must be able to endure the unendurable.' He was determined he would outlast Entwistle and remain true to the Way. He would endure and come out on the other side not only intact but stronger.

Well, that was the plan anyway.

Why Entwistle had chosen such punishment as gibbetting, Quintus was unsure, but he simply reminded himself it could be worse. It wasn't a dark dank dungeon, and it was not as extreme as the crucifixions he witnessed as a centurion.

In the cage, he had at least the days and nights and the four seasons to keep him entertained. Apart from decaying skulls below him, he found the view quite pleasing. On sunny days, the lake and its surroundings were beautiful enough to help him forget his predicament and to disregard the pain.

As the years went by, Quintus got to know each and every tree around the lake. He watched some sprout and saw others fall to rot and feed the soil.

The closest thing he had to a social life was befriending birds, especially bullfinches, who he taught to sing. He welcomed the white swans visiting for winter and generations of swallows who built mud nests under his gibbet's beam during warmer months.

Even a bunch of fairies — who watched him for years before making themselves known — offered their friendship. Several of these diminutive folk occasionally visited him at night, their flapping silver wings shining in the dark.

While Quintus saw such fantastical sights, he saw no people, not a soul, not at least during the first seven years. He presumed Entwistle had made the lake off-limits. It felt at times as if he was the last person on Earth.

The Wall

During Quintus' seventh year in the cage, a single rowboat manned by Entwistle's two provost guards came out onto the water and rowed close enough to check that he indeed remained in the cage. They noted that the naked, bearded, and longhaired man was alive and then rowed back to shore.

A week later, more men arrived, this time laborers who began cutting down trees around the shoreline. After the trees were cleared, another gang of laborers began building a 10-foot-high stonewall circling the lake. It took them three years to finish the wall, which threw the natural dynamics of the lake out of kilter. The water silted up, and an algae bloom killed the fish. The swans and the bullfinches no longer visited him, while the swallows went elsewhere to build their nests. The fairies lost their home among the trees, and they, too, had to relocate.

To fill the vacuum, hundreds of crows arrived. They

insidiously cawed day and night, taking turns to perch on the gibbet or on the wall.

Quintus rightly assumed Entwistle was behind the building of the wall, which he grudgingly recognized was weakening his resolve. A gnawing sense of unease began to chip away inside him, and by the time of his 10th winter on the island, cracks finally began to appear in his mental state. The monotonous horror of it all had become like sandpaper upon his soul.

The first thing to go adrift was his perception of time. Everything seemed to slow down, which magnified his suffering even more. Short periods of mental instability and acute restlessness followed. The shells of what remained of the skulls below began to haunt him, as did the incessant caws from the crows. A mild form of simmering panic set in.

Sometimes Quintus thought he saw soldiers patrolling the wall, tossing rocks at the crows, but he wasn't sure if he was hallucinating or not. On other occasions, he thought he heard the music from an erhu just as he did way back on White Dragon Mountain. It seemed to drift in on the northerly breeze, pushing out the nightmarish tones of the crows. It brought him some comfort. Revitalized him to a point.

He likewise began sleeping, something he hadn't done for centuries. It was another way for him to escape the misery and mind-numbing boredom he faced. Be it in his dreams or his waking hours, more than once, he called out to his teacher, Tai, for help. However, by his 11th year, it got to the stage where he wasn't sure if anyone was listening or not.

Midway through the last month of the year 1664, one of the coldest in a century, the rope that held the cage snapped. He and the cage dropped to the stony ground. The cage smashed the remains of the skulls of his friends before it came to a rest in an awkward position between two slabs of dark rock.

Gravity pushed his body into the top of the cage, which now was pointing in a downward direction. How he had been for the previous 12 years was positively more comfortable than what he now had to deal with. Quintus attempted to summon his abilities of levitation to budge the cage, but it was useless. Not being able to do his exercises or meditation for so long left him worn out and disconnected from his talents.

As for the crows, they just laughed at him.

An hour after his fall, it began to rain lightly, heralding what would be five days of non-stop drizzle and sleet. As the cold began to further soak into his bones, Quintus asked himself how much more slow-motion obliteration he could endure. He didn't dare answer himself. His sanity was now hanging by a thread.

A day after the rain ceased, he finally had visitors.

Given a Choice

As he lay in a semi-consciousness state, Quintus heard two separate sounds. One was of agitated crows; the other was of paddles hitting water. He opened his eyes, tilted his head towards the noise that was not so typical. Moments later, three rowboats emerged from the morning mist, scaring a half-dozen crows off the gibbet.

At the bow of the lead boat was Entwistle, who wore a

fancy collared cloak trimmed with braid. Now aged in his 50s, his thinning grey hair was mostly hidden underneath a beaver hat.

A shivering, naked Quintus could do naught but stay fixed to where he was and wait for them to land. The first on the island was Entwistle. His two provost guards and five other soldiers followed. Soon enough, they found Quintus wedged among rocks in the rusty cage.

'Oh dear, oh my, did the rope fail you saint?' Entwistle asked, not expecting an answer. 'You look a right mess, in fact, more like a filthy animal than a man. What are we going to do with you, eh?' he mocked. 'How about you have a bath or a splashdown?'

And with that, Entwistle pulled out his private part and urinated on Quintus.

'Splashdown it is,' Entwistle mocked.

The urine bounced off Quintus' matted hair and beard. Dribbled off his cheeks, his chest, and shoulders. The humiliation of it all brought him to his senses, but he refused to respond, instead choosing to bury his rage.

Entwistle finished urinating but continued his heckling.

'If you plan on hanging there for another dozen years, I should have a chain made of iron,' he taunted. 'But until then, we will have to make do with some more rope.'

Entwistle nodded for three soldiers to pick Quintus up and carry him back to the gibbet, where a soldier with a fresh coil of rope waited.

Entwistle followed, talking as he went.

'In old age, I find myself softening, so I'll offer you

something saint. Let me end your needless suffering, all of its loneliness,' Entwistle said.

As the soldiers got to the gibbet and stood Quintus upright in the cage, Entwistle drew out his thin-bladed sword.

'It would only take a quick pierce to the heart to finish it all or are you fine with rotting away some more in the cage? This is the opportunity of a lifetime here.'

Quintus remained silent and blank-faced.

'So, what's it to be saint?'

Quintus still didn't reply. Instead, he turned his head to look at the soldier applying the rope to the cage. This infuriated Entwistle.

'Give me an answer!' he screamed. 'A liberating death or more of the cage?'

Quintus then looked squarely at Entwistle. From somewhere deep inside himself, he discovered his long-neglected voice.

'I will never give up. I will endure,' he whispered.

'Endure? A fool's reply, but as you so wish,' Entwistle snorted. 'Either way, I will grind your bones to dust one day.'

Entwistle ordered his men to rehoist Quintus onto the gibbet. He next told his two provost guards to retrieve something from a rowboat.

Moments later, they returned with a large basket filled with severed heads. They upturned the basket, spilling the heads onto what remained of the old pile of skulls just below the rehoisted Quintus, who let out a moan of distress.

Delighted to get a reaction, Entwistle burst into a fit of laughter that lasted for at least a minute. His jackal-like howl dug into Quintus, niggling away at the mass of emotions that now simmered inside.

The still laughing Entwistle gestured towards the heads.

'Now, if you look closely, there's an Italian among this collection,' he said. 'A priest sent by Rome to confirm rumors of your pathetic existence.'

And with that, Quintus snapped.

'You butcher! I will follow you to Hell if that's what it takes. Mark my words, Entwistle. You will pay for what you have done!' he exploded.

Everyone, including Quintus, has a breaking point. The mass of fury he'd stored away had nowhere to go but out. Unrestrained, he screamed, he shouted, he shook his cage with what strength he had left.

After the initial surprise, Entwistle began to enjoy the moment for the victory he perceived it to be.

'Finally, where's your goodness now?'

Quintus roared and shook the cage some more.

'Goodness? Goodness has nothing to do with it!' Quintus screamed.

'Oh, yes, it does. For you, it means everything,' replied the man below him.

Quintus spat at Entwistle, but the phlegm went nowhere near its intended target.

'A saint no longer, just a madman stuck on a rock. My work is done!' laughed Entwistle, who waved for his men to return to their boats and leave the island.

Quintus continued screaming and shaking the cage as they rowed away. It was pure rage, uncontrollable anger. Something he'd never felt before to such an extreme. He would go on in such a manner for the rest of the day until he blacked out from exhaustion.

Three days later, he woke to find his small island and the surrounding countryside dusted with snow. It was the first time he had seen anything like it since being in the cage. It was a novelty, but it was certainly no comfort. It was just another indicator of the harshness of that winter.

The sight of the fresh heads below him, now speckled white, renewed his loathing for Entwistle. The hatred, the disgust, consumed Quintus day and night like a fever, at least until the arrival of spring when it stealthily retreated somewhere inside his humanity.

By the time summer arrived, his exhausted soul was as fragile as a gossamer thread. Luckily for him, sometime midyear, he had another visitor but one more benevolent.

The Visitor

The lake was chilly a foot beneath the surface, and Alba O'Malley caught her breath as the water rose above her chest. At her feet, cold mud squished between her toes until she lunged forward to swim. The 22-year-old managed to keep her head above water as she dog paddled towards the small rocky island where the gibbet stood. She paddled as fast as she could, mindful that a patrolling soldier might see her.

Earlier from the shoreline, Alba could see that there was a human figure inside the gibbet's cage. But the young woman knew she had to get onto the island to learn beyond doubt it was no myth that the 'saint' was still alive.

Twelve feet from the island, she could see the caged man was breathing. His chest sucking in and then expelling air. He was filthy, long-haired, and naked. The legend wasn't pretty, but it was true.

With such information, Alba hoped to rally family and friends to free the saint. No longer would they allow him to remain in such an evil condition.

The crows on the gibbet ignored her as she got onto the island, and as for Quintus, his mind was so scrambled it took him several minutes to register he had a visitor. Eventually, he managed to open his eyes. Initially, he could only make out a blurry profile. Whoever it was, they began saying something, and initially, it was difficult to understand. *It sounds like a young woman praying*, Quintus thought.

A minute later, his eyes adjusted, and he saw Alba. Her head was lowered while she recited prayers. He noticed that her underclothes were soaked and muddy and that she quivered slightly. The morning sun's rays highlighted her auburn hair.

Upon finishing her prayers, she looked at him in the cage. *What a pathetic sight I must be*, he thought.

Quintus wanted to call out to her but found he couldn't utter a single word. He could only look at her and meet her gaze. He noted her strong jawline and her kind eyes.

After several minutes the young woman softly spoke in Gaelic.

'I'm sorry I'm unable to help you now; forgive me,' she said. 'But we will be back to rescue you. I promise.'

Alba then turned away and searched the shoreline for

patrolling soldiers, and once confident there were none, she began her return.

Just as she reentered the water, Quintus found his voice.

'Thank you,' he said, but it was far too soft for her to hear.

He watched her paddle and then wade back to the shore, where she put on her jacket bodice, and petticoat that were waiting for her on a rock.

Once dressed, she returned to the wall where a crudely made nine-foot ladder awaited. She climbed up it, and when she got to the top of the wall, she pulled it over with a short rope, so she could use it to get her down to the other side.

And then she was gone.

The important thing about Alba's visit is that it gave Quintus hope. After living so long in that cage, hope in himself, others, and his mission had nearly run dry. Without hope in goodness, a human is prone to, sooner or later, smash themselves to pieces. No matter how mythical or mystical he or she may be.

Quintus now had enough hope — in himself, in the Gods, and his master — but only just. Despite Alba's good intentions, he had two more years alone on that small rocky island.

Free

It was just after midnight, and the glow of a full summer's moon guided two small rowboats toward the island. Each boat carried three young Irishmen. Among them, a large red-headed individual named Seamus O'Malley held a lantern.

The boats reached the island, and the men hopped out. They made their way toward the shadowy outline of the gibbet. Yes, they were fearful and cautious.

They were likewise appalled when the lantern's light revealed the pile of rotted and crumbling skulls under the cage. More than one of them made the sign of the cross across his chest.

Seamus lifted the lantern up high. Its light allowed him to see Quintus' figure in the cage. The 17-year-old cleared his throat.

'You have suffered the unimaginable. Finally, we have come to set you free,' Seamus said.

Quintus was unable to reply. His sanity, by this stage, was frayed. He remained detached from reality. Even as they freed him from the rusty cage and carried him to one of their boats, he was unsure if he was hallucinating or not.

Saint or No Saint

Sitting in a wooden bathtub half-filled with water, Quintus leaned forward as a stout woman of age used a sponge to scrub layers of filth and dead skin from his back.

Using a sharp knife, she had already hacked away at his matted hair and beard, which were both filthy with a vast array of minute critters.

The water in the tub would have to be changed five times that day to clean him properly.

The tub was set up under an apple tree in between

the stone hut that sheltered the animals during the winter months and two larger windowless cottages that housed the O'Malley clan.

There was no way that the ruddy-faced woman was going to permit such a grimy body into their home in such a state. Saint or no saint.

Quintus did not protest. In fact, he had not yet said anything since being freed from the cage.

Midway into his third bath, Seamus brought another pail of water and some fresh clothes for Quintus to change into. After putting them aside, he sat on a stool and pulled out a clay smoking pipe from his pocket. He offered it to Quintus, who, with a shake of the head, declined while saying his first word to them, which was 'no.'

'Yes! Good, you can talk,' Seamus said, grinning.

The woman rolled her eyes at her nephew.

'And where'd you get that tobacco from, Seamus?' she asked.

'It's from Youghal in County Cork.'

'Who gave it to you?'

'Can't give away all my secrets now, can I? I only thought that maybe our good guest would fancy some.'

'Have some respect; he doesn't want, nor need your pipe or your silly ways,' she scolded him.

Seamus' grin only got bigger.

'Oh, now Aunt Mary, he can surely make up his mind on that; he's a big fella and now a man of liberty,' he cheekily challenged while packing tobacco into the pipe.

'Don't mind the boy, sir; he knows no better,' the aunt told Quintus.

Seamus good-naturedly winked at Quintus.

Such unabashed friendliness forced the filthy man not only to smile but to burst out laughing and then laugh some more as it truly dawned on him that all the horrors of the cage were now behind him.

Quintus' laughter continued for 15 minutes and was so contagious that Aunt Mary and Seamus joined the hysterics. Other family members, ranging from toddlers to the elderly, exited the cottages and joined in laughing with the saint. They laughed the way only survivors can appreciate.

The Church Ruins

It took Quintus and Seamus ten minutes to stroll from the cottages to the ruins of the parish church. While they walked, the young Irishman did most of the talking. All the O'Malley clan were talkative, but Seamus was the best of them. They were a rowdy and cheerful bunch, despite what they had endured since Cromwell's armies first arrived.

Beyond 'yes' or 'no,' Quintus had spoken little during the past seven days since he was cleaned in the bathtub. He just wasn't used to talking yet. Seamus' aunt told the family to be patient, as the poor man had suffered unimaginable horrors.

From the youngest to the oldest, they understood Quintus was more than a man. He was considered a saint, set apart by Heaven. Someone able to survive years in a gibbet. But given their salt-of-the-earth qualities, the O'Malleys naturally viewed Quintus as one of their own and not someone to be revered. They quickly and quietly accepted his perceived oddities, his strange standing exercises, and how he would sit eyes shut with his legs folded upon each other under the apple tree for hours on end.

Seamus' childhood was full of stories about the saint locked in the gibbet cage. A legend now living with his family, it was the finest thing that had occurred in his short life thus far. So, it was a welcome development when Quintus began talking just as they arrived at the eastern side of the church ruins.

'Last time I saw the church, it had been set on fire,' Quintus said quietly, nodding at the ruins. 'They'd already put the priest to the sword, laid waste to most of this side of the river. It was horrific. This whole area was once prosperous and peaceful. Hopefully, one day it will be thus again,' he added.

'There have been whispers about rebuilding the church, but there's little chance of that happening any time soon,' Seamus said. 'Whether we like it or not, we're a subjugated people.'

That simple fact left a silence between them for several minutes until the sound of a large bird landing nearby took their attention. By the heavy beat of its wings, Quintus knew it was a crow. From the corner of his eye, he saw it perched on the remains of the church's sole remaining spire. He picked up an acorn-sized stone and threw it at the bird, which flew off unharmed, cawing as it went.

'I loathe crows,' Quintus said.

Seamus grunted in agreement.

'Aunt Mary believes they're a servant of the devil,' he said. 'Hand reared and trained by Entwistle himself, she'd say.'

It was the first time anybody had mentioned Entwistle's name in Quintus' company.

'Entwistle — what happened to him?' he asked. 'I've been under the presumption he's dead. The air is lighter, and there's less dread than there once was.'

The young Irishman scowled.

'That feckin' fop and his two lackeys are no more. Some say the fairies got to them, others say it was his own men that did them in after discovering he was in league with the devil,' Seamus said. 'It's a pity they didn't end them earlier. Some believed they'd been already cursed because of what they did to you,' he added and then continued. 'After Entwistle was gone, some of his soldiers opened the wall's gates so we could come and get you. There were earlier attempts by others to free you or to even just see if you were alive, which mostly failed,' he said. 'Some doubted you even existed. But Alba, she never doubted the truth of the matter.'

Quintus looked at Seamus and asked a question he intuitively already knew the answer to.

'Who is Alba?'

'She visited you out on the lake around two years ago. She swam out there to see if it was true about you. You remember?'

Quintus softly gestured, acknowledging that he did.

'I initially thought I was imagining things,' he replied.

'She wanted to free you, but us — all da boys — were hesitant, afraid of Entwistle if I'm, to be honest. By herself, she couldn't do it, but she could learn the truth,' Seamus said.

'She family?'

'Older sister who was truly the best of us. She died three months after visiting you. Plague got her.'

Learning of what happened to the young woman cut Quintus deeply. She was like an angel to him when she visited. He subtly shifted his stance and turned so to hide his sadness while offering commiserations.

'I'm truly sorry to hear that,' he said.

Seamus nodded.

'Before she saw you, she'd been dreaming of a funny old man with a long beard riding a half-dragon half-lion looking kinda thing,' he said. 'This old fella was talking to her in Latin, she said. Begging her to go see you,' he added.

Quintus mulled over what Seamus had just told him and the significance of it, but he didn't share his thoughts. Instead, there was sad quietness between them that lasted for several minutes before he spoke.

'I'm in your debt Seamus, and I'll be eternally grateful, but I'm putting your family in danger. I should go soon,' Quintus said.

The Irishman shook his head.

'The English now no longer bother us so much. Unlike Entwistle, the new man in charge is not the murderous type, he knows he needs laborers for tilling the land, so you're welcome to stay as long as you like. Y'know, you're the perfect guest — you don't eat food, and you don't need a bed,' he quipped. 'We'd love you to stay forever.'

That made Quintus smile.

'I will have to leave one day, but I'll never forget what you and your family have done for me,' he said.

'Where will you go to Quintus? France or Spain?'

'I'm not sure.'

Further South

Quintus was in no great rush. He never was. Time, he had plenty of it. It would be another five years before he left Ireland and the O'Malley family behind.

On the day he finally did depart, he was taken in a dingy by two Spanish sailors to a galleon anchored not far off the port city of Kinsale. Watching from a rocky beach was Seamus with two of his cousins.

Earlier, it took Quintus and his friends eight days to travel from Wexford county to reach the rendezvous point at the beach where they said their final farewells. Plenty of district folk wanted to be there for the sendoff, but they didn't want to attract undue attention from the English.

Quintus was well-loved by the people of Wexford who he offered hope to. He set up a secret school that gave Irish children in the area a chance at an education. There he taught Latin, history, reading, writing, and calculation. For a dozen or so adults, he also taught advanced building techniques, including masonry. To assist those seeking a new life abroad, he gave Spanish lessons. In all, it made it possible for the O'Malleys and other Irish folks to one day become industrious and respected citizens in the Spanish city of Malaga.

As for Quintus, he was going in the opposite direction, somewhere into the unknown. Seven weeks after leaving Ireland, he landed in the New Kingdom of Granada (today's Colombia) and steadily made his way north, biding his time for the end of days. He just hoped he'd never run across Meng's reincarnation again.

CHAPTER IV

A Murder of Crows

QUINTUS WAS SEATED on a train that made its way westwards through Nevada. The year was 1871, just seven years since the state became part of the Union. He was seated in a second-class carriage beside a loquacious middle-aged man with the surname of Green, who was fascinated by a newspaper report on the discovery of giant skeletal remains.

'These half-dozen giants were from nine to ten feet tall, and they had six digits on each of their hands and feet,' Green exclaimed, holding his newspaper. 'Incredible. Who knows how many other things are under all those mounds in the Midwest,' he said.

'But then again, they'll print anything to sell penny papers these days,' he added.

Quintus nodded. He was familiar with the mounds and the Indian legends of giants made extinct because they lacked a sense of decency. He had no doubt that giants once existed, Roman historians, such as Titus Flavius, wrote as much as well. Other cultures likewise had similar tales.

As Green continued to read his newspaper, Quintus looked out the window at the passing high-desert country. Decades before large numbers of Europeans arrived, he passed through the region on saddleback. It was then a land inhabited by remnants of three tribes — the Paiute, the Shoshone, and the Washoe — those who survived introduced diseases. He was not there to see how the sparsely populated tribes later fared against the powerful pale-skinned newcomers. He correctly guessed the likely outcome. The clash of cultures he witnessed in the Americas over the course of 200 years was not a pretty thing.

But that is how history rolled, and he had to roll with it whether he liked it or not. He had to wait until he was called upon. Whenever that was to be.

It was as if Green read Quintus' mind when he began talking about the misery he'd witnessed in displaced native communities.

'Man, or beast, all shall suffer. But "It is through much tribulation that we enter the kingdom of Heaven," so says the Apostle Paul,' Green said before shifting the conversation to Quintus.

'So why are you going to San Francisco for, work I presume?'

'Yes, to help with some building there, a new city hall,' Quintus answered.

'It can be a wild city, so be on your guard. I know of a rooming house on fashionable Kearny Street if you need one.'

Before Quintus could respond, a mustached conductor passed through the carriage, making an announcement as he went.

'Okay folks, two minutes and we will pull up in Reno. We'll be stationed there till 3 o'clock, and when the whistle blows, we then continue on,' the conductor said. 'What's more, it looks like it might rain outside; storm clouds are gathering, so don't wander off too far without an umbrella or coat.'

Soon enough, the coal-fired locomotive and its carriages pulled up at the Reno train station. Once it stopped, Quintus stood from his seat and stretched his body. He hadn't been able to exercise or meditate since the train left Nebraska three days earlier.

As the steam engine calmed down, he heard the familiar swoop of crows landing on the station's timber roof just outside. It wasn't long till several of them were cawing.

Given his Ireland experience, such sounds got under his skin. No matter if it occurred ten or a thousand years ago, he could recall everything as if it only happened yesterday, which could either be a blessing or a curse.

The crows' cawing rebounded inside the carriage, forcing him out of his seat and wanting out, away from the noise. Green offered some advice as he moved past, carrying his sack coat and a wide-brimmed hat.

'Remember, at 3 o'clock, the train departs,' Green said. 'Have a nice stroll around town.'

Terrible Trio

Sherman Chivington was a mean man, as loathsome as they came. Ever since he was a boy, he had enjoyed inflicting pain on living creatures, people included. His heartbroken mother was mystified why her third son had such a cruel streak about him.

It was perhaps a small blessing in disguise that she was no longer of this world when he committed his first serious crime at the age of 23. Somehow, he managed to avoid a conviction for the stabbing death of a Boston saloon owner, a crime he'd drunkenly brag about over the years that followed. Chivington still kept the bone-handled knife he used as proof of his supposed fierceness and flashed it around while recounting his tale to anyone willing to listen. It was during such a bragging session that he met George and Karl Grossman — twin brothers just shy of 40 — who had escaped from a lunatic asylum near New York City.

For reasons mysterious to all three, they hit it off and became a tight-knit gang committing acts of wickedness across five states, with Chivington leading the way. Most of their lawbreaking was committed in the bigger cities on the Atlantic, where it was easiest to find prey, mostly fresh-off-the-boat immigrants.

Now they were heading west, seeking to somehow strike it rich in San Francisco's lucrative gambling scene. To get there, they chose to travel by train, which happened to be the very same one that Quintus was on in 1871. They were third-class passengers in the seventh carriage on a journey that was meant to take four days.

In a bid not to attract attention, they tried being on their best behavior, but on day three, they began drinking. By the time they got to Reno, they'd been blind drunk for six hours, and things, well, they got out of hand.

The Fury

With hat in hand, Quintus twice walked up and down Reno's dusty main street. Such an exercise was meant to help clear his mind, but he was shadowed by the crows first seen back at the railway station. They cawed at Quintus and made short flights from roof to roof to keep pace with him as he strolled. It was as if they were blaming him for the approaching thunderstorm that threatened the town.

The crows followed Quintus until he returned to the station's timber building which he entered and cut through to get to the platform where he found a drama unfolding, one ugly enough to make him promptly forget annoying birds.

Right there in front of him, on the platform, the Grossman brothers were bashing a family man who stood little chance of defending himself. He was cowering on the ground, holding up his arms for protection as fists rained from above.

Chivington was standing to the side and cheering on the fight. He'd been assigned to ensure no one would try intervening in the one-sided brawl. He'd already shoved the family man's 11-year-old son away and warned off the wife. She was now holding her crying boy while pleading for help from any of the dozen or so other people on the platform and from anyone inside the carriages. When Quintus stumbled onto the scene, she turned to him.

'Stop them, please. They're killing him!' she begged.

Chivington cut in, screaming drunken threats and pointing at Quintus.

'Don't even think about it. If you come any closer, I'll kill you. I'll kill y'all!' he yelled.

For several seconds Quintus stood holding down Chivington's mad stare, which had something familiar to it.

'Yeah, I'll kill y'all!' Chivington repeated.

Since Quintus left the mountain, there'd been a half-dozen times where he used the fighting skills his master taught him. On each of those occasions, he did as little harm as possible, and he left those he fought with no long-term injuries. Before it got to that stage, he always sought a peaceful resolution to any situation, but sometimes this met mixed results, like in Ireland.

Initially, he was unsure how to handle what was happening on the platform, but the sight of the innocent family being terrorized infuriated him.

Chivington sensed that Quintus would not skulk away, and he yelled to his partners, still bashing the family man.

'Fellas! Just finish with that chump and give me a hand ripping the head offa this clown, will you!' he yelled, referring to Quintus.

'It will be fun, come and join in,' Chivington manically laughed.

That mad laughter. It was the same as Entwistle's. *Is it him?* Quintus thought.

'Right there, Romeo, just don't stand there — come get

me,' Chivington taunted as he pulled out his bone-handled knife from his pocket and readied to use it.

'C'mon now, don't be shy!' Chivington yelled while laughing some more.

It's him, for sure. Even looks like him.

The memory of Entwistle and what occurred in Ireland now hit Quintus like a ton of bricks. A swell of emotion began at his feet; ran up through his gut and into his brain, where it exploded, and he snapped. He let his wide-brimmed hat fall from his hands, and he advanced towards Chivington. By the time the hat landed on the platform, he was in striking distance of the madman, who had little time to react or dodge what would come — a furious right hook punch.

It was hard and blunt. Much more powerful than what a mere man could throw. There was little art or technique to it, but it knocked Chivington off his feet and onto his back. It also shattered his jaw and knocked out four teeth. If he lived beyond that day, the punch would have permanently disfigured his face.

In a daze, Chivington somehow managed to sit himself up. He'd dropped his knife, and it was now nowhere to be seen. He spat out the loose teeth and looked at Quintus standing above him with fists raised, fire in his eyes.

'Hell of a punch. Why'd you go do that?' Chivington managed to slur from his broken mouth.

'I'm your comeuppance,' Quintus told him.

Chivington chortled at the reply, blood and saliva dripping from his lips.

There was enough time for Quintus to step back and

deal with the brothers beating the family man. He also could have left Chivington as is. The drunk was no longer a threat. There was no fight left in him. But Quintus didn't move, nor did he drop his arms. He kept them raised, primed for another swing. Chivington offered Quintus a sneering smile that dared him to throw another punch.

'C'mon, tough guy. Don't just stand there. Do it,' he mumbled.

The loathing in Quintus was more than willing, but before his downward punch hit, Chivington had a look of triumph about him. A glint in his eyes. The same mad glint that both Meng and Entwistle once had.

This punch was even more powerful than the initial blow, and it killed Chivington outright. He slumped over into a lifeless pile on the platform with Quintus standing over him.

The brothers belatedly saw what had happened, and they went to rush Quintus, who quickly dealt with them just as brutally. Powerful blows to the head, the temple region, killed them both. He now found himself standing over three men who he killed with his bare hands.

It wasn't long until numbness replaced the rage that drove him to commit what a judge would undoubtedly rule as either murder or voluntary manslaughter if it ever came to that. Soon enough, dread mixed with doubt emerged. A sense of shame followed. He could hear Tai's words in the back of his mind warning against this type of madness.

A grey shadow cast over him. Thunder rumbled above, and heavy rain cursorily followed. Through the downpour, Quintus saw the woman assist her beaten-up husband to his feet. She glanced at Quintus, and he saw the fear still in her eyes.

Now drenched and doubting himself, he began feeling tired, and sapped of energy. He left the dead bodies and made his way up the platform. He felt someone looking at him, and he turned to a carriage, where at a window, Green was wearing a look of disbelief.

'Mister, what have you done?' Green asked.

Quintus ignored the question, and, through the downpour, he made his way off the platform. At the front of the station, he stole a horse, a chestnut American Saddlebred, and rode away, heading south. Our hero was now a killer and a thief. A fugitive.

Decision to Be Made

Quintus placed a shard of mirror on the outside windowsill, so it could best capture the light of the early morning sun to help him shave. Next, he lathered soap and spread it across part of his face. After shaving off his stubble with a straight razor, he hand scooped water from a leather bucket and splashed it across his face. Drops of water fell to the sandy Mexican ground.

With a cotton rag, he patted down his cheeks and took one last look at his reflection in the mirror. Five years since the events in Reno, he'd aged equally as much. His hairline had climbed back an inch, and there were a few wrinkles on his forehead. He now looked like a typical gringo around 40 years of age.

It was a superficial reminder of how much of what Tai

had trained him for had been lost. Likewise, he now had no supernormal powers to speak of. No ability to do without food or sleep, and he certainly couldn't free float down any mountains. His limited celestial eye vision, which allowed him at times to see fairies and ethereal beings, disappeared as well. Not that the Franciscan monks who took him in were aware of these issues. To them, he was a shy, sincere character of few words. They were somewhat more doubtful when he first stumbled upon their mission, in a half-dead state on a half-dead horse, half a decade earlier.

Despite occasional drunkenness during his first year at the mission, in time, this man, who the Franciscans knew as Quintus Acardi, gained their trust while remaining an enigma. He did not talk of his past, nor did they enquire. They were though impressed by his knowledge of construction and use of Latin. Quickly, he became their go-to man capable of any building repair work, and in that way, he earned his keep. He was busy and often in demand.

The Franciscans had nine mission churches in the Sonoran Desert area, a few constructed during the 1600s with sun-dried mud bricks or stone. A series of repairs at one of them — a two-day ride away — was planned after that morning shave. There, Quintus would spend several weeks repairing the church's interior and building an exterior wall.

Following his shave, he took the soapy water to a small garden at the front of the mission, where he used it to water a lemon tree. It wasn't much, but every drop counts in the Sonoran. As the water disappeared into the soil, he heard a young squeal of laughter behind him. Three native Tohono

O'odham children from the village served by the mission ran up to him, wanting his help to squash a black scorpion they had cornered in the nearby cemetery. He waved them off with a smile, he knew they were savvy enough to handle such things themselves.

After packing supplies, building materials, and tools into a horse-drawn cart, Quintus left the mission. The horse that pulled the cart was the very same chestnut American Saddlebred he stole in Reno. But he didn't need to be reminded by the horse about his killing of the three thugs. Internally he'd been stewing over it for the past five years. The guilt was there when he woke up. It was there when he fell asleep. Who really was that first madman killed at Reno? Likewise, who were the other two killed?

During his trip to the church needing repairs, he mulled over more. *Was everything now in vain? Was there any hope of clemency? Was there still a purpose?* His questions may have gone unanswered, but Quintus was now at the point where he had to make a choice himself.

It could also be fair to say it was one forced upon him by circumstances. You see, his once acute memory was now fading fast, and for someone like Quintus, that was fatal. On occasion, he wasn't even sure who he was. He now only had vague recollections of his life as a Roman soldier, and his memory of his time with Tai was starting to dim. Quintus knew if he lost White Dragon Mountain, if he lost those memories, then there was no hope of his resuming the Way. He would live and die as any normal man does. If that were the case, then he'd be dead within several decades. *And then what?* he wondered. *Eternity in Hell?*

By the time Quintus and his horse-drawn cart reached an overnight camping area situated on a dry riverbank, he had made up his mind. Ultimately, he knew he had to resume his practice. He had come too far to throw in the towel. He could not give up. The crimes he committed in Reno had to be left behind, somehow reconciled if that was at all possible.

After lighting a fire and eating dried beef, he sat to meditate and then did his Tao Yin exercises for the first time in five years. As he did so, he was somewhat rusty. He just hoped his master, if he was watching, would take him back and that the Gods would forgive him.

While it was the beginning of a comeback, I must tell you, he remained among those destined for Hell over what he had done. Once you're condemned to such a place, it's no small feat to have it reversed.

The Great Unseen

In another realm — yet physically still meditating in his cave — Tai was exultant when Quintus returned to the Way. Since the Reno incident, he had been more than concerned and worried. Despite what occurred on the railway platform, he remained by his disciple's side. He was unseen and mostly unnoticed but was busy, often blocking other unseen beings that sought to harm his disciple. These beings are what you would describe as demons. If you could perceive them, you'd see they come in all shapes and sizes.

After Quintus decided to return to the Way, these nefarious creatures sent by Hell attacked in droves but luckily for Quintus, Tai was able to fend them off, much to the displeasure of the 13 demon kings. What was once just a passing interest in Quintus had become an obsession for the 13. Following what transpired in Reno, the demon kings thought he was now theirs. He'd already been given as much mercy as Hell could possibly muster, they reasoned.

If these sinister beings got cheap thrills from anything, it would be watching a good man fall, especially one of which there was so much expectation. If he was among the best examples of humanity, then there is little hope for the rest of them, something they repeatedly told each other after the punching deaths of Chivington and the mad brothers.

It is true that the demon kings had a point, to an extent at least, but it was self-serving. The incident in Reno was actually a setup. The demon kings planned it all. They even called in the crows to set the mood. Another test of worthiness for Quintus, they said, just like Ireland and the gibbet, which they argued was inconclusive.

But now that's history.

Thanks to his master's unseen protection, Quintus successfully returned to the righteous path, back to the Way. After the decision on the dry riverbank, he spent another five years helping the Franciscans. Then he moved on and drifted around Mexico for several decades. His abilities quickly returned but plateaued to a point where they weren't as powerful as before the Reno killings, and his celestial eye vision never returned. As for sleep or food, if compared to regular folk, he was supernormal, but he needed some. A meal every second day was fine. Two hours of sleep daily was best. His aging stopped, and he regained the appearance of someone around the age of 30.

Just prior to World War I, he left Mexico and returned to the United States. He may not have served in that conflict, but he did in the second one as a U.S. Army medic. Given the scale of that fight, he found it hard not to get swept up in it. After 300 or so years of absence, he was back in Europe, this time patching up the bodies of soldiers and civilians from both sides.

At the war's end, Quintus returned to America. Unimpressed by modern building methods, he took advantage of the GI Bill and got himself an education, and became a history teacher.

In early 1952 he again changed his surname, this time from Hill to Sheehan, and he ended up in the quiet city of Boise, Idaho. There he met a woman named Kaitlyn, who he married in 1957. It was his first intimate relationship ever. Tai earlier warned him about sentiment but getting married seemed to Quintus the fitting thing to do at that time and place. He was tired of wandering and waiting for something that had yet to happen, plus he fell head over heels in love with her. But yes, there'd certainly be complications that he'd have to somehow navigate in time.

Nevertheless, in 1961 they had a daughter and named her Abby.

One thing he discovered was that being a parent and the head of a family changes everything.

From below, the demon kings were increasingly furious at what they saw. They couldn't stomach the fact that Quintus was living everyday life in what was one of the most prosperous and freest societies in history. Now they had to destroy him to prove a point amongst themselves that no one was beyond their reach if they so deemed it.

At first, the demon kings shrieked, cursed, and moaned about it.

'How dare he!' 'Send him here, down to us!' 'I want to flay his soul!'

In time, they calmed down and figured they needed to take another course of action, one they felt was more proactive. They knew they had to be cautious; they didn't want a wrathful Tai and his White Dragon revisiting them, despite promises made centuries ago.

For some time, they argued how to carry it out, eventually deciding if they were to decisively destroy Quintus without risking Tai entering their lair, they'd need to take the old Taoist out in advance. It ended up being something that all 13 of the pit agreed they should have done much earlier.

Urban Life

It was early-fall 1966. Quintus rode his English racer through a middle-class Boise neighborhood. He was conservatively dressed as a high-school teacher would be in Idaho during that period. As he pedaled, he turned into a street lined with trees in the beginning stages of shedding their leaves. He rode past four pampered homes until veering into the driveway of number 45, a timbered double-story house painted off-white. His home.

Under the house's attached carport, Quintus stopped his bicycle and dismounted just to the side of the parked Buick Invicta station wagon. He waved to his neighbor, a squat humorless retiree called Andrei Vasiliev, who was next door up a ladder mending a broken gutter.

'Afternoon Mr. Vasiliev, another beautiful day,' Quintus said.

Vasiliev gruffly nodded while continuing his repairs.

Ignoring his neighbor's frostiness, Quintus made his way to the house's back entrance and entered a living space connected to the kitchen.

'Daddy! Yay!' exclaimed a 5-year-old girl clutching her favorite stuffed teddy bear.

'Hello there Abby girl,' Quintus said warmly.

She tackled him around the legs and looked up at him, this man who was half of her world.

'Mommy and I went to nan, and pop's and I ate cake!' Abby said.

'Aren't you lucky, did you bring me home some?' her dad asked as he playfully picked her up.

'No, all gone. None left,' she said.

'Tasted good, huh?'

'Yep.'

As Quintus held her, he looked over to his wife, Kaitlyn, who was preparing dinner in the open kitchen. She winked at him. He winked back.

'Then she spent the afternoon feeding squirrels and gossiping with the fairies in the garden,' Kaitlyn said.

'So how are those fairies?' Quintus asked his daughter as he put her down.

'Good! They said to say "Hello" to you. They think you're very, very special,' Abby said.

'Well, you must be special if they let you see them.'

'And they love mommy's poems, and when she plays the piano, they love, love, love that a lot.'

'A lot? Mommy's poems and piano?'

'Yes, and they love Dean Martin like mommy does.'

'Oh, do they now?'

'Yep.'

'Any song of his in particular?'

'Nope.'

'What about Sinatra? They like him?'

'Don't know.'

'Well, either way, those fairies have exceptional taste in music,' Quintus said as he ruffled her hair, which had the same blonde hue as his wife's.

'Dinner in 30 or so minutes, Quintus Sheehan, so you'd better go wash up and then grace us with your company again,' Kaitlyn said.

Quintus playfully lifted Abbey up again, and she squealed in delight.

'Now you stay here, princess; keep your mom company while I go shower and clean up,' he said as he put her back down.

'Yes, daddy, but hurry it up!'

'I'll certainly be fast.'

As Quintus left to go upstairs, his wife called out to him.

'After showering, can you please light the fire? It's going to be chilly tonight,' Kaitlyn said.

'Will do,' he replied, already halfway up the stairs.

'And Abby, you want to do some more drawing while

you wait for your daddy?' Kaitlyn said to her daughter, who nodded.

China Televised

The warmth of the lit fireplace in the living room took the edge off the cool night. Quintus was with Abby sitting on a rug, drawing pictures of fairies on paper with crayons. He wondered about his daughter's ability to see and communicate with these special beings who called their garden home.

Just behind them, Kaitlyn played a soft tune on an upright piano — one of Chopin's nocturnes. It was one of eight classic pieces that Kaitlyn enjoyed playing.

The music she played was soft enough to allow Quintus to hear the television situated in the corner. A news program about chaos in China was being broadcast.

'Gangs of Red Guards, most of whom are no more than teenagers, are destroying religious institutions, long-cherished traditions, and so-called antirevolutionary elements,' the program's narrator said.

The TV displayed grainy footage of fanatical young Red Guards adulating Mao Zedong, the then-chairman of the Communist Party of China. The program went on to show monasteries being looted, statues of deities being desecrated, and nuns being publicly humiliated.

'China, dear viewer, is continuing its downward spiral into Hell.'

Politics of Hatred

Like others nominated in his village, Chang Boyang was proud to be entrusted with the knowledge of where the ancient sage was hidden on White Dragon Mountain.

As a 13-year-old, he and five others of about the same age were taken by three elders to be shown what remained of the Taoist's sanctuary. At the end of their four-day trek-climb, they maintained a respectable distance from the immediate area of the terrace so as not to disturb holy ground.

The boys, now considered custodians, earlier swore to protect the sanctuary and keep its location a secret. It was expected, if need be, that they would lay down their lives to keep the sanctuary safe. Their village had numerous tales of how their ancestors built up their merit by doing just that.

But Chang and his vow were tested when the communists came decades later. In the fall of 1966, two truckloads of Red Guards, led by a tall thin 20-year-old sociopath nicknamed 'The Hammer,' arrived at the village.

The Hammer got his name due to the pickaxe he always carried. When he wasn't swinging it around, he was fond of stroking his delicate mustache. He also made it a habit of seeking shade so that his skin would remain fair.

He and his fellow Red Guards weren't welcomed in the village, but no one was brave enough to tell them so.

The villagers had viewed the Maoists as thuggish followers of an insane ideology since day one. But despite what the communists had committed throughout much of China, the valley, up until then, had managed to avoid the worst of their depredations, including the mass collectivization of rural communities and the Great Famine that followed. The villagers believed their good fortune was due to having a Taoist in the mountain as their otherworldly protector. And for the most part, they were pretty much right about that.

However, with the arrival of The Hammer and his Red Guards on that October day, it appeared to them their blessings had run out.

Not that our now middle-aged Chang understood or comprehended such things as the Red Guards arrived. Like lambs to the slaughter, Chang and the other elders gathered in the village center as ordered. There, The Hammer lectured them.

'We are not here to make friends! Chairman Mao has ordered us to rid society of old customs, old culture, old habits, and old ideas,' he shouted in a creepy squeaky kind of way. 'Elders, you must prove your worth, or the ever-glorious party shall smash you and sweep you aside!'

The Hammer then demanded that they tell him the location of the sanctuary. When no one told him what he wanted, that's when the torturing began.

Remorse

Chang wondered how the Red Guards learned of the sanctuary's existence in the first place before the torture began. Had someone in the valley unknowingly told a party snoop or a scheming official from a nearby district? But that was irrelevant now as he led The Hammer and six of his Red

Guards up White Dragon Mountain. With each step, Chang asked Heaven's forgiveness for betraying the vow he had made as a boy. He felt there was little choice when The Hammer ordered children to be tortured. The older men had earlier managed to endure.

Chang had already led the Red Guards up the mountain for four days, and their ruthless fanaticism dismayed him. Two other villagers had been tasked as porters to lug food supplies needed for the trek, and both were summarily executed once their purpose was spent.

At their last rest stop before reaching the sanctuary, Chang looked at a young Red Guard named Zhou Lijun, who sat nearby massaging a sore foot. *Perhaps this boy has some conscience left*, he thought.

Zhou felt Chang's gaze on him, and their eyes met.

'Do you really want to destroy what the Heavens have given China?' Chang quietly asked the boy.

Zhou did not immediately reply. He initially looked sideways at his nearest comrade, who was reading Mao's Little Red Book, and then returned to Chang and offered the older man a rancorous look.

'Save your talk of Heaven you old clown. All of us despise your feudal superstitions,' Zhou said. 'Great Chairman Mao has promised to lead mankind to communism. The purification process begins with the annihilation of the likes of you and the end of all your lies.'

With that, Chang knew he would not see his family again.

A minute later, The Hammer ordered them all to continue with their climb. It wasn't long till they reached the sanctuary.

Desecration

It was pitch black inside the cave, but the sound of steel hitting stone from outside could be heard. There were also muffled yells in Mandarin. Soon enough, cracks of light emerged as a pick and iron bar broke through what Quintus had built centuries earlier.

The incoming wind unsettled a layer of fine dust that covered everything inside the cavernous room. Little by little, Han Dynasty period artifacts and murals emerged.

When the cracks became the size of a small window, The Hammer and his Red Guards stopped their efforts and momentarily peered inside the cave.

The room's largest object appeared to be a life-size sculpture of a man meditating, sitting in the lotus position. As the entering breeze cleaned the statue's surface, they noted that it wore decayed clothing and that it had long hair and protruding fingernails.

The Hammer cleared additional stones and plaster from the wall, resulting in more light filling the cavern. It quickly became obvious to the Red Guard leader that the figure was not a statue but a living man — a Taoist sage in trance. Just as the villagers believed.

Such ways must be wiped from the earth, The Hammer thought as he put in extra effort to widen the entrance.

It didn't take long for the Red Guards to make a gap big enough for them to enter the cave, and once they were inside, they began trashing and looting the room. The Hammer approached the still Taoist — Tai in a meditative state.

'Take everything out, including him!' yelled The Hammer pointing at Tai.

Zhou was one of three Red Guards who dragged Tai out of the cave and onto the terrace. They unceremoniously dumped him beside the dead body of Chang, who they had clubbed to death before they began work opening the cave.

As his spiritual and physical bodies reunited, Tai slowly emerged from his deep meditative state. The three Red Guards stood over him, each unsure of what to do with this wizened, disorientated remnant of the past.

The Hammer exited the cavern, pulled out his pistol, and gave it to Zhou.

'Shoot him,' The Hammer ordered.

The teenager hesitated.

'Zhou! Battle with Heaven, fight with the earth, struggle with humans — therein lies endless joy!' The Hammer shouted.

Zhou cocked the pistol, as per how he was shown how to do a week before, and then aimed it at Tai's heart and pulled the trigger.

The shot rang out across creation.

The Funk

Quintus awoke with such a shudder he initially thought the house had just been hit by a tremor or a minor earthquake. Quickly the stillness of the room convinced him otherwise. *A dream perhaps?*

A feeling of oddness — bordering on unease — made

him sit up. Next to him, Kaitlyn slept soundly. She could sleep through a tornado without stirring if need be.

After switching on the small bedside lamp, he looked at his wristwatch. It was just before midnight. He'd only been asleep for an hour, but that's half of what he usually needed anyhow.

The bedroom door creaked open, and Abby waddled in. Without an invite, she got into her parents' bed. Quintus moved over and gave her room in the center. He puffed up the pillow for her.

'It's cold, daddy.'

'I know bubby, try and sleep.'

After two minutes, she was doing just that, and Quintus got out of bed and went into the adjoining study, where he sat at its timber desk. He put his head in his hands, trying to figure out what was amiss, but he couldn't pinpoint what.

By default, his thoughts shifted to the situation he had put himself in by losing sight of the long game. Marriage and having a family are wonderful. It was the best thing he had ever done, but one day, his wife would eventually figure he wasn't aging. How could he explain it away? Could she handle the truth and watch him stay young as she became old? The only other option was for him to abandon his mission and not follow the Way and subsequently get old and die with her. Things he should've decided on before he proposed to her. People do the darndest of things sometimes, Quintus included.

He was like this, thinking useless human thoughts, sitting in a funk, until 1 a.m. when he slipped into a slumber that lasted five fuzzy hours. Despite being at his desk, it was his longest stretch of sleep for some time. Something was indeed amiss.

The Asmodeus

In telling you this fantastical tale I'm somewhat limited in what I can convey. I must frame certain things in a way that you can relate to them, so I'll start this part of the tale by telling you about a Catholic priest who was an exorcist by trade. No, he wasn't a wayward cleric. He was legit and recently was on record describing a demon — called 'Asmodeus' — that attacks the family. Yes, there is such an entity. It's a wicked creature first mentioned in the Old Testament. The Book of Tobit, if I remember correctly. The priest said that he had fought such a fiend many times.

Tai had done so as well, but in a different reality. In other dimensions, he fought off more than one Asmodeus. Many of them had been sent by the 13 Demon Kings of the Pit to attack Quintus and those he loved after he got married.

However, Tai had found the Asmodeus easy enough to block. This, of course, changed following his death, much to the delight of the demon kings. After he was killed, the sage was separated from his body, and he was sent spiraling through the universe. In such a state, he could no longer provide protection for Quintus and his family.

This allowed the demon kings to send in an Asmodeus one last time. As instructed, it arrived early in the morning, two hours before sunup. This creature was unseen, of course, at least to the human eye. It tried to enter Quintus' house but was repelled by the goodness within it — or, to be more exact, from the love of the family who called it home. For an Asmodeus to be effective, there needed to be an existing gap in a family's relationship to take advantage of. There was no gap among the Sheehans.

The Asmodeus had been forewarned this may have been the case, so it took the next recommended course of action and entered the neighboring house of Andrei Vasiliev.

Given the disgruntled widower had a cruel past, he proved easily manipulated, as all wicked individuals are. The Asmodeus whispered dark tidings into one of Vasiliev's sleeping ears for about an hour and then departed.

When he awoke, Vasiliev was primed to do any dirty business required. As the sun emerged, the 68-year-old, wearing grubby pajamas, paced around his filthy kitchen in a silent rage until he saw Quintus exit the house next door dressed in gym gear. Vasiliev muttered evil deeds as he watched his neighbor begin exercising.

Reluctant Champion

Still dressed in pajamas, Abby played with the sparkling, wonderful things in a bronze jewelry bowl that usually sat on top of a chest of drawers in her parents' room.

Her mother was close by, making up the double bed and tucking in sheets. As Kaitlyn pulled up the cover, her thoughts were of her husband, whose only fault, she believed, was his lack of ambition. Recently he declined an offer from his school that would have made him deputy headmaster. If he took it, the next promotion would have naturally been headmaster, and she knew that is what the school wanted.

A year earlier, Quintus had reluctantly taken on the role as head of the history department. Everyone admired him for his obvious qualities both as a teacher and person. Everyone but himself.

But his humble nature was likewise one of the many manly traits that she loved about him. He never had a harsh word to say about anyone. Never in their time together had she seen him lose his temper, nor had they got anywhere near having an argument.

Yet he was an enigma in other ways. Kaitlyn was sure he knew everything there was to know about her, but she felt that was not the case the other way around. She did not know much about his youth apart from how he was an orphan. He rarely discussed his backstory, including his time in the war. Nor did he care much to talk with her about those oriental exercises he did, typically very early in the morning when she was still asleep.

'They're something I just picked up and like to do,' Quintus said when she first asked about them. No conversation followed. He instead preferred to talk at length about their life together or about their daughter, who she now noticed was pushing a footstool towards a bedroom window.

'Where are you going with that young lady?'

'To watch daddy,' was the matter-of-fact reply.

Upon getting to the window, Abby stood on the stool and looked out the window to see her father below in the garden doing his Tao Yin exercises.

'What's daddy doing?' Abby asked her mother, who came up alongside her.

'He is exercising,' said Kaitlyn.

Abby wasn't fully sure what that meant, so she pushed open the window.

'Daddy! What are you doing? Are you gardening?'

Fairy Talk

Dressed for work, Quintus tipped the last dregs of his coffee into the kitchen sink. As he wiped his hands, he felt a tug on one of his pant legs.

'The fairies want me to tell you something,' said Abby, who stood beside him, chewing on a piece of toast spread with honey.

'And what's that, Abby?'

'They think you are very, very old. Like super-duper old. Dinosaur old,' she said, emphasizing the last description with a dramatic facial expression.

'Well, you inform those gossiping fairies that I'm certainly not that old,' Quintus said while winking at her.

He then kissed her on the head and made his way toward the back door.

'See you after school, Abby girl. You look after mommy,' he said, nodding towards Kaitlyn at the kitchen table finishing her breakfast.

'Quintus try to be home early, please,' Kaitlyn said. 'Theo and Julia and the kids are coming by at five-ish for dinner, okay.'

'Roger that,' he replied. 'You want to go to Lake Pend Oreille for our next week away?'

'Sure. You'd better go, or you'll be late. Enjoy work. I love you.'

'Love you too,' were his parting words.

News from Charlie Simpson

Sitting at his staff-room desk, Quintus corrected essays submitted by an ancient history class about how the modern world was influenced by the Romans. He was midway into marking one focusing on the calendar, when he heard someone running down the hallway outside.

It didn't sound like the run of a teenager. It was labored and untrained. It was Charlie Simpson, the slightly overweight biology teacher. He came to the door, sweating profusely. His bulging eyes searched the room. His stare fixed on Quintus, who he frantically waved to.

'Quintus!'

'What's up Charlie?'

'Your house, it's on fire!' Charlie yelled, somewhat louder than intended.

The dozen or so other teachers in the room turned their heads to watch Quintus exit the room with Charlie, who would drive him to his home.

The next day the house fire was on the front page of the city's newspaper. It wasn't that a house had been burnt down that gave it the newsworthiness as a front-page lead. It was the distressing fact that the fire killed Kaitlyn and Abby and that it had been lit by their neighbor Vasiliev who later hung himself from a beam in his own house before police arrived.

Out of respect and real sorrow for Quintus, the school closed for the rest of the week, but he never returned to teach.

To Wander

In the shade of a large elm tree, Quintus sat near the roadside somewhere in rural Washington state. His clothes were filthy. He had a motley beard and unkempt hair. That's what happens after three weeks of walking country roads like a lonely ghost.

The day after his wife's and daughter's funeral, he grabbed a small rucksack that survived the fire and just took to the roads, rambling his way north. Within one week, he'd ambled out of Idaho and into the top of Oregon and then onwards some more.

Now, in Washington, he didn't care that the coming winter bit through his clothes. Physical discomfort and deprivation at this stage mattered very little. He just wanted to walk and outpace his misery.

By the time he reached that roadside tree, the pain in his heart had dulled a bit. He had a shoe off and was trying to fix a hole in it with a bit of cardboard when a police cruiser pulled up on the opposite side of the road. Its driver, a middle-aged state trooper, wound down his window.

'Hey buddy, what're you doing out here, all alone?' he asked.

Quintus didn't reply. His attention remained on repairing his shoe.

'Hate to say it, but there's no vagrancy in this county, so you will need to move on,' the trooper said.

Vagrant, derived from the Latin word vagari — to wander, Quintus thought as he wedged the cardboard further into the shoe's toe.

He looked up at the cop and gave him a half-hearted smile.

'Yeah, I'll be on my way shortly. Just fixing something,' he said.

'Okay, I'll be driving back this way in about an hour. I sure don't want to find you still here. If I do, I'll have to put you in a cell for the night, and I don't want to have to do that,' the trooper said, not expecting or wanting a reply. He then drove off.

Quintus put his shoe back on, got to his feet, and shouldered his rucksack. He readied himself to resume his walk while thinking about the last time he saw Kaitlyn and Abby. Kaitlyn was talking about friends coming over, while Abby was talking about the fairies who shared their backyard. He wondered how the fairies were feeling now. They'd still be grieving, he guessed, for such little creatures, they were certainly big-hearted.

Quintus pushed out such painful thoughts. He looked to the mountainous horizon ahead and began to walk towards it. Within ten days, he was in Canada.

CHAPTER V

Today

In the cabin of the hovering Bell helicopter, a family of five South Koreans, all with face masks on, took holiday snaps of Athabasca Glacier below them. Upfront in the cockpit, their heavily bearded pilot deftly handled the controls. It was Quintus.

When the half-hour joy flight over this part of the Canadian Rockies finished, Quintus landed the chopper at the Alpine Heli Tours' helipad, where the tourists exited to be escorted to a waiting minivan.

After the Bell's engine cut, he got out and made his way to the company office, a somewhat quaint building in the clichéd fashion of a small Swiss chalet.

Inside the office, framed photos covered the wall showing the company in better times. Some featured the bearded Quintus and Frank, the 76-year-old chain smoker, who sat at the manager's desk talking on the phone as he entered.

'So, there's no other course of action I can take?' Frank said on the call while waving Quintus to go grab something from the kitchen area. To give him some privacy, Quintus did so. He knew Frank and the company were in dire straits; things had been coming to a head for some time ever since the Covid-19 pandemic mauled tourism.

Drawing hot water from an electric urn, Quintus made a cup of coffee. Not far away, Frank's 13-year-old grandson, Zac, surfed through channels on a small television.

'Hey Quintus, how're you doing?' the boy asked.

'Good Zac and you?'

'Wi-Fi isn't working anymore.'

'Wi-Fi not working. Embrace it. Read a book.'

'Nah, I'll watch TV, which Grandad calls the idiot's delight. Got a joke?'

'Of course,' Quintus said. 'What do you call a pig who knows karate?'

'Dunno. What?'

'Pork chop.'

The boy laughed. 'That's dumb, but I like it,' he said while stopping on a news report featuring an on-the-street interview with an obese middle-aged balding man dressed in a suit. The supertitle at the bottom of the screen identified him as Chuck Goyette.

'The Australians are in a pickle with what's occurring to their agricultural sector, something I prophesized months ago, and I can add that it's only going to worsen,' the televised Goyette said. 'Famine is moving his way through the Aussie outback but, to be honest, a bit too slow for my liking, yet it is what it is. However, Famine is really the least of your problems,' he said.

'What do you mean by that?' asked the off-camera reporter.

'Well, you can wait and see, or you can do your research and check what I have posted online at Temple Science Ministries.com or read my social media feed. It's all there, at least everything that I've said thus far. The world's end is coming very soon, just around the corner in fact but whether you can accept it or not is not my concern.'

Disinterested, Zac grunted and changed channels.

More news.

This time a goose-stepping military parade in North Korea was accompanied by the voice of a news anchor.

'The White House has accused China's government of handing over advanced missile technology to the North Koreans,' said the anchor. 'It's a dramatic turnaround from a month ago when officials from Pyongyang and Washington were talking up prospects of a summit.'

Zac changed the channel again; this time, he stopped on a rerun of the American game show Family Feud. He sighed in relief and stayed with that.

Quintus heard Frank finish his call. He looked over to see his boss peering outside at the tourists driving off in the minibus. Frank lit up a cigarette as Quintus approached.

'What's the latest?' Quintus asked with a kind tone.

'No surprises. It's just now official, we're totally fin-ished. As of a minute ago, we're no more,' Frank replied as he began to shuffle some papers. 'The bank is sending in their evaluators tomorrow, and they'll end up taking everything. Three decades and it's come to this. Such are the times that test men's souls.'

Quintus was Frank's last full-time staff member. Others had long gone.

'They'll be managing severance pay for you,' Frank continued. 'I'm no longer allowed to touch the books it seems.'

'No need. For that, just tell them I don't want it,' Quintus said as he sat in a chair in front of the desk opposite Frank.

'Quintus, take it. And I owe you money from that personal loan,' Frank said.

'Forget about that, Frank, seriously. We've spoken about it. I'm in a good position. I got plenty of cash but nothing to spend it on.'

'Damn it, it's no small amount I owe you, Quintus.'

'Yeah, but it's been canceled, Frank. It's settled.'

'C'mon Quintus.'

'Frank, you don't owe me anything. Not a cent. You and Linda; you're like family. Don't think about it. There's no need to burden yourself over it. You've got other things to worry about.'

Frank sighed again and took a moment to compose himself and then looked at Quintus and nodded in thanks. 'If I win the lottery, you'll be the first to know,' Frank said. 'Meanwhile, the whole world's going to hell in a handbag. Just don't get old and jaded like me, Quintus.'

'Well, you're not alone there,' Quintus replied.

After a brief pause of silence, the two men went on to talk some more and did so for half an hour, mostly about better times before the virus. Frank predominantly did the talking, and just as dusk arrived, he passed Quintus a slip of paper.

'Hope you don't mind, but I've phoned around,' Frank said. 'Don't feel obligated; they're just some suggestions.'

Quintus looked at the contact details scribbled on the paper.

'Not in Canada but in the States. They're good operators, both who'd like to meet you about flying choppers for them if you wanted,' Frank said. 'They're a bit of a way from here, but they're trustworthy and solid enough despite the last couple of years. One's in Reno, Nevada and the other is in southern California.'

The mention of Reno stung Quintus a bit, but it didn't show in his manner.

'Reno?' Quintus asked.

'Yeah, Reno, nice place in parts; a guy there by the name of Johnny Pence runs a recreational helicopter fleet,' Frank said. 'You been to Reno?'

'While back,' Quintus said. 'The gesture is appreciated, Frank, thanks.'

'Least I could do. Johnny is with Flying Cowboys, a good outfit, they say, even if it has a silly name. I can't vouch for the pay, though. Heck, you're a fine pilot plus a mechanical whiz; you could get a job anywhere on the planet,' Frank said as he stubbed out his cigarette. 'Besides, it'll probably do you a world of good to get off that mountain of yours.'

Rare Dreams

Given he no longer had a job to go to, Quintus, the next day, sat on the porch of his mountain cabin and soaked in the view. Its outlook and peaceful seclusion reminded him of White Dragon Mountain. To the rest of the outside world, it may as well not even have existed, and that's how he liked it. There was no road directly leading to the cabin. He had to park his pickup truck some two miles away in an old farm shed and then hike from there.

His quaint abode had neither phone nor electricity, let alone the internet. It was simple. Handmade. Old fashioned. Like him. It went well with his beard and shoulder-length hair. Here he could do his exercises and meditation without being disturbed.

Quintus didn't bother to get a permit to build the cabin eight years earlier, mostly because he loathed the modern world's compulsion for regulations. There were many things he didn't like about modernity and its resulting delusion. It tended to ruin everything it touched, he believed. It was a time when great numbers lived in nihilism as if Gods didn't exist, something that he was even guilty of for a time. For a decade after the deaths of Kaitlyn and Abby, he lived the life of a dejected tramp. Broken. Cynical. Defeated. It was pitiful what he'd become, he later realized.

It was all desperation and darkness until the spirit of Bruce Lee came along. He saw the late Hong Kong martial arts superstar on television sometime in 1976 using nunchucks in a game of ping-pong. It was an odd 'road to Damascus' moment, but Lee's simple yet exceptional act of skill shamed Quintus enough to have him consider returning to the path, and that's what he did.

In effect, it was a similar decision to what he made in Mexico a century or so earlier. With his last shreds of bravery and discipline, he trained alone again as Tai had once taught him. He worked on himself and sought peace, a pure heart. Slowly, yet steadily, he became unstuck and regained much of what was lost.

In the practical world, he had several identity changes and went from his first Canadian job as a truck driver to becoming a helicopter pilot. Not long after he started flying for Alpine Heli Tours, he built himself the log cabin.

It may have been Quintus' version of paradise, even during the winter months, but he was now pondering if he should up and leave it behind. He had long recognized how comfortable he was there and knew that in itself was a distraction. His master did not train him for all those years to live a life of ease and isolation.

But the idea of abandoning the mountain wasn't over the guilt of a laid-back lifestyle or that he no longer had a job to go to. Instead, it was due to a recurring dream he had several times during his short sleeping spells.

In each dream, Quintus walked along a ridge just above the tree line during the night. He saw what appeared at first to be a falling star hurtling across the ink-black sky. It descended, hitting the earth some 20 miles away from where he stood.

BOOM!

It was nuclear. A flash. A harrowing roar. Then another 'falling star' plunged to earth but much closer.

KA-BOOM!

Blinding white light was followed by a fireball. Everything was vaporized. The sound that followed was the incessant screaming of the world's people. The only thing moving in this bright fiery void was a silhouette of a flying seven-headed dragon. It circled Quintus. It got closer and closer, its dark mass increasingly glowing, becoming redder. As its features became clearer, so did the evil resolve in its beady eyes.

And with that, Quintus would wake up, typically in a cold sweat. He was not sure if such dreams were a harbinger of what Tai had trained him for, a duty that he had long thrust from his mind. A task that he sometimes assumed had run flat.

But as he sat on his porch, Quintus felt he was perhaps at another crossroads in his long-drawn-out life.

Over the course of history, he had faced more than one instance of people believing the end was nigh. The Plague of Justinian of 541–542 AD and the Black Plague of the mid-14th century were just two examples. There was, of course, the Millennium Apocalypse that saw various Christian clerics, including Pope Sylvester II, predicting the end of the world to occur in 1000 AD. It caused riots in Europe and sent thousands of pilgrims traveling to Jerusalem, where Quintus was living and working at the time. More recently, he remembered all the hoo-ha caused by Halley's Comet in 1910 when some believed it was going to poison the Earth's atmosphere.

In none of those cases did Quintus feel like the end was upon the world, and of course, it wasn't, yet now, he had a nagging sense that humanity was sleepwalking into oblivion.

Fate, he felt, was pushing him in a certain direction, but whether it would take him all the way back to White Dragon Mountain — as Tai once said it would — was another thing.

As the sun dipped, and its dying glare blanketed the ranges, he again studied the piece of paper that Frank gave him. Among the jumble of words that made up the address details, one stood out like neon.

Reno.

The Nevada city was, he guesstimated, about an easy two-day drive from where he sat.

I'm no good to anyone just passing time here, he thought. Fate, he believed, would reveal what would come, for better or worse. If revisiting Reno was a part of that, then so be it.

Early Morning, Heading South

The shale of the Canadian Rockies crunched under Quintus' boots as he walked the trail for what may be the last time. Wearing well-worn denim jeans, a t-shirt, and a baseball cap, he carried a duffel bag and shouldered a backpack.

After five minutes, the trail stopped at the lip of a cliff that dropped some 50 feet or so before rejoining another track further down. Without a second thought, Quintus stepped over the ledge and floated down, landing at the bottom as soft as a butterfly.

From there, it was another five-minute walk till he reached his aged Ford F-150 pickup parked in a shed just past a grove of trees. He got into his vehicle and turned the engine over. He backed out and drove off, heading towards the border, which was just over an hour away. Despite its closeness, it would be his first time inside the U.S. in over 50 years. He planned not to attempt Reno in one trip. He was first driving to Boise, Idaho, to pay his respects.

As he approached the first bend of the road, he came into radio range, and he found an American news channel which he turned up.

'Scientists in Australia have yet to determine any causes behind either the widespread crop failures or the mass live-stock deaths witnessed across inland regions of the eastern state of New South Wales,' the radio said.

'The affected communities have been through years of prolonged drought and battled the odd bushfire, but nobody expected or has experienced anything like this before, locals say,' the radio reported.

'U.S. officials are in contact with their Australian counterparts, and there have reportedly been discussions about the possibility of quarantining Australian agricultural products coming into America as a precautionary measure.'

Deadly Mumbles

There was a full moon in the southern night's late fall sky. Underneath it, a gaunt, tall, middle-aged man shuffled along the side of a quiet dirt road. He was somewhere between the small Australian cities of Albury and Wagga Wagga.

His skin was a sickly yellow. His eyes deeply set. His

hair was thin and scraggly. He wore a dirty trench coat, from which flies and other insects escaped.

He was mumbling an incantation, and if you could hear it, it would raise the hair on the back of your neck. It was spooky. Foreign. Incomprehensible.

Under such utterances, something else could be heard; a collective groan coming from the fields of young wheat on either side of him. Life was being sucked from the crops. Their death was perceptible. For miles around the mumbling man, wheat just wilted, gasped, and crumpled.

Beyond crops, any nearby animal raised for food likewise just keeled over and breathed their last. In this part of the country, that meant cattle, sheep, the odd goat, and pig, even a few kangaroos. For some reason, their deaths were more discreet. It was the crops that died the loudest.

Back to Boise

Quintus arrived in Boise earlier than anticipated, allowing him to exchange some Canadian for U.S. dollars and buy some tulips, which were Kaitlyn's and Abby's favorites. At the city's main cemetery, he laid the flowers at their neighboring graves. He sat by their headstones, recollecting the good times while trying not to dwell on the loss.

If you, dear reader, have lost loved ones in tragic circumstances, you would appreciate how Quintus felt. The sorrow of losing his girls remained raw, but everything he learned on White Dragon managed to keep him evenly keeled.

After an hour, Quintus left the cemetery and drove

to his old address. He didn't plan it, but the idea of finding some closure pushed him in that direction. Once he got there, his old street seemed smaller and duller than he remembered. Instead of driving through, he pulled his pickup over to the curb and parked a few houses down from where he previously lived.

He exited his vehicle and unhurriedly walked towards number 45, where his home once stood. Now there was a modern boxy-looking dwelling with dark green walls punctured by tall vertical windows. *Hardly inviting*, he thought, when compared to the double-story timber house that his family once called theirs.

Quintus did his utmost to avoid looking at the neighboring house — the past address of the murdering arsonist Andrei Vasiliev — which was likewise a different building from what used to be there. After what occurred in the fall of 1966, Vasailiev's house was bulldozed. No one wanted to live in a house where a murdering madman had hung himself, especially next to where he committed his dark deeds. Number 47 was left as an empty plot for 25 years or so. Probably just enough time for people to forget what happened there.

As Quintus got to the front of his old address, three girls, all sisters under the age of 12, playfully ran from the side of the house into the front yard. A fun-loving barking Labrador followed. The youngest of the girls saw the bearded and scruffy-headed stranger on the other side of the fence and promptly started shrieking. It started a chain reaction of hyped-up hysterics that all three joined in on.

'Weirdo! Weirdo! Weirdo!' they chanted as they turned and ran back to where they had come.

But the Labrador, sensing the man behind the beard was no threat, did the opposite and remained behind, wagging his tail.

'Howdy pup,' Quintus said.

The dog jumped up and placed his front paws on the fence so Quintus could scratch the side of his neck.

The house's front door clanged open noisily, revealing the girls' father, who was ruddy-faced, balding, and suspicious.

'Buster get inside,' the man said. 'Can I help you?' he inhospitably asked the stranger who the dog now abandoned.

'Sorry. Don't mean any harm. I used to live here. Sometime back,' Quintus replied.

'I'll call the cops if you keep loitering and scaring my kids,' the father said.

'Sure, on my way. I mean no harm,' Quintus said as he began to make his way back to his pickup.

'Yeah, so you said,' the man replied.

Quintus felt no malice towards the man. *He is protecting his family as any decent father should*, he thought.

As the dog brushed past the man's leg, he glanced back at Quintus, who, as he walked away, nodded at him. It was a simple and unexpected gesture of respect that melted some of the man's hostility.

'You hear about Venice?' he asked in a softer tone.

'No,' Quintus replied.

'You will,' the man said as he went back into his home, shutting the door behind him.

Tsunami TV

The Italian city of Venice had nearly been wiped out by a tsunami. The television in the motel room that Quintus was staying in had been on non-stop for the past 12 or so hours showing nothing but coverage of the disaster. There was ample video footage, most of it initially posted online by survivors. TV commentators by this stage were speculating fatalities, but I can tell you the massive wave took with it 80,000 plus souls.

Quintus pulled himself away from the TV and went to the bathroom, where he unpacked the hair clippers he bought from a department store not long after he visited his old street.

As he began clipping his hair to a half-inch from the scalp, the morning's sun snuck through the small bathroom window. After he finished with his hair, Quintus shaved off his beard. *Barba non facit philosophum*, he thought in Latin. 'A beard doesn't make a philosopher.'

Next, he showered and afterward watched more television. He flicked through channels, stopping on one that featured Chuck Goyette, that portly 'prophet of doom', being interviewed by two hosts, Ryan and Chloe, in a studio.

'You have stated that only your members will survive doomsday,' said Ryan, who was then interrupted by Chloe.

'We should also inform everyone that membership to your organization requires individuals to pay ten percent of their take-home income,' Chloe said.

Anyone watching the program would have noticed

Goyette purse his lips at the innuendo of it all, but he allowed her to continue.

'How many members do you have?' she asked.

'I can tell you both it's a good number, and it is sky-rocketing, but I think you're missing the point here, that being my prophecies, like the tsunami obliterating Venice, are consistently —' Goyette said before being interrupted by Ryan.

'But the details you give,' Ryan said. 'Such as the descriptions of so-called mystical mantras or incantations setting off these disasters, it just sounds like you're making it all up as you go along.'

Before Goyette could refute the claim, Quintus turned the TV off. There was little to gain from watching anymore, he felt. In his solitude, he sat on the bed and tried unsuccessfully to clear his mind. Instead, thoughts rushed in about his several past visits to Venice, the last being in 1396 when he helped build pedestrian bridges across canals.

He got off the bed, sat on the floor, and folded his legs into the lotus position. Again, he tried purifying his thoughts as he began his meditation.

Just over an hour later, he would check out of the motel, leave Boise, and make his way to Reno.

CHAPTER VI

Black Hearted

A WALLED TELEVISION showed news coverage of Chuck Goyette leaving a TV station and walking to a waiting stretched limousine. 'The controversial cult leader stated he personally knows the Four Horsemen of the Apocalypse,' said accompanying audio. 'Resulting in several Christian groups accusing Goyette himself of being the Antichrist.'

A man in a charcoal grey Italian suit was the only one in the large office watching the broadcast. His name was Aaron Marx, a stern-looking 48-year-old hedge fund manager. He was lean, mustached, and cold-eyed. He had an air of sharp, efficient cruelty about him.

'This is embarrassing,' Marx said, critiquing the broadcast.

He threw the TV remote onto his desk and walked towards his office windows, passing a large portrait of murdering tyrant Mao Zedong as he went. In fact, right across his walls were pictures of unsavory characters and horrifying scenes.

Marx reached his office windows that offered views of New York's financial district. For five minutes, he stood there looking over eight blocks of money, power, and corruption. He could stand there doing that all day and night if it were at all practical.

On the street opposite, he could see his nightclub, The Devil's Pleasure Palace, which he'd owned for three years. A bit further along, he could make out the inconspicuous entrance to a local coven of the Order of International Satanists, of which he was a prominent member.

The intercom on his desk buzzed, and the voice of Kristen Goode, his personal assistant, followed.

'Good morning Mr. Marx. Did you hear about Venice?'

'Yes, I did. What do you want?' he abruptly said.

'Mr. Irfan and Mr. Vacher are on their way up in the elevator to see you, sir.'

'Fine, send them straight in when they arrive.'

A Pair of Maniacs

Tony Vacher and Sabre Irfan were hard-looking but well-dressed men. Aged in their late 30s, they shared the elevator as it climbed to the penthouse level. Both were ex-military from their respective countries, France and Pakistan. Due to some extremely depraved behavior, they each earned dishonorable discharges.

More broadly, it could be easily said no one in their home countries missed them or wanted them back.

The smaller of the two was the Frenchman Vacher. He was completely bald-headed and squat in form. He was fixing his foulard necktie in the lift's mirror.

'You ever consider wearing a tie?' Vacher asked tie-less Irfan, who was scrolling through perversion on his iPhone.

'No,' Irfan replied without looking up from his device. 'I don't want to appear like a peacock.'

'And screw you too,' Vacher bit back. 'The more time I spend with you, Irfan, the more I can see why you nearly ended up as a whack-job jihadi.'

Irfan rolled his eyes, but just months earlier, he had indeed sought to join a radical Islamic militant group. More for the possibility of unbridled violence than for anything else.

A week before his planned recruitment, Irfan left Karachi and flew to the Thai seaside city of Pattaya for five days of depravity. After he befriended Vacher at a seedy hotel, this turned into a month, and the idea of jihad fell to the wayside. Together they ran amok in the city's places of disrepute until the Russian mafia and the Thai police chased them out.

From there, Irfan managed somehow to get into the States, where Vacher made a work referral for him to Marx. Irfan was surprised when he was offered a high-paying security consultant position with Black Crest Management.

Not that Irfan, the son of a high-ranking Pakistani general, wasn't qualified. He served in Pakistan's special forces and military intelligence for around 15 years. He spoke fluent English and some passable Mandarin. His amoral tendencies similarly made him an ideal fit for Marx, as did karmic reasons.

Their elevator journey came to a halt upon reaching the penthouse floor. Vacher took one last glance at his reflection, and Irfan switched off his iPhone. Both men got out and made their way to their employer's office.

Mess in Reno

Vacher and Irfan entered the office to find Marx seated at his desk, typing away on his computer keyboard.

'So, what is it? Why do you two have to see me at such short notice?' Marx said without looking at them.

'It's Peach, sir, he's having difficulties in Reno with your Mexican investors, Mr. Hector Herera in particular,' Vacher said. 'Some kind of random altercation with rival cartel gang members, apparently.'

Marx now looked at his minions, who he had earlier asked to report to him any issues related to account manager Albert Peach chaperoning his clients from the Amado cartel.

'What kind of altercation?' he asked.

'Some words exchanged, a bit of screaming, someone waved around a gun,' Vacher said.

'In public?'

'Broad daylight,' Vacher said while nodding. 'Sounded like a case of road rage.'

'Another cartel, you say?' Marx asked.

'Yeah, I know, what are the odds. Apparently from Baja California. Criminals are everywhere these days,' Vacher said, laughing a bit.

The Frenchman went on to describe how trouble started when one car bumped into another in a parking lot.

'Peach said it quickly escalated but, in the end, nothing much eventuated with cool heads managing to prevail, which he took the credit for. No cops involved, no one hurt, but threats were made, and so he's a bit spooked,' Vacher said. 'He says Hector Herera is a wild one and a bit batty.'

Marx nodded.

'That is putting it mildly,' he said.

'And so, Peach would like some backup, if possible, in case things got further out of hand. There's a private eye in Reno I know of who could help,' Vacher said. 'An old guy by the name of Jack Day.'

Marx shook his head.

'What about some guys from Black Crow, some with time on their hands?' asked Vacher, referring to a subsidiary security company owned by Marx.

'No, it needs more of a personal touch. It's not really a security detail, so I want you two to handle it,' Marx said.

The order surprised Vacher. It wasn't a typical request.

'Sure, okay, Herera is just looking to buy a gambling machine factory, isn't he?' he queried.

'Yes. The business aspect is straightforward but leave that to Mr. Peach,' Marx said. 'This firm's association with the Amado cartel has been long-standing, and I need it to remain that way and so I want Herera to be happy.'

'And what do you want us to do?' Vacher asked.

'Hopefully, nothing. The Amado cartel has a few hot-heads in its ranks, and Herera is the worst of them. He is also an idiot of the highest order, but he's a nephew of Alfonso,' Marx said, referring to the cartel's drug lord. 'You are to ensure things don't go further awry and that he has a good time within boundaries. It may appear to be just a babysitting gig, but it's extremely important that nothing goes wrong,' he said without offering additional details.

Marx hit the intercom.

'Kristen, book Mr. Vacher and Mr. Irfan flights to Reno. They need to be back by Friday. They're on the way out to see you.'

Kristen acknowledged the orders.

Vacher and Irfan took that as their cue and exited.

The Call

Still at his desk, Marx brooded over how his well-laid plans were threatening to unravel. The news from Reno reminded him how fragile his task was, or at least appeared. He dialed his desk phone and five seconds later somebody at the other end answered.

It was Chuck Goyette, the cult leader. He was traveling in a stretched limousine while enjoying a foot massage from a follower dedicated to such tasks. He was on the call hands-free, not that Marx could see that.

'Mr. Goyette, I've been watching you on TV,' Marx said tersely.

At the other end, Goyette rolled his eyes.

'Yes, I've been busy. How may I help you, Mr. Marx?' he asked in a nonchalant tone.

Marx held his breath for a second before responding to ensure his voice didn't betray signs of irritation.

"I'm just very surprised that certain issues, such as mystical mantras, are being so casually discussed on television,'

Marx managed to say with a steady voice. 'No one will take you seriously.'

'Time for you to just chill,' said Goyette. 'It's important to have some fun along the way, Mr. Marx, and besides, you shouldn't worry yourself so much. I'm just playing and toying with them all. Besides, I'm in Los Angeles, and they love that kind of talk down here; all the supernatural, so let's keep it in perspective, shall we?'

'I'm still responsible for you all, Mr. Goyette. That's my singular perspective. This, what you're doing, is not part of the plan and as such, it puts things at risk,' Marx said.

Goyette chuckled before replying.

'Mr. Marx, I think you're overlooking some fundamentals. You're merely the middleman, that's it, and yes, your services were appreciated upon our arrival, but that was then, and this is now,' he said. 'Regarding the future, we all know how it is going to pan out, so there is no point in making a fuss about what method is best.'

'Well, Mr. Goyette it appears we still have an issue with how to approach this. It would be beneficial for everyone if we meet again,' Marx said.

Goyette offered a loud sigh that spoke volumes.

'Marx, that's unquestionably impossible,' he replied, dropping the Mr. 'Ever since day one, Death has been independent, and I know you don't stalk her. Not that anyone in their right mind would.'

Marx abruptly cut in.

'Enough of the schtick. As agreed earlier, let's refer to her as Trudy when speaking via phone,' Marx said.

'Oh, keep your pants on, Marx. Call her whatever, but

I'm sticking to character,' Goyette said. 'And then there's Famine, and yes, he is behind schedule, but at least he is still wandering around doing his thing Down Under, drawing at least some media attention. What did you want to call him? Bruce wasn't it?'

'That was the name we settled upon,' Marx said.

'You say Trudy, I say Death, you say Bruce, I say Famine. What was War again, Ivan, wasn't it? It's preposterous,' Goyette said.

'Again, it was something we agreed upon. Let's just stick to the plan.'

'You need to relax, Marx. You're only the middleman, and you're way overboard on this matter.'

'Without me, you'd have nothing. I could cut off your funds in a heartbeat,' Marx bit back.

'Now you're being rash. Look on the bright side Marx. You have War in your stable, don't you? Is he depressed? I hope not, but if he is, it's probably because he's so, so idle,' Goyette said. 'Is he still cooped up in your boardroom? Is he still drawing like crazy? I hope so, it helps keep him evenly keeled in this realm — you don't want him unkeeled, that's for certain.'

It was then Marx's turn to sigh.

'Look, this is childish,' he said.

'Yes, I certainly agree,' Goyette shot back.

'Look, we just need to meet. Fly to New York.'

'I'm sorry, Marx, but my schedule will only get busier after today. I've now arrived at ZBS, so I can't talk anymore. Just make good on you and War's visit to China and North Korea. Ensure that you fulfill your end of the bargain,' Goyette said. 'That's all you have to do at this stage. Everything else is out of your hands.'

Goyette ended the call just as his limousine pulled into a parking lot at ZBS TV.

At his end, Marx hung up the phone and shook his head in frustration. It was a desperate conversation, and he wasn't surprised how it eventuated. He was at the point of giving up on trying to reason with any of the four otherworldly types. They were entirely on another level when it came to stubbornness.

But he had to push on and stick to the plan as he knew it to be. He stood from his desk and exited his office.

War

As Marx entered the reception area, he caught a last-second glimpse of Vacher and Irfan disappearing behind the lift's closing doors just before it went down.

'Can I assist with anything, Mr. Marx,' said a female voice from behind him.

Marx didn't bother turning to Kristen, who remained seated at the reception desk. 'You book their air tickets?' he asked, his tone typically unfriendly.

'Yes, sir.'

'I hope you're looking after him,' Marx said, nodding towards the glass-walled boardroom where a dark-haired man aged in his 30s sat alone at a long table. He had a full beard and was powerfully built, not that that was evident under the surplus-army jacket he wore. He was sketching on blank pieces of paper. Nearby on the floor was a bedroll that he'd slept on for the last ten nights.

'Has he eaten anything today?' Marx asked.

'Yes, he had what I got him this morning,' Kristen said, referring to some pulled-pork sandwiches. 'I'll get him some lunch soon.'

'What has he been doing?'

'The same. Just drawing.'

The hipster-look alike had been drawing aplenty. Littered on the table were piles of drawn-on paper and used sketchbooks.

'Has he said anything?' Marx asked.

'Nothing beyond general courtesies,' she replied.

Marx looked at Kristen's generous and pretty face for the first time that day. He knew she was a decent person, and that made him wary of her. *She's 100 percent Middle America*, he thought. Typically, he hired people on the darker side or recommended by the coven, but for her, he made an exception. She was useful to him for other reasons.

'Have you talked to him?' he enquired.

'No, you asked me not to. He's just been sketching like always.'

Marx left her and went back into his office. He shut the door loudly behind him, leaving Kristen wondering how much longer she could last in a job with such an unsettling boss. She looked at her watch; it was time to get the sketcher some lunch.

Deli Viewing

Kristen was oblivious to the hustle and bustle of orders being taken and delivered in her favorite Lower Manhattan café delicatessen. She was too busy dealing with the million and one thoughts running through her mind as she waited for her own take-out order to be made. Her workplace was understandably upsetting her. It was a bizarre office to be a part of.

More than once over the past six months while working at Black Crest, the 29-year-old told herself she should get back to Texas, where her family was.

Her boss was the biggest and rudest jerk she'd ever met. Not only did she have to endure him, but there were his two security consultants: Vacher and Irfan. They all gave her the creeps, particularly the Frenchman, who sent shivers down her spine.

This fact alone disturbed Kristen. In essence, she was a no-fuss type who generally got on well with others, no matter their creed or color. She didn't like not liking people, but in these three, she saw little to admire.

She also found it odd that Vacher and Irfan were the only two Black Crest employees who Marx allowed into his office. The hundreds of others working in the building's lower levels never ventured up or directly dealt with their director and employer. What's more, Vacher and Irfan acted more like bodyguards half the time.

Such oddities resulted in her researching online about Marx, Black Crest, and the subsidiary Black Crow. What she found wasn't flattering. Parts of it were downright disturbing. Go to Hell kinda stuff. How much of it was true or false, though, she was unsure.

Now adding to the weirdness of working at Black Crest was 'Ivan' camped out in Marx's boardroom. Kristen didn't know much more than he was Marx's cousin who needed somewhere to stay, which she judged a falsehood given her boss owned apartments throughout Manhattan. She didn't see the two men interact much, and they certainly didn't look related. Ivan looked positively Arabic. *But at least he ate whatever I brought him*, she thought as her deli order arrived.

As she took the bag of tuna and avocado sandwiches, a staff member turned up the volume of a television mounted on the deli's wall.

Some customers and staff called for people to be quiet.

Kristen paused, wondering what the fuss was about.

'What's going on?' she asked a young guy next to her.

'It's Chuck Goyette, the cult guy who predicted the tsunami that hit Italy,' he told her.

Someone shushed them to be quiet.

She looked at the deli's television, where ZBS hosts — Robert and Anne — were interviewing Goyette.

'So just to be clear, Mr. Goyette, you're suggesting an additional earthquake will hit, one bigger than what caused the Venice tsunami?' Robert questioned.

Goyette nodded and then spoke with confidence.

'I'm not suggesting anything. Let's not weasel around, I'm specifically telling you that Death will strike again in Italy, and at 8 p.m., that's Pacific Standard Time, Rome will crumble,' Goyette said.

'Tonight? Rome?' Anne said, checking her watch.

'Correct, you got a scoop. Death will shortly do her mantra there, and soon it will cease to exist,' Goyette said. 'Of course, the Vatican will be reduced to rubble as well. That's a given at this stage.'

Despite sniggers of disbelief in the deli, most eyes remained glued to the TV as Goyette went on to describe what would happen to Rome. Summed up, it sounded horrific.

Then came the kicker.

'The catastrophes will, soon enough, move westwards, and in less than a week, what we will see in Rome will occur in New York.'

'Say what?!' someone in the deli shouted.

In the TV studio, Robert interjected.

'An earthquake in New York City in less than a week?' Robert asked.

'Yes, Death will arrive in New York in advance of that date to again perform her incantation, which will seal the city's fate,' Goyette explained.

It was Anne's turn to cut in.

'Excuse me, did you just say Death is a woman?'

Goyette smiled, raised his eyebrows while enjoying the drama of it all.

'I did, but she could take the form of a rabbit if she wanted to, but that would hardly be dramatic, now would it?' he said.

He noticed Anne frowning at him.

'Or, if she so chooses to, she may self-identify as a Labrador,' Goyette said, laughing at his own folly. 'But let's just call her Death for old times' sake, shall we?'

Another customer in the deli yelled at the TV.

'This fat jerk is nothing but a fraud,' the customer shouted. 'Turn this fake junk off.'

Others told him to be quiet, they wanted to hear Goyette describe how Death operates.

'Being in human form, Death has to travel wherever she needs to get to by whatever means she can,' he explained. 'It's a part of the challenge the four face, and they do face challenges in what they are doing. It's the nature of this realm. It's a tough gig. It's not easy, you know.'

Anne, now wide-eyed, squirmed in her seat.

'Can you describe her for us?' she asked.

'I can, but I won't,' Goyette said.

There was stunned silence in the deli. It seemed like an eternity for Kristen and others watching before Anne asked another question.

'Many of our viewers may not be so familiar with the Four Horsemen of the Apocalypse, can you at least briefly describe them for us? It's Death, Famine, War, and the Antichrist, isn't it?'

Goyette rolled his eyes.

'Look — Death, Famine, War, and the Antichrist or whatever you want to call them — they aren't human, but they're neither demons nor divine beings,' he said. 'They have been assigned this purpose; the destruction of humanity, or at the very least, they volunteered for it. But really, the biblical term the Four Horsemen of the Apocalypse is just a reference point for them. Strictly speaking, they're not the four as described in the New Testament. They may have been inspired by these old things and from it taken a form that mankind can accept, so they have borrowed these ancient things.'

By now, Robert had had enough.

'Okay, so they're like a cover band?' he joked sourly.

Goyette gave Robert a look of disapproval.

'It's to help you understand. That's all. Hell, I'm not even a Christian,' Goyette exclaimed. 'I'm totally moral free. Sicko perverts, liars, and thieves are all welcome. My sole worry is that I may be infringing on some copyright issues, but my lawyers assure me I'm not.'

Anne was perplexed.

'So, help me here, what is your Temple Science Ministries about?' she asked.

'Survival. Nothing more, nothing less,' Goyette replied. 'And I'll take anyone with me who has the cash.'

Robert folded his arms and shook his head in disbelief but continued with his questioning.

'Well, Mr. Goyette, that's heartening to hear. Now the agricultural crisis in Australia, I presume, is due to Famine, one of the four you have been referring to, right?' Robert asked with a large dollop of mockery in his manner.

'Yes, but he is very slow and not living up to expectations,' said Goyette, non-plussed by Robert's attitude.

'Could what we see there in Australia just fizzle out then? You know, not eventuate to much?' Robert asked.

'That is conceivable.'

'So, if Famine goes to the wayside, becomes a bit of a Mr. Do-Nothing, and makes a mess of it all, then obviously things aren't set in stone, right? And so, presumably, these great disasters you're speaking about can also be averted. Am I accurate in presuming that, based on what you have just said?' Robert said.

Goyette then waffled on for half a minute, explaining why it was possible but improbable.

'If Famine falls short, the other three will simply take up the slack. It's just hard to see any other outcome apart from the end that I have seen, which I will speak about more at a suitable time.'

'Probably on another network,' Robert said.

'Probably,' Goyette responded.

Anne butted in.

'So, what gender is Famine? And what about War — girl or boy?'

By now, Kristen had seen enough. *This is bonkers. Either the world or ZBS has lost the plot*, she thought.

Kristen exited the deli, and ten minutes later, she gave the tuna and avocado sandwiches to the odd bearded sketcher in the boardroom, the guy known as War to some and Ivan to others.

CHAPTER VII

Reno Arrival

WHEN QUINTUS KILLED Chivington and the mad twins, Reno had just come into existence. Today it's known for its casinos and the nearby great outdoors. It may have been just over 150 years since Quintus was last there, but I'd be lying if I told you he wasn't a bit unnerved as he arrived at the city's outskirts.

During his drive, he recognized some of the country-side where he rode that stolen chestnut horse to escape the law. In a bid to avoid such recollections, he mulled over how he'd again have to alter his identity within the next five years. A process that was increasingly becoming difficult and complicated.

His current Canadian identity was Quintus Bremmer. Going by the date of birth on his fake passport and all his other counterfeit documents, he was a young-looking 42-year-old. His internet research at his last place of work told him he might have to go as far as Thailand to acquire quality replacement forgeries.

Such a scenario had him toying with the idea of visiting nearby China for old times' sake. He'd earlier used Google Earth to find what he once knew as White Dragon Mountain, which was situated near what is today called the Toudou River, not far from the city of Leshan in Sichuan province. Google Earth even showed him where he believed the sanctuary was and how two blurry blobs, which he thought were probably very large boulders, had slipped and lodged where the terrace once was. He calculated that the sanctuary might be a two-day walk from the nearest road as shown on the internet.

For several minutes, Quintus mulled over his master's words: 'When the time is right, you will return to White Dragon Mountain.' He just wasn't sure what his teacher said was still valid.

But as he drove towards the city's center, he pushed China and any doubts from his mind. Instead, he focused on finding a hotel to book into before finding somewhere to eat, something he hadn't done for several days.

The Diner

Reno's Last Great Diner was old-school Americana. Elongated and spacious, with large glass windows and slide-in booths. Built in 1962, you know the type.

Inside it, the diner's manager, Bill, a large friendly-looking 38-year-old with a wild mop of red hair, worked an espresso machine at the counter's end. The kitchen phone rang behind him. Someone picked it up and called out.

'Excuse me, Bill, it's Lauren; she is calling in sick.'

Bill, steaming a pot of milk, mumbled something about Gen-Z before offering a reply.

'Okay, do me a favor and call Tina. Her number is above the phone. See if she can work today; tell her she'd be doing me a huge favor,' he said.

The doorbell chimed, but he didn't look up at the elderly couple exiting the diner. Outside, Quintus held the door open for them, and once they were through, he entered. He cut through the near-empty eating area and sat on a swivel stool at the counter.

A mid-40s black guy named Lance, who was halfway through a late lunch, was seated two seats up next to him and scrolling through a cellphone.

A waitress, Gabriela, approached with a 'what will it be' smile and a menu.

'An Americano coffee to start with, please,' Quintus said as she handed him the menu.

A minute later, he gave a food order.

Three minutes later, Bill delivered the coffee.

'And there you go, one Americano,' he said.

'Many thanks,' Quintus said.

'You're welcome. You're Canadian; your accent gave you away, all two words,' Bill said in a friendly manner. Speaking with customers was the highlight of his working day.

Quintus nodded.

'You visiting or living in Reno?' Bill asked.

'I'm seeing a guy tomorrow about a job, so could be here for a while if all goes well.'

'Awesome. Good luck with it. What kinda job? Casino work?'

'No, helicopter pilot.'

'Alright. I spoke with a guy once, and he said learning to fly a helicopter was one of the hardest things he'd ever done.'

'Yeah, they take some getting used to, but in the end, bit like riding a bike once you know how.'

The two men talked some more, and soon enough, the conversation broadened out from helicopters, and Quintus learned Bill was married to a woman named Erin. They had two kids and were originally from Kansas.

Their attention was eventually drawn to the walled TV behind Bill, showing images of cult figure Chuck Goyette.

'What do Canadians think of this guy?' Bill asked.

Before Quintus could reply, Lance, the other customer, offered his opinion.

'The dude makes doom an' gloom sound like Disneyland,' he said with half a mouthful of food. 'I'm over all this Apocalypse talk. You'd be doing us all a favor, Bill, by leaving the TV on mute.'

'Sure. Well, his credibility hangs on what occurs in Rome tonight. I hope he's just full of BS. I don't want to see Rome go to Hell, it's an awesome city,' Bill said.

The mention of Rome naturally caught Quintus' attention.

'What's happening in Rome?'

Lance, grabbing a napkin to wipe his mouth, looked sideways at Quintus.

'According to the overweight dude, Rome is going to be wiped off the map by an earthquake,' Lance said. 'He also predicted the same for New York City, which by his account has got less than a week before its gone-bye-bye.'

'This the same guy who predicted Venice?' Quintus asked.

'The one and only. Everyone knows Goyette, man. Where have you been?' Lance asked.

'Living on a mountain with no TV or internet,' Quintus replied.

'And no smartphone?'

'No smartphone. Off the grid. Go online on a need-only basis. I'm one of those folk who thinks the world was better pre-digital.'

'Yeah, you might be onto something. I should try some of that; I'm addicted to this thing,' Lance said, referring to his device. 'One day, they'll discover they're worse for you than cigarettes.'

'And more addictive than crack,' Bill added.

'We're all under some magic spell,' Lance said.

Bill nodded at the TV, which still featured Goyette.

'But the media must be making a fortune out of this guy; been doing their darndest to make him a rock star,' he said.

'Media are pushing us all back into hysterics as they did with Covid. Anyway, what else has Goyette prophesized?' Lance asked.

'Something about the killing of crops and livestock in Australia,' Bill said.

'I heard something about it on the radio yesterday,' Quintus added.

'He foretell Covid? How long's Goyette been around for?' Lance asked.

'I don't know but doesn't seem that long,' Bill replied. 'Earliest prediction of his I'm aware of that came true was one about the last election,' Bill said as the TV showed Goyette getting into a limousine. 'That was enough for my sister-in-law to join his cult, not that there is much to it apart from taking a chunk of money from her,' he admitted. 'She did it all over the internet. Now she's trying to convince me to do likewise before so-called Judgment Day arrives.'

'Sounds like a Ponzi scheme. Judgment Day, isn't that a Christian thing, though?' asked Lance as he pushed away his now empty plate.

'Yeah, but is he even Christian?' Bill responded.

'Don't know, but he's milking it; he's ripping off the Bible, and the media is spoon-feeding it out to us all like we're 2-year-olds,' he said.

Bill smiled, agreeing while Quintus listened on.

'He was quoting the Bible earlier about the Four Horsemen or whatever of the Apocalypse,' Bill said. 'I'm certainly no expert. Who are they?'

'Who are who?' Lance asked.

'The real Four Horsemen of the Apocalypse? Individually? I know there's Death; that's at least one,' Bill said.

'Well, there's also Famine, War, and taxes. Altogether,

with Death, that makes four all up if I count correctly,' Lance joked. 'And out of all of them, taxes is the worst and by far the evilest.'

'Inflation, that's up there as well,' Bill added with a smile.

Lance laughed and then said more.

'Seriously though, who is the fourth dude?'

Bill shrugged, he didn't have a clue either, but Quintus did.

'It's Conquest. Some see him as the Antichrist,' Quintus said.

Lance clapped his hands.

'Damn right. Yeah, the false messiah!' he cried.

Bill took Lance's finished plate from the counter.

'At least Goyette hasn't mentioned a plague of zombies yet. You wanna drink or some dessert or something else?' he asked Lance.

'No, I'm good, but Goyette, he's just making up all his BS as he goes along,' said Lance. '

Bill offered some thoughts.

'Given how back-to-front everything is these days, it's unsurprising everyone's going on about the Apocalypse,' Bill said. 'Things have been weird for a while and getting weirder.'

'Yeah, okay, I'll agree; the world is upside down, and we're being told what to do by self-serving charlatans. We can take that all as fact, but I'm ignoring all this hip pessimism. World ain't ending, not just yet anyhow, especially with the likes of this Goyette at the head of it all,' Lance said. 'In fact, I predict I'll be here next year. Same old same

old: eating your burgers, sweet-talking your waitresses —
platonically of course — and drinking your coffee.'

Quintus had by now finished his first cup of coffee.

'And I gotta say it's superb coffee,' he remarked.

Bill gestured in thanks.

'Made from the finest Fairtrade coffee on the planet,
from northern Thailand to be exact; suggested by one of
my staff. Just enjoy it while you can; it's getting harder to
buy,' he said.

'Supply issues?' Lance asked to which Bill nodded.

'Better make me another one then,' Quintus replied.

The Gift

IT TOOK TINA Phetung around 15 minutes to ride her
mountain bike from her shared-student house to the diner
to fill in for the waitress who called in sick. Due to her
easygoing nature, the third-year college student was more
than happy to help, especially seeing Bill was okay with her
returning to Sacramento to spend time with family for a
month or so during college break.

Not that there'd be much in the way of rest, given
she'll be waitressing at her mom's busy Thai restaurant. Not
that the 22-year-old minded. Working in a restaurant was
second nature to Tina, who enjoyed helping her mom out.

Being first-generation Thai-American, there was some
pressure on her to study something other than the art-ed-
ucation course that she eventually chose. For a while, it
looked like she may instead have chosen to be a language

teacher, given how she excelled in both her Mandarin and French high-school classes.

But either way, both her parents knew their daughter well enough not to push her in a direction against her will. Her mom and dad knew she wasn't like others, including her elder brother Jeremy who favored business and computers. Like his father, he was introverted, fastidious, and ambitious. Tina was the complete opposite, but neither was she like her mother.

If I had a couple of words, to sum up Tina, they'd be kind yet cautious. These qualities were largely an indirect result of a hidden talent that she had. In fact, Tina's secret gift gave her a head start in most things in this human world of yours when it came to understanding people, at least. With one glance, she could make out those of you who were good-hearted and those who weren't. Based on that, she could further appreciate what really mattered; a lot of that was simply about being virtuous.

Now I can see you are thinking, what could be such a gift?

You may shrug it off as something New Age or paranormal, but Tina had the ability to see other people's auras, a phenomenon recognized by many spiritual traditions — Christians call them haloes as an example. Perhaps one out of every 50,000 people can see them.

Without getting distracted by the history or theory of it all, I will just stick with what Tina could see when she looked at someone, which for a decent individual is a subtle, luminous glow, sometimes mixed with vibrant colors, surrounding the body but typically centered on the head. The more virtuous the person, the greater the glow.

However, if someone was of a lesser character, then the field that she saw was correspondingly weaker. For those who are horribly depraved and corrupted, she instead saw they were covered by a dark haze.

Given she could gauge such things, Tina chose her friends well. On the surface, they were an eclectic mix of different races, ages, and beliefs, but they had one thing in common, they were decent people. That's one reason why Tina liked working at the diner; from the light that shone from Bill and staff such as Gabriela, she knew she was in good company.

Bright

After dismounting from her bike and chaining it up, Tina entered through the diner's back service entrance. She cut through the kitchen and made her way to a small staff zone where she stowed her personal items in a metal locker. As she put on her apron, Gabriela passed carrying dirty plates.

'Tina, thanks for coming in so quick.'

'No problems. Busy yet?'

Gabriela shook her head.

'But in an hour, it will be.'

Prompted by the noise of the diner's front-door bell, Tina went out to the dining area to begin her shift. She approached a newly arrived family of four and seated them at a window booth. After leaving them with menus to review, she stopped to pick up some used plates off a table, and it was then that something caught her attention from the corner of her eye.

Something glowing.

She looked towards the glow and saw a man seated at the counter who had the brightest and largest aura she'd ever witnessed. It was mostly golden in color with traces of silver. It also contained streaks of reds and blues, which she had seen in others before, typically the elderly or those who may have experienced trauma, such as military servicemen and first responders.

Then Bill's voice took her attention.

'Tina, I appreciate you coming in at such short notice. You're a star!' he said.

She smiled at her boss at the espresso machine, not far from the glowing man. She gestured that it was nothing. Then the glowing man casually looked her way. His face was radiating so much that she barely noticed that he was softly smiling.

The only way I can describe to you how she felt at that moment was that it was as if an avalanche of warmth hit her. Such was its force, it nearly brought on a surge of tears. Quickly she composed herself and went to the kitchen with an armful of dirty plates.

'Super shy but a heart of gold and full of life,' Bill said to the glowing man, who was, of course, Quintus. 'This year I've mostly been blessed with awesome staff, other years only so so.'

In the kitchen, Tina delivered the dirty crockery to the dishwasher and then went to a mirrored window that allowed her to peer into the dining area unnoticed. Gabriela came up beside her and joined in staring at Quintus.

'Yeah, he's sure super cute in an old-world charmer kinda way,' Gabriela said as she playfully elbowed Tina in the ribs.

Yes, but it wasn't his fetching looks that fascinated Tina.

Live from Rome

The television behind the diner's counter was going live to a reporter in Rome.

'You guys mind if we hear this?' Quintus asked.

'Guess we're looking at it, may as well hear it,' Lance said.

Using the TV remote, Bill upped the volume.

On the television, a ZBS reporter named Jake talked to the camera.

'It's after midnight here, and we're in the city's historic center, and most people are asleep,' Jake said. 'As you can tell, there are not many about.'

Behind the reporter, in the shot's background, was the floodlit Trevi Fountain in all its Baroque grandeur. The vision cut to the U.S. studio where Teresa, a news anchor, was asking questions.

'It may be late, Jake, but is there yet any indication of what the mood in the Italian capital is like?'

Back in Rome, Jake shrugged.

'Well, Teresa, y'know, the Italians are still coming to terms with the tsunami that hit Venice less than 18 hours ago. So, it is somber, the mood is somber, that's how I can best summarize it,' Jake said. 'Now, despite Chuck Goyette's prediction about the Venice catastrophe being correct, he still, surprisingly, remains relatively unknown here in Italy.'

'That so?' Teresa asked.

'Yeah, I told one person about Goyette and his predictions just earlier, and he only laughed, saying, you Americans are crazy!'

From here, dear reader, I'll focus on things that occurred off-camera some six blocks away from the TV crew of three to out the front of the Pantheon, a former Roman temple, now Catholic church and tourist attraction. There, a thin woman, aged in her 20s, was walking in circles around the façade with her eyes shut while murmuring in a trance-like state. She was wearing black skinny-fit jeans and a dirty t-shirt. Her arms were covered with hard-core tattoos, and she had piercings in her nose, lips, and eyebrows. Her unruly hair was peroxide blonde with dark roots showing.

Eventually, she stopped her walking and stood still on the cobblestone. There, standing as stiff as a soldier on parade, she continued her chants for a further 20 seconds until becoming quiet. After a moment of silence, a tremor shook the city.

Back at the Trevi Fountain, the reporter Jake nearly wet his pants when the buildings rattled around him and his two crew members.

'Holy mother of…' he exclaimed.

After the tremor subsided, Jake resumed talking to the camera, somewhat frazzled.

'Teresa, I presume you're still with us,' he said. 'I'm not sure how that looked back in the studio, but we just experienced a tremor maybe or perhaps even a small earthquake.'

Meanwhile, at the Pantheon, the thin woman opened her eyes and sighed as her task was done. She then walked off in search of a taxi stand which didn't take her long to find.

When she got into a waiting taxi, the elderly driver — a man named Antonio — got a shock. Her body odor was putrid. *It smells of death*, he thought. Like something dead on his nephew's farm. But Antonio wasn't going to complain, he was grateful for the fare, and he was also polite. He looked back at her, trying his best not to grimace, and asked where she wanted to go. He was surprised that her reply was in faultless Italian. He had presumed she was from elsewhere.

As instructed, he drove her to the Leonardo da Vinci international airport. During the drive, he did all the talking, some of it about his family but most of it about the tremor that occurred just minutes before she got into his car and the tsunami that had recently devastated Venice.

When they finally arrived at the airport, the woman gave him a generous tip and some parting advice.

'Get out of Rome within the next four hours, or you will die.'

That left Antonio in a cold sweat. He didn't drive off straight away; instead, he watched her thin figure enter the airport's departure area.

After five minutes of contemplation, he picked up his cell and phoned his wife. She eventually woke from her sleep, and he informed her what had occurred.

'Pack your bags and get ready to leave,' he added.

Antonio then tried phoning and warning others — friends and relatives. Despite the time, most answered their phones, but no one took notice of what he had to say. It wouldn't be long before they wished otherwise, just as he regretted not being more convincing or forceful.

Traveling in his taxi, he and his wife, their two pet cats, and whatever they could grab were out of the city limits by daybreak and making their way to his nephew's farm. By then, the thin woman — who others called Death — was onboard a 9-hour flight to New York City.

CHAPTER VII

Countdown

BY 7 PM, the diner was half full of customers. Bill was busy making drinks, and Lance was long gone; the tremor in Rome seen earlier on the TV was enough to send him home to his family. Quintus, however, remained at the counter, watching TV and drinking umpteen cups of coffee. Luckily, he was impervious to the effects of caffeine. In the past 24 hours, he'd already watched more television than he had in the past decade. It was an extraordinary time.

Quintus checked his watch again. It wasn't long until the big quake was due to hit Rome, according to Goyette's prediction. Over the course of history, he had seen many ruined towns and cities, especially the wasteland of Eastern Europe following the Mongol invasions and later in Western Europe during World War II. The thought of something similar befalling Rome soured his gut, but he had to see if it would eventuate.

If Goyette's quake did transpire, it was evidence enough that what Tai had trained him for had come. In such a development, he'd cancel his job interview scheduled for the next day and get himself to an international airport to catch a flight to China. The only thing that his teacher told him was that when the end times arrived, he would have to return to White Dragon Mountain. He wasn't sure if his mission remained valid, but Tai's words were all he had to go on.

Quintus sensed the people in the traffic outside the diner were driving home or at least somewhere with a TV or WiFi to watch what would transpire, to see if the end really was nigh. But he failed to pick up that among them, there were some, like those in a white Humvee and a following black limousine, who couldn't care less about the fate of the world.

Unsavory

A downside of my telling you this story is I must listen to or be inside the heads of some unsavory characters. On this occasion, I was an unseen witness to a conversation between five men in the back of the stretched limousine that had just driven past the diner.

All of them were simply appalling individuals, including 34-year-old Albert Peach, the account manager from Black Crest. He was as spineless as he was morally corrupt. Among the others were Marx's henchmen — Vacher and Irfan. You should already have a fair idea of who they are.

Seated opposite the Black Crest staff were the Amado

drug cartel's Hector Herera and his sidekick Antonio Chavez. The Amado were sadists; beheadings were their trademark.

Fueled by alcohol and other substances, all five were full of loose talk and bravado.

Despite the 'jolliness' of it all, Irfan was looking back, checking for tails. Herera slapped him on the knee.

'You're making me nervous tipo! No one's going to tangle with us,' the cartel lieutenant said.

Herera thumbed towards his driver and another tough-looking brute in the front.

'My warriors are former Mexican special forces, same as the guys in the Humvee. All U.S. trained,' he said with exaggerated pride. 'No doubt Marx hires quality also, eh?' he said, referring to Irfan and Vacher.

'Yeah, these guys were both black ops,' Peach said way too eagerly.

Vacher gave Peach a displeased sideways glance.

'Who said anything about black ops?' Vacher asked Peach. 'Do you even know anything about black ops?

Herera butted in.

'C'mon, no one cares. Relax guys,' he said. 'I'm hungry; let's eat.'

Herera tapped his driver on the shoulder and issued orders in Spanish.

'Felix, find us somewhere to eat. American food is okay. In fact, go back to that old-style diner we passed before. Tell the Humvee to follow.'

The FBI

Three FBI agents from a special surveillance team were in the back of a moving unmarked van. The one calling the shots was 42-year-old Chris Pena. He and the other two watched monitors showing chopper vision of the cartel's Humvee and limousine.

A brief crackle of static was heard before a voice from the police surveillance helicopter came through a speaker system.

'Both subject vehicles pulling over, turning around on Ryland,' said the voice.

Pena's cellphone vibrated, and after checking the caller's identity, he took the call.

'Agent, what've you got for me?' he asked Joseph Rose, who was phoning in from an FBI strategic information and operations center somewhere in Virginia.

'Zero information so far on the two new arrivals,' Rose said, referring to Vacher and Irfan. 'But I have something on Herera's preppy chaperone.'

Pena, still watching the monitor, switched on the phone's speaker so all could listen.

'His name is Albert Peach, a business development manager for Black Crest, a hedge fund management firm based in NYC. He is pretty dull, but his boss, Aaron Marx, is plenty colorful,' Rose said.

'Pad on the Hamptons, I presume,' Pena said.

'Bit darker than that.'

'How dark are we gonna go?'

'Forget Wall Street, pal, this freaking guy is a member

of several secret occult societies, funds an annual witchcraft event in Georgia, and is a practicing Satanist.'

Pena raised his eyebrows.

'You never cease surprising me, agent Rose, on what you can dig up.'

'Depending on your worldview, he also backs some dubious causes, among them the Hindley chain of abortion clinics, and finances some inane woke causes.'

'But any ideas why his employee is in Reno with cartel maniacs?'

'Yeah, let me get to it; this next point will mean something if you've been watching the TV recently; this guy Marx provided the startup money for Temple Science Ministries and its founder Chuck Goyette.'

'Sure, so he has a diverse portfolio,' Pena said.

'But listen, it's understood he's made most of his billions off the radar through the likes of the Amado cartel,' Rose said.

'Is he under investigation by anyone?'

'Not currently. He has friends in high places. After the last global financial crisis, he was under investigation for security fraud, but it went nowhere. That was as close as anyone got to him.'

Then Rose delivered what he thought was more juicy stuff.

'But if we go east, it gets even more sinister. Marx has made a lot of dough in China, where he's well-connected with Communist Party elite. He is even on a couple of Chinese state company boards in some advisory capacity. He also has a subsidiary called Black Crow that is set to provide logistical, operational, and security services in some of China's border areas. Some say he's the most powerful white guy in China. I guess it helps that he is fluent in Mandarin and six other languages.'

Pena, by this stage, was ready to move on.

'Joe, we're getting information overload here. Any details on his links with the Amado?'

'Yeah, let me get to it. Marx is on extremely friendly terms with some high-ranking party members and one PLA military official, in particular, a General Zhou Lijun.'

'C'mon Joe; I'm running out of time,' Pena said.

'Yeah, yeah, just listen. This General Zhou has an upstart son named Lin who recently became a suspect in the production and shipping of precursor chemicals to Mexican drug cartels.'

Now we're finally getting somewhere, Pena thought. He knew the Amado cartel uses precursors shipped in from China for manufacturing meth, most notably fentanyl which is 50 times more potent than heroin.

'There's more information, data, and details about it all which I'll email you,' Rose added.

'Sure, Joe, much obliged,' Pena said as the call ended.

A minute later, an encrypted email arrived for Pena with more information about Marx. Needless to say, what the FBI thought it knew about the hedge fund manager and his associates in China was merely the tip of a very large and sinister iceberg.

Phone Call

Marx stood alone at the window of his office. Shirtless and barefoot, he took in the nighttime view of New York City. The only thing he had on was his suit pants. Satanic-themed tattoos covered his bareback.

In one hand, he held a lit cigarette and in the other an Atomos smartphone which cost him $15,000. The Atomos was secure enough to give him the confidence no one was eavesdropping or taking his data. The person he was about to call had one as well; in fact, it was a gift he gave him the last time they met.

He scrolled through names and stopped on one that simply read: Lin.

He hit the dial button, and the call went across the globe to southwest China.

A ringtone broke the silence in a patient's room at a Chinese military hospital. Its sound didn't disturb the deathly pale General Zhou Lijun, who lay unconscious in the room's bed, nor did the two elderly women, sitting by his side, show any annoyance. That was left to hard-faced Colonel Deng Jia at the foot of the bed. He gave an evil-eye glance at the expensively dressed Lin, who pulled the ringing Atomos from his jacket pocket. He answered it, fully aware of who was at the other end.

'Mr. Marx, there's no good news,' Lin said in near faultless but accented English, the product of a college education in the U.S.

Back in his office, Marx grunted in frustration.

'Why? How is the general? I need to speak with him.'

Lin made his way out of the room and into the hallway so he could talk more freely.

'My father is sleeping. The transplant was not a success,' he said. 'The doctors call it an acute rejection. It should be treatable with drugs, but they're not working.'

This was the last thing that Marx wanted to hear. He was dependent on the general's goodwill in fulfilling his plans. What's more, he did not trust Lin to have his own father's best interests in mind.

'Your father is as strong as an ox. Can't he just get another liver?' Marx asked.

'Yes, and within a few days if he so chooses to do so, but he doesn't want to kill any more fellow Han Chinese, no matter even if they are enemies of the state. He thinks killing them is bringing him ill fortune,' said Lin, who heard Marx sigh in exasperation.

Yes, Marx knew killing innocent people for their body parts is a fire and brimstone offense that brings on retribution like no one's business, but that was not his concern. For all practical purposes, Marx needed the general alive and useful, if only for just a bit more time.

'Lin, there are over a billion people in China to choose from. Your father is high ranking PLA. What about Tibetans or Uyghurs?'

'We're trying to source other suitable liver donors in the prison system, but time is running out,' Lin replied.

Marx tried to hide the displeasure in his tone.

'Have you had time to follow up on my North Korean arrangements? Your father made some —'

Lin had the phone snatched from his hand. It was Colonel Deng. He bellowed Mandarin into the phone.

'Call back at a convenient time!' he yelled before ending the call.

The military officer thrust the phone back into Lin's hands and re-entered the general's room.

Marx knew who it was; the voice and the manner were giveaways. He also knew Deng had a deep distrust of foreigners, especially well-connected ones.

Back in the hallway, Lin was exasperated by his cousin's behavior. He gathered his thoughts. He feared losing his broader connections with Marx. His lucrative business, shipping precursor chemicals into Mexico, relied on it. Thankfully Deng was not included in that, he reminded himself, but his cousin was a part of this new North Korea deal. *Maybe Deng shouldn't be involved with what Marx wants*, he thought. *Is it too late to have him exit?*

Lin's cell rang again, interrupting his thoughts. He answered it and listened to what was said from the other end. He nodded several times and then walked back inside the general's room, where he approached Deng and offered him the phone.

'Cousin talk to Mr. Marx,' Lin pleaded. 'There's a lot of money at risk.'

Deng reluctantly took the call.

'I have nothing more to say,' Deng said into the phone in Mandarin. 'We can communicate later.'

Marx wasn't in the mood for impertinence, and time was pressing.

'I know you comprehend English, Deng, so listen up,' he said.

'And you speak Mandarin,' Deng replied.

'I do, but that's not the point. The point is — do you want in on the North Korea arrangement?'

'Yes, of course.'

'Then act like it. For the next week, you work for me. You are mine to do as I will. Make no mistake about that. When I tell you to do something, you will do it.'

There were a few moments of silence before Deng replied.

'I will honor our agreement, but your threats only mean something while the general is alive,' he said before ending the call.

No One Laughs in Hell

With the call finished, Marx flung his phone onto the desk in disgust. Several options ran through his mind, but he knew, given the general's condition, he needed to get to China and then North Korea sooner rather than later. The schedule had to be moved forward.

While figuring out how they now needed to travel within the next couple of days, he poured himself a stiff drink. As for Deng, he had thought earlier that he needed him, but given his behavior on the call, he was no longer sure. The colonel may prove to be a liability, but his options, at this stage, were limited.

Grumbling to himself, Marx, now drink in hand, sat on a leather sofa in front of the large, framed portrait of

Mao that was a gift given to him by General Zhou some 20 years previous.

Back then, Marx was a young intern with an international corporation setting up an office in Beijing, where he fell in with a crowd of debauched Communist Party princelings that the older Zhou was a part of. I won't put into your head what they got up to.

Yes, Marx has quite a checkered past. Much more than what the FBI was aware of and even more than what you think you already know, so I'll get to the point.

Marx has made a deal with the devil. The 13 Demon Kings of the Pit to be spot-on exact.

I hope that didn't come across as flippant.

There's nothing amusing at all about Hell, believe me, and that's something Marx was aware of.

I may have taken you to a scene in Hell earlier in this tale, but it was limited by design. If I could convey to you just a bit of Hell's reality, you'd probably never be the same again. Believe me when I say — no one laughs in Hell.

Fundamentally most of you, to varying degrees, are decent people, even if you forget it at times. As for Marx, he's evil to the extreme, and he knew that. In fact, like a small minority of humans, he embraced it. Indeed, he believed he had much in common with the demon kings. A shared hatred of creation is just one example.

But he only became aware of his deal with the demon kings eight years earlier after he went into a deep trance during a ritual at his local coven of the Order of International Satanists. When he came to, he could recall the deal, where, in a bid to join their ranks, he agreed to be the human facilitator for the end of times, a version at least that the demon kings wanted to see played out in their favor and on their terms. They got the nod from their boss Satan and just went for it. Their goal was for everyone to end up in Hell, and Marx, as he recalled, agreed to help with whatever was required.

Undeniably, the fund manager was proud of the 'bargain' he made with the demon kings, a deal which, if he were successful, would see him enthroned as the 14th king upon his return.

If he failed, however, there'd be no throne waiting but instead, an eternity spent at Hell's deepest level. Despite his bravado and wickedness, that thought horrified him and drove him onwards to play his part in bringing on humanity's demise.

He presumed that was why, ever since the ritual, he was permitted to have such memories of not only his time in the abyss but, more importantly, of all his past earthly existences as well. The demons believed Marx had to be fully aware of what was at stake for him to perform optimally. The only risk was that such memories could send him insane.

As for the coming earthquake in Rome, that was actually Marx's idea based on a throwaway suggestion made as he bargained with the demon kings, who surprised him by taking it onboard.

A large digital clock on a cabinet told him it wasn't long till that would transpire. He finished his drink and then found his TV remote, and turned on the walled television in preparation.

For a moment, he thought of asking War, who was probably busy drawing in the boardroom, if he wanted to come in and watch Rome be destroyed but quickly changed his mind. For some reason, Marx found War's presence unsettling. Otherworldly types have a habit of doing that, he supposed.

Hungry Henchmen

Away from prying eyes, Tina and Gabriela flipped a coin in the kitchen to see who would deliver Quintus his order of carrot cake and ice cream. Gabriela won the toss and whooped in delight. Tina laughed, going along for the fun of it. Privately, she was only captivated by the stranger's striking halo. She only wished to talk with him to get to know who he was and what he was about.

'How long's he been here for now?' she asked Gabriela.

'It's been hours since he first walked in, 'bout mid-afternoon.'

'He a friend of Bill's?'

'Not sure, but they've been chatty.'

The subject of their attention remained seated at the diner counter, waiting for the aforementioned dessert. He was checking his watch. It was just a little over 20 minutes until the anticipated destruction of Rome.

Given that the diner was now three-quarters full, Bill was busy making drink orders by the coffee machine at the counter. But, like pretty much everyone else, his mind was on what could happen to the Italian capital and what that would mean for the rest of the world.

'Tell me if something happens, okay?' Bill asked Quintus regarding the TV.

'Sure, will do.'

'It's surreal, isn't it, that the end of the world could end up being broadcast live?'

'That it is.'

Then on the TV, the chubby but well-dressed figure of Chuck Goyette appeared.

'Okay, Bill, they're back interviewing that guy Goyette,' Quintus said, nodding towards the walled television. Bill paused what he was doing and grabbed the television's remote to increase its volume.

Everyone in the diner turned to watch. Tina and Gabriela even exited the kitchen to see Goyette being interviewed outside a chic hotel in LA's West Hollywood. Bill had the volume up just in time, so all could hear the news reporter's one and only question.

'It appears Rome's residents have largely ignored your prediction; most of them are reportedly remaining in the city. How do you feel about that?' the reporter asked Goyette.

'Of course, I feel sorry, I do feel sorry for them, and it's only natural that I feel this way as I made the announcement in advance for their sake and no one else's, certainly not mine. I doubt the people of New York City will be as foolish,' he said before walking off, leaving the reporter.

The news broadcast cut to a commercial break. Bill muted the sound.

'He didn't sound too sorry,' Bill remarked to Quintus as he went back to making drinks.

A split second later, the hair on the back of Quintus' neck stood up. It wasn't a delayed reaction to the TV interview or any pre-quake nerves. He just felt something very wicked come his way. Instinctively he half-swiveled around, and the first thing he saw was Vacher entering the diner. Their eyes met. For several seconds both men held the other's stare.

Quintus then shifted his gaze onto those who Vacher accompanied; Irfan, Peach, Herera, and Chavez. After they walked past, he noted four additional suspicious-looking types — Herera's bodyguards — loitering outside by a parked Humvee and a limousine.

Meanwhile, Tina took Vacher and the other four to a window booth. Vacher couldn't help but notice how nervous the young woman was and how she avoided eye contact with them all. As she handed him a menu, he gave her a gruff look while eyeing her nametag.

'Why thank you Tina,' he said curtly. 'You can get us five coffees for freaking starters.'

Tina nodded as Vacher and the others gave her more details on what types of coffees they wanted, and she then mumbled about returning to take further orders. She left them, gave their order to Bill, and then went to clear another table. Before collecting an armful of plates, she patted down her brow, wiping away beads of sweat.

The amount of darkness she saw entering the diner with the five men startled her. She'd never seen such a concentration of wickedness. Each of them was covered by a dark haze to the point their figures were nearly obscured. The four men outside waiting by the vehicles were likewise swimming in darkness. It was the opposite of what she saw in Quintus.

DING!

Time was moving quickly, and Bill hit his little call bell by the coffee-making machine. He placed three coffees on the counter, and Tina came to pick up.

'For table 13. Espressos to follow,' Bill told her. 'Be careful,' he added, referring to the ominous five.

Quintus watched Tina take the order to the booth. He noted how they gawked at her as she handed out the coffees.

'Hey, chicka that's three. We ordered five,' Herera said menacingly.

'Yes, two more are coming; the espressos, they're being made now. Won't be long,' she softly replied.

As Tina turned to leave, Herera gave her a noisy slap on the behind.

'Be quick then chicka. Ándale! Ándale!'

The others in the booth cackled, but the act caused a hush throughout the rest of the diner.

Tina walked on, red-faced.

At that moment, Quintus wanted to deal with the men in the booth there and then but instead restrained himself. He remained seated out of concern that any intervention would only escalate matters, making it worse.

However, Bill had had enough. He left his coffee machine, came around from the counter, passed both Tina and Quintus, and approached the men in the booth.

The five stopped snickering and looked up at the owner-manager with the big mop of hair in front of them, hands on hips.

'Excuse me, you can't mistreat my staff,' Bill said.

Herera rolled his eyes and moaned.

'C'mon man! You hire people like that; what do you expect, huh? The chicka has a nice rump,' Herera said. 'Smokin' hot!'

Bill glared squarely at Herera.

'Take your trash talk somewhere else. Finish your coffees, then get the hell out. If you're not gone in ten minutes, I'm calling the police,' Bill said.

Herera quickly stood up and got in Bill's face.

'Hey, you show some respect tipo!' Herera yelled as he began to poke Bill in the chest with a finger. 'What do you want, huh? You want me to get loco on all your people here?'

Behind them, Vacher didn't want trouble. He leaned over the booth's table and tugged on Herera's shirt.

'Hey, not here, not now,' Vacher said quietly. 'We can sort this out by other means, another time.'

Herera swatted Vacher's hand away, and he continued harassing Bill, who was now wondering if this guy was all bluff or just downright crazy. He was beginning to realize that it was probably the latter.

'Best you leave now. No one wants trouble,' Bill said, trying not to look or sound alarmed.

'I'm fine with trouble,' Herera said. 'Bring it on!'

And with that, Herera raised his right hand above his head and made a signal to three of his four henchmen outside in the parking lot to come in.

The three saw their boss' signal and assertively rushed into the diner.

Quintus saw them each pulling out pistols as they

moved. They were going in the direction of Herera, and along the way, they'd have to go past Quintus, who was closer to the door entrance.

Once the three were positioned in the diner, Quintus knew these thugs would take further control of the situation. He figured it was now or never to deal with this mess before it got any worse. As the first of the three thugs rushed past, he put out his foot.

'That's enough,' he said steadily.

The first thug tripped over Quintus' foot and fell hard, face first. Quintus next dealt with the two following. His punches were swift and exact, hitting acupressure spots that would result in both being paralyzed for at least 12 hours. After they crumpled to the floor Quintus returned his attention to the thug that he tripped who was now trying to get off the floor. With a right hook, Quintus smashed him again to the floor and then followed through with two sharp jabs to acupressure spots, immobilizing him.

Nearby the coffee machine, Tina watched Quintus then move across the dining area towards Bill and Herera by the booth. To her, he was an orb of magnificent golden light cutting through a fog of darkness.

Once Quintus reached the booth, he pushed Bill out of harm's way and then tried to take out Herera but was blocked by Vacher, who sprung from the booth with pistol in hand. Quintus responded with a powerful roundhouse kick that connected and knocked Vacher off his feet and onto his back on the floor.

Herera tried to flee, but Quintus grabbed him by the collar and yanked him around, and then jabbed him sharply in the armpit, directly pressuring a sweet spot. Herera was now frozen in a crouch-like stance. As a follow-up, Quintus did the same to Chavez, who toppled over onto the floor.

With a knife in hand, Irfan sprang at Quintus from the booth only to be sideswiped by Bill, who came back into the fight with a three-punch combination. Irfan dropped dazed to the floor.

BLAM! BLAM! BLAM! BLAM! BLAM! BLAM!

Things went up a notch as someone outside began firing an automatic weapon into the diner. Tina saw that it was the thug in the parking lot who was now armed with a bullpup assault rifle.

Bullets slammed into glass, furniture, and walls. Diner patrons and staff screamed and dived for cover. A bullet smashed into the coffee machine just a few feet away from Tina as she ducked behind the counter. From there, she couldn't see much; she could only listen to the commotion. Shots being fired. People screaming. She heard one person yell in pain — it sounded like Bill.

BLAM! BLAM! BLAM! BLAM!

More shooting. The chaos appeared to up a notch as a firefight erupted outside. She was unable to see it, but the FBI agents from the van had appeared on the scene; it was now one cartel thug versus four well-armed feds.

Amidst the confusion and clamor, Tina saw at the end of the counter two bad guys scurrying past in a crouch; it was Irfan and Vacher with their dark aura mists trailing. They didn't look in her direction, they were too busy fleeing into the kitchen. Meanwhile, unknown to her, the thug from outside was making a fighting withdrawal into the diner, bringing with him the firefight and all its noise.

Tina similarly couldn't see that from the kitchen, Irfan and Vacher managed to exit the diner via the backdoor to escape into the night. By the time they'd jumped a fence beyond the parking lot, the gun-wielding thug back in the diner was shot dead by the FBI.

It was the last bullet fired for the night.

The madness was over.

Still, behind the counter, Tina could hear people whimpering and crying. She could also hear Quintus tending to Bill.

She crouched up and peered over the counter to witness all the carnage of the dinner. There were prostrate bodies of frightened people everywhere. She saw Isabella towards the back, hiding behind a table. Their eyes met, and each gave a wave indicating they were both alright.

Miraculously, the only two who looked dead to Tina were the gun-wielding thug lying near the doorway and Peach, whose lifeless body was slumped in the booth he was in. Both men now had no auras.

She saw paralyzed Herera frozen in his crouched stance. It made little sense to her why he was that way, but she didn't dwell on it as her attention was taken by the glowing light of Quintus tending to Bill, who had been shot in the upper thigh. Quintus was already in the process of using strips of tablecloth to cover the wound that Bill was holding a napkin on to stem the loss of blood.

Thinking quickly, Tina grabbed a first aid box that was under the coffee machine and took it around to Quintus and Bill. Once she got next to them, she opened it and passed Quintus a bandage.

'This help?' she asked.

'Sure will,' Quintus replied.

'How's he doing?'

'He's lost some blood, in a bit of shock, but he'll pull through.'

'Hang in there Bill,' she said as Quintus began wrapping the bandage around Bill's thigh and over the cloth already covering the wound.

'Freak show over?' Bill faintly asked through his pain.

'Yeah, no more drama. Those lunatics won't be doing anything nasty for a while,' Quintus replied.

Tina pulled her phone out from her pocket and began dialing a number.

'I'll call an ambulance,' she said. 'Actually, sounds like some are on their way, maybe,' she added.

Indeed, distant but approaching sirens could be heard. Around the same time, Pena, the head of the FBI team, entered the diner with his weapon raised.

'FBI. Everybody, please stay down, remain as you are, don't move until we say otherwise,' Pena said.

He saw Quintus and Tina tending to Bill.

'But you two folks keeping nursing that wounded man,' he said. 'Ambulances will be here soon,' he added.

'Everyone else, just keep your hands where we can see them, just till we get everything sorted.'

Everyone else complied except for Herera, who remained frozen as he was.

As the sound of ambulances came nearer, Quintus tightened the bandage a bit more and gave Bill a smile.

'You're gonna be fine Bill. Paramedics will be here soon, they'll give you something for the pain.'

Quintus then looked to Tina by his side.

'You okay?'

She nodded yes and managed to smile just as two ambulances pulled up outside. The glare of their flashing lights bounced off the diner's windows.

Then someone screamed.

'Oh, no, oh my gosh!'

It was a diner customer, a middle-aged woman. She was lying on the floor but still managed to point at the walled television that still worked despite being hit by a bullet.

'It's happening!'

Quintus looked up at the TV and what he saw made his blood run cold. It was dawn in Rome. Video was being shot from the safety of a helicopter. The earthquake had begun. The first thing he saw was the collapse of the Colosseum, then the Roman Forum. Nearby ant-like figures of people on the streets tried in vain to outrun falling debris. Not far away, the quake reduced the Vatican to rubble.

The video from the helicopter panned, offering a broader panorama of the city. Seismic waves spread. Wide-scale devastation followed.

'It's the end! It's no joke! It's the end of everything!' the woman screamed.

CHAPTER IX

Sketches

THE 9.7 MAGNITUDE quake that destroyed Rome was the largest in recorded history. Now that it had transpired, Marx was strangely disappointed. He'd anticipated it would have given him much more satisfaction than it did. After five minutes of watching the televised disaster, he was bored. Nothing could fill his void. He turned off the television, got properly dressed, and then exited his office.

On his way to the lift, Marx made a detour to the boardroom where War was alone drawing with a pencil in a sketchbook on the table. The bearded man looked up at his visitor, who stopped at the doorway. Neither smiled at the other.

'Rome is no more,' Marx said coldly. 'Death certainly makes the rest of you three appear lackadaisical.'

War ignored the comments and returned to his drawing.

Marx entered the room.

'Do you know what the definition of lackadaisical is?' he asked War, who ignored him and kept drawing.

'Of course, you don't. Lackadaisical — lacking enthusiasm or being spiritless,' Marx said as he began looking at some of the drawn-upon single pages spread on the table. One was of cult leader Chuck Goyette talking into a microphone, and another was of an unsmiling Death in her skinny-fit jeans. Then he saw a sketch of himself seated in a chair with the picture of Mao looming behind him.

'Cute,' Marx commented sourly. 'Why do you draw like this? Stop yourself from going mad? That's what Goyette thinks. He implied you can't handle this realm's reality.'

War still didn't reply or react. He just continued drawing in his book.

Marx dropped the sketch of himself back onto the table.

'Our schedule has moved forward. Day after tomorrow, we leave for China and North Korea. There, your input is finally required,' he said before turning to go.

Marx exited the room and made his way to the elevator.

On his way down, he thought about the lack of emotion he saw in War, just as he'd earlier witnessed in Famine and Death. All dullards. Chuck Goyette, though, was another thing. He came in advance of the others, spending two years fronting Temple Science Ministries. From day one, he was as emotional as any typical American, if not more so.

Marx considered such oddities as he left his building, crossed the road, and entered his multi-roomed nightclub, The Devil's Pleasure Palace. He waved away two bouncers who usually hung around him to ensure he wouldn't be bothered by club patrons. Usually, the club was bursting with clientele on mind-bending substances, some doing deviated things. Tonight, there was hardly a soul about. The broadcasting of the end of one of the world's most iconic cities on TV kept them away.

After getting a drink, he sauntered into the club's dimly lit dance area. The large space was near empty save for dancers in two gibbet-like chrome cages that hung from the ceilings. Arty versions of the device that imprisoned Quintus centuries earlier. The space around them blared techno music. A youthful but overweight DJ in a booth was responsible for that. It was just how Marx liked it and somewhat reminded him of a softer version of the sounds he heard in the first ring of the fourth circle of Hell.

Marx felt his cellphone buzz in a trouser pocket. He took the call. It was Vacher calling from Reno. He sought out a quiet room in his club to talk.

The Playground

On his cellphone, Vacher was hiding behind playground equipment centered in a dimly lit park. Beside him, Irfan tried listening while keeping his eyes open for police. The Pakistani heard some yelling at the other end of the call after Vacher briefly explained what occurred at the diner. When Marx calmed down, Vacher switched on the speaker so Irfan could fully listen.

'And where is Peach?' Marx asked.

'We lost Peach, he might be in custody,' Vacher said while Irfan shook his head.

'No, he's dead. Stray cartel bullet to the head,' Irfan said.

'Oh yeah, that's correct, Peach is collateral damage. Sorry, Mr. Marx, I've got a slight concussion,' Vacher said.

Back in New York, Marx swore further. After half a minute of that, the fund manager steadied himself and began to explore options.

'The Reno private investigator you mentioned, is he dependable?' he asked.

'Jack Day, yeah. Ex-cop, bit long in the tooth, not cheap, but he's discreet and well connected,' Vacher said.

'Sound him out, and if he wants the work, get him to phone me ASAP. Tell him we will triple his usual rate and pay it wherever he wants. At this stage, money is no issue. I just need you two out of there and back in New York,' Marx said. 'Get to it and call him.'

The Cartel Boss

Marx hung up on Vacher only to have another incoming call. He noted the caller ID and knew he had to answer it.

'Hello, Senor Lazcano,' Marx said as he began to pace around the dark empty room he had relocated to.

Some 2,000 miles away, Amado cartel chief Alfonso Lazcano was at the other end of the line. He was lying on a massage table, being kneaded by a masseur in the comfort of his mansion. He watched TV coverage of the Rome earthquake while he spoke on the phone.

'Mr. Marx, I've been told about a shooting incident at

a diner in Reno. The details are vague, so I'm calling to ask if you know anything,' Lazcano said.

'Yes, I have only learned of it, so I'm trying to get to the bottom of it as we speak, but from what I know, there are at least two dead: one mine, one yours,' Marx replied.

Lazcano grunted and cleared his throat.

'I will send some men to Reno; they will also make enquiries. Mercenary types. Tough hombres,' he added, just for the drama of it.

'I'd appreciate it if we could work together on this matter,' Marx said.

'Of course, my friend,' Lazcano said. 'Call me when you find out more, and we will see how we can sort out this mess.'

'I won't rest until I do.'

'Yes, Mr. Marx, no rest for the wicked. That's what I admire about you. Are you watching the news about the fall of Rome?'

'I was.'

'How will it affect the markets?'

'It will be worse than anything in living memory, they may even close the markets for a period.'

For a further ten minutes, Marx told Lazcano what could happen in global markets over the short and mid-terms. There seemed little point for Marx in discussing the long term.

'Very interesting,' Lazcano said. 'Will it affect our China supplies? Can they still deliver, do you think?'

'Of course, it won't be an issue. It's a priority for us and my Chinese associates,' Marx said.

'I'm glad you see it that way. Time will tell, I guess, my friend,' Lazcano said. 'But the million-dollar question is, Mr. Marx do you believe the end of the world is coming?'

'Maybe for Italy, but for the rest of us, I think it'll just be business as usual,' Marx lied.

'Yes, well, let's see what happens to you New Yorkers in a few days. To be on the safe side, you should go on holiday, even come visit me in Matamoros,' Lazcano said.

Marx sensed it wasn't a genuine offer, not that that mattered.

'Speak with you soon,' Lazcano said as he hung up.

The Email

Marx left the nightclub, and five minutes later, he was in the large entertainment room of his penthouse apartment, one floor above his office. There, he sat on a black leather sofa and surfed the net on his laptop, monitoring market reaction to the earthquake out of interest.

It wasn't until just after midnight that he received a call from Vacher telling him that private investigator Jack Day was onboard. Day had already picked up Vacher and Irfan and had them safely hidden.

Vacher put Day on the call, and an agreement was struck to get both men to the local airport in the morning. There they'd be put on Black Crest's corporate jet, which would take them back to New York. As the call wrapped up, Marx asked Day to find out what the cops knew about the diner fiasco. He could use such information to appease his cartel client.

Following the call, Marx slumped into the sofa's corner and took several sleeping pills. He promptly fell into a deep dreamless sleep, one that wasn't disturbed until a fair bit of time later when his cellphone beeped, letting him know a text message had arrived.

He sat up and noted the sun coming through the curtains. Before reaching for his phone, he checked his wristwatch and cursed after seeing how late it was. It was just before eight in the morning.

He picked up his phone and read the text message that said: 'Check email,' and he turned on his laptop. He opened an email with the subject line: 'From Jack Day.' Inside it was a link for a video from the diner's CCTV.

Marx clicked on the link and watched the video of the incident, which began with Herera taunting Bill, followed by Quintus intervening. More than once, an excited Marx replayed what he saw.

Jack Day's Dreams

For Jack Day, the deal with Marx was like all his Christmases had come at once. As the 59-year-old sat in his stationary van opposite the FBI's Reno office, he could only chuckle over the easiest money ever made. He had been promised a half-million to shelter the two guys from Black Crest and then deliver them to the airport later that morning.

Then the deal got even sweeter when Marx promised more money if he could find the 'karate guy' with the short haircut featured in the CCTV video of the diner incident. Another half-million there.

Day had FBI and local police sources, so he had no problem getting the right information — the karate guy's identity, his vehicle details, and why he was in Reno — which he forwarded to Marx as soon as he got them.

All so easy, Day smugly thought. Now he couldn't help but daydream about what he'd do with all that money. Either early retirement in Panama or Colombia. He had zero time for all the headline chatter about a pending Apocalypse.

The guy that Day was additionally hired to find was a Canadian national identified as Quintus Bremmer. He was ordered to follow him undetected until told otherwise. When he spoke with Marx, Day also made it clear that he would not approach or confront 'Bremmer'.

He had watched the diner video. There was no way he was getting physical with him. At his stage of life, Day knew his limitations.

As he dreamed of things he hoped to come, his cell-phone rang. It was from New York. It was Marx again. Day, of course, took the call, and with money on his mind, he did so with a smile.

'Mr. Marx, how may I help you sir?'

'Any developments?' Marx asked sharply at the other end.

'I'm pretty sure he is still with the feds. I'll call you when there is any movement,' Day said. 'But there's one more thing about payment. If you want to give it to me in cash today, I'm fine with that, but if you would prefer to transfer it to my Panama bank account within the next hour, that's fine too,' he said, hoping he wasn't sounding too greedy. 'Just need to be clear on these things, sir. Nature of the game, I'm afraid to say, and I hope you understand,' he added.

Marx didn't hesitate to reply.

'I'm flying to Reno, I'll give you your money myself,' he said. 'Where are Vacher and Irfan?'

'Back at my place, keeping low until they fly out,' he said.

'Fine. There is one more thing related to Quintus Bremmer. I have some associates currently traveling to Reno by road,' Marx said, referring to the Amado cartel team sent by Alfonso Lazcano. 'They will link up with you, and they will take care of Bremmer. Is that clear?'

'Clear as crystal, sir.'

'They have your number, they will be in touch soon enough,' Marx said.

FBI Offer

It was a call from the hospital confirming the paralysis that immobilized Herera and some of his thugs had worn off, which meant Quintus could leave the FBI building. The authorities were holding him in case the paralysis was permanent because if it was, the feds assumed a vengeful cartel would spare no effort in tracking him down.

Now given that Herera and his thugs weren't paralyzed, the feds judged it was marginally safer.

But it must be said, like most of the world with access to a TV or the internet, the feds were preoccupied with the idea that doomsday was just around the corner. This was in the back of Pena's mind when he and two other tired senior agents made Quintus one last half-hearted offer in the interview room they were in.

'So Mr. Bremmer, again, I can't stress it enough — the Amado cartel is brutal, they're animals; we'd like you to reconsider and take the agency's offer of protection, even if on a temporary basis,' Pena said.

'As I said, I'm fine,' Quintus said.

'Additionally, there are the guys who work for the New York financier, one of whom is now dead. The other two you helped beat up before they got away, they may also be wanting some payback,' Pena said.

'Thanks, but I can look after myself.'

Pena had now heard enough. He had other things to do.

'Okay, if that's the case, then I think we're done here but contact us if you have second thoughts. One of our guys will drive you to your hotel.'

Quintus nodded in thanks and left the room with an agent who'd be his driver. As they walked, he battled trying to keep Rome's obliteration from his mind. He had to focus on getting out of Reno and flying to China as per prophecy. Humanity, he presumed, still needed saving.

From the FBI building, the agent drove and dropped Quintus off at his hotel, where he washed and changed. He made a phone call canceling his helicopter job interview, meditated for half an hour, and then checked out.

After that, he drove his pickup truck to one of Reno's hospitals, unaware that along the way, he had a tail following him. Day's white van.

Hospital Visit

Quintus was thinking it'd be best to fly from San Francisco to China as he walked through the hospital's reception after visiting Bill in his sick bed. Near the exit, he was intercepted by Tina the waitress from the diner.

'Hi there, were you just seeing Bill?' she asked.

It was a moment before Quintus recognized her, given she was dressed in sporty clothes and carrying a bike helmet.

'Hey again, yeah, I was. He seems to be doing okay. Doctors say he'll be out of hospital in a few days, which is good. You on your way to visit him?'

'I already have, just a bit before,' she said, smiling.

A half-hour earlier, Tina was leaving the hospital after visiting Bill until she saw Quintus. She first saw his glowing golden aura enter the reception area, followed by his physical self. He was unaware of her presence as he passed through on his way to see Bill. Not wanting to miss the chance of speaking to him again, she sat and waited for his return which, as you know, just occurred.

'I was about to go, then I saw you and thought I'd say hello, see how you're doing,' Tina said.

'I'm fine, and you after that mad circus last night?'

'Took a while to get to sleep for sure,' she said. 'At least Bill is in good spirits despite everything, but he's pretty much always like that: chilled. But it still looks like he's getting out of town,' she added.

Quintus nodded.

'Yeah, he mentioned he and his wife are already

planning to take their two kids to stay with her brother in Montana, who's into prepping and survival,' he said.

'The Rome earthquake has everyone spooked. It's all they're talking about,' Tina said. 'I told my friends what happened at the diner, and they're like: "Who cares — New York is gonna be destroyed in a week!"'

'Yeah, it's bizarre,' he said. 'You staying in Reno?'

Tina shook her head.

'I need to get to Sacramento to be with family, hopefully via bus or a train whenever one was next available,' she said.

'Well, I'm heading to San Francisco today, and I have to go through Sacramento, so I can give you a lift if you want,' he said. 'It's only a few hours' drive from here, I think.'

'Yes, two and a bit, but my mom and dad would kill me for traveling with a virtual stranger.'

'Well, we don't want that to happen,' he said, smiling.

But Tina knew what Quintus was made of and understood she was safe in his company. What's more, she wanted to spend more time with him.

'But dang it! It's the end of everything, so some rules now no longer apply. So, gosh, yes, I will take you up on your kind offer,' she said. 'I can go this morning if that is what you had planned or whenever, but I just need to get some things from my place on the other side of town, if that's okay.'

'Sure, not a problem. I'm glad to have company,' he said.

They left the hospital building and made their way to his pickup in the parking lot. Unknown to them, Day was taking their photos from his parked van. After putting Tina's bike into the rear of the pickup, they drove out of the hospital grounds, and an hour later, after going via her student house, they were on Dwight D. Eisenhower Highway heading towards California. Meanwhile, Day was following.

The Crow

It was midday and Marx was halfway across America, flying west in his corporate jet. It was painted black, his corporate color. Unsurprisingly, it was nicknamed the 'Crow.' The lavish $53 million aircraft was divided into five sections, including a walk-in cargo area.

Typically, the Crow could take 13 passengers, but on this occasion, Marx was one of three. Behind him, at the very back, just out of earshot, were two of his Black Crow soldiers for hire.

He looked out his window down upon the Great Plains with unfocused eyes. He held his Atomos phone to an ear while waiting for the private investigator Day to pick up at the other end. When the connection was made, he drew down the window shade.

'Hello, Mr. Marx,' Day said.

'Did you link up with my associate's men?' Marx asked about Alfonso Lazcano's own mercenary types, the tough hombres.

'Yes, two teams in separate vehicles. They are now tailing the subject who entered California some 20 or so minutes ago,' Day said. 'I'm on my way back to Reno and will see you at the airport after I pick up your two guys from my residence.'

'Good. I'll see you soon enough,' Marx said before ending the call.

He picked up his iPad and revisited a breaking news report he had seen earlier. Its headline read: 'Cult Leader Brings Forward Doomsday Prediction, New York City Now Only Has Three Days.'

Marx could only sigh and shake his head at what was Chuck Goyette's first media interview since the Rome earthquake. Out of frustration, Marx regathered his phone and dialed it. Someone at the other end picked up, a Temple Science Ministries staff member.

'I need to speak to Mr. Goyette; it's Aaron Marx calling,' he said.

The staff member handed the phone to Goyette, who was with his team behind a stage inside a jam-packed sports stadium,

'Greetings and salutations from Los Angeles. How are you today, Marx?' Goyette asked.

'Somewhere between frustrated and baffled. I've been reading the news, and according to at least one New York publication, the schedule has been altered,' Marx said.

'I presume you are talking about that article with the overly sensational headline,' Goyette said. 'But yes, the doomsday schedule has been brought forward because you're the one zipping off to China earlier than expected. Thank you for the notification, by the way, about changes to the so-called plan you always harp on about,' he added.

'There have been complications. It certainly wasn't

done on a whim, but it doesn't really affect what you are meant to be doing,' Marx replied.

'Look, I don't care for lame excuses. You should have consulted with me first,' Goyette said. 'Stick to the plan, isn't that what you like say?"

'It's happened now, so just tell me your amended schedule,' Marx said, now not even trying to hide his sullenness.

'Marx, how about you just follow the news like everyone else? I see no point repeating myself to every Tom, Dick, and Harry. You're the delivery boy, so just get War to the Far East, as you're supposed to, and let nature take its course,' Goyette said. 'This venture is bigger and more finely tuned than you think. I'm surprised the demon kings failed to spell that out for you.'

A large chant in the stadium began, making it hard for Marx to hear Goyette and vice versa.

Some 10,000 people in front of the stage were now chanting: 'Chuck! Chuck! Chuck!'

'What's that appalling racket? I can hardly hear you,' Marx asked.

'Oh, ignore that; it's just the sound of well-earned adulation,' Goyette said. 'But look, I, for one, have no doubts you'll also be an outstanding king of the pit and that you'll be as cruel as the best of them.'

'This is straying from what I want to discuss,' Marx said.

'I just wanted to say you could've got so much more if you negotiated with a bit of gusto,' Goyette said. 'The demon kings of the pit are not really that bright y'know. Anyway, your loss.'

An exasperated Marx could hardly restrain his ever-increasing hatred for Goyette.

'I got what I bargained for,' Marx said.

'Ha, yes, you did; driven by a fusion of terror and near-ancient grievances, no doubt. Either way returning to Hell must be a horrid predicament, king or no king,' Goyette said.

Marx tried reining in his emotions which he knew could send him over the edge if he let it. He breathed in deeply and waited a few seconds till he could reply in a steady manner.

'Yes, and a multitude of words, Mr. Goyette, is no proof of a prudent mind,' Marx said.

But this only made Goyette burst out in laughter.

'Dear me, resorting to pilfering Greek proverbs now, are we Marx? How pitiable,' he said, chuckling away. 'You know what else I heard? That you're planning to conduct a coup once you get to hell, get rid of the demon kings, and make yourself top dog.'

'Ridiculous,' Marx said.

'Yeah, maybe, but don't tell me you haven't fantasized about it. Now my people are waiting, and I dare not test their patience anymore. Time to go. Just do your bit and just get War to the East,' Goyette said as he hung up.

Goyette gave his phone to one of his assistants, who, in exchange, handed him a microphone. The crowd on the other side of the stage was still chanting his name. He walked up some steps onto the stage and made his way to the front into full view of the crowd, who gave him a rock-star reception.

He lapped it up.

'Well, hello, Los Angeles! My oh my, this truly is west coast hospitality at its finest. Isn't this a grand occasion?!' Goyette yelled. 'No matter what has happened halfway around the world in Italy, it's still an awesome day if you are a member of the Temple Science Ministries!'

The crowd roared back in the affirmative, and a new chant began circling the stadium. 'Survivors! Survivors! Survivors! Survivors! Survivors!'

Moms Know Best

Tina did most of the talking for the bulk of the trip right up until her mother called her cellphone to check on their progress.

'He's a Reno friend,' Tina said in response to her mother's question about who was driving the vehicle. 'Don't worry, mom, he's a very responsible driver plus a super nice guy,' she said, shooting a grin at Quintus at the wheel. 'We're still an hour and a bit away, so maybe we'll be too late for lunch. Yes, mom, okay, mom.'

She lowered her phone and looked at Quintus.

'Do you like Thai food? Bangkok Thai, to be precise? Not so spicy. Mom wants to know if you would like to have a late lunch with us.'

'Thank your mom for me, but I gotta keep driving to San Francisco.'

'You hear that, mom?' Tina said into the phone and then listened to her mom's reply. 'Mom said a man's gotta eat. She'll have some food there at home for you.'

'Well,' he said. 'Sounds like I can't say no, so count me in.'

'All right, mom Quintus is in, so we will see you soon. What? Ha, ha, err okay mom, I'll check,' Tina said. 'My mom wants to know what kind of name is Quintus?'

'It's an old Latin name.'

'There you go, mom, you hear that? No, he's not Latino.'

'Italian heritage.'

'Quintus is Italian, mom, not that it matters where he is from!'

For the last 30 seconds of the call, Tina and her mom said goodbyes in Thai.

After ending the call, she looked at Quintus.

'My mom is the best cook in the world. You're one lucky guy,' she said.

'I'm sure I am. Did you tell your mom about what happened at the diner?'

'Not yet. She'd worry too much if I just blabbed it out over the phone,' she said. 'I'll tell her in person after we arrive.'

'Wise girl,' said Quintus.

'But given the events in Italy and what that's all about, she was pretty chilled. Heck, she mightn't even be fully aware of what's happening. Mom has never been a fan of watching regular news, maybe she tunes into Thai language news now and then.'

'You speak other languages apart from Thai and English?' he asked her.

'Some high-school Mandarin and French. How about you?'

'Some Spanish and bits of pieces of others.'

From what she could see, Tina knew Quintus was great. Going by his aura, he was unsurpassed as far as she was concerned. But he was very guarded in what he said. So far, he had offered few real details about himself. She wanted to know more, but she was too well-mannered to intrude, so she just stayed on the obvious topic of conversation.

'It's hard to fathom the end of the world might be soon,' Tina quietly said.

'Let's hope it doesn't come to that,' Quintus said.

In a bid to lighten the mood, he asked Tina about her art education studies. And from that, she was gladly surprised to find that they both shared a love for the Renaissance and the culture that it created. Quintus, of course, experienced that glorious period, not that he could share that with Tina. For decades he actually helped drive the Renaissance with his architecture, first in Florence and then through Italy and elsewhere in Europe.

Quintus spoke in moderation, saying about as much as he thought she could accept. In turn, he listened to her talk about her admiration for the likes of Raphael, Andrea del Sarto, and of course, everyone's favorites, Michelangelo and Leonardo da Vinci.

The flow of the conversation stopped when Quintus noticed the pickup truck's temperature gauge was higher than usual. It wasn't extreme, but he didn't want to risk it. A month earlier, the radiator needed repairs which he did himself, but he wasn't overly confident in what he did. After passing through the town of Colfax, he pulled up at a small gas station that was devoid of customers.

'I better check under the hood,' Quintus told Tina as he parked the pickup. 'And get some backup coolant while I'm at it. Won't take long.'

'Okay, sure, do what you gotta do,' she said.

'You like anything from the gas station store?' he offered her as he stepped out of the vehicle.

'No, I'm good. Hope you don't mind me not coming out, I have to speak with some friends who have been messaging me all day,' she said. 'With the Apocalypse, they're freaking out somewhat.'

'No problem,' Quintus said before he popped the hood to check on his engine's coolant levels, which he promptly found were in order.

After dropping the hood, he went into the shop, where he was greeted by a young shop clerk armed with a price gun.

'Excuse me, buddy, I'm after some coolant,' Quintus said.

'Yeah, over in that corner. I haven't been there yet, so it's still reasonably priced. So be quick; I'm bumping everything up by 70 percent today,' the clerk said. 'With the world going to end, the manager reckons prices are set to skyrocket.'

Group Chat

In the parked pickup, Tina was talking on her phone in a group chat with four of her friends; three girls and a guy. All were engrossed in their conversation.

'I tried getting on the website for Temple Science Ministries earlier today and couldn't,' said one of the girls.

'I heard it crashed with so many people trying to visit it after Rome,' said another.

'Hey, everyone! Chuck Goyette is actually live on TV right now from Los Angeles,' chipped in the third girl.

'I'm not going to watch him just out of principle,' the guy friend said. 'Goyette gives me the creeps. He is the Walmart version of the Antichrist.'

Laughter.

Tina was so occupied with the conversation she didn't notice as two vehicles — a van and an SUV, both black — parked to the left side of the pickup. Nor did she register two men getting out of the van and quickly approaching.

It was only when they yanked open her door did she realize she was in trouble. They grabbed her and hauled her out of the pickup's cabin.

'Make noise, and you're dead, do as we say, and you'll live,' one of them said to her in accented English.

As they dragged her towards the van, her phone spilled out of her hands. Her online friends yelled hopeless concerns until a thug crushed the phone under the heel of his boot.

A hood was placed over Tina's head. The last thing she saw was the murky blackness of the thugs' auras.

After forcing her into the van, they waited.

Gold Tooth

Carrying his coolant purchase Quintus exited the store and promptly saw that Tina wasn't in the pickup. A split second later, he saw thugs around the van where Tina was inside with her head covered. She sat near the open side door. Beside her, a thug — with a gold tooth — had a pistol thrust into her ribs.

Quintus had, by this stage, stopped in his tracks. He counted seven thugs, one of whom was behind him. The one with the gold tooth smiled in a not-so-friendly manner.

'Machotes, you've caused an awful mess, and now we gotta clean it up,' said the thug with the gold tooth. 'No matter. It's our job. Nothing personal, okay? So, take three steps to your left, and then get down to your knees,' he ordered.

Quintus may have performed wonders at the diner the night before, but he couldn't repeat them under these circumstances and risk Tina's life. There was little choice but to do as instructed and hope to do something when odds improved.

After dropping the coolant, he stepped to the side and got to his knees. As he put his hands on his head, the thug behind him approached and walloped him on the head. Quintus went down semi-stunned. Sprawled on the ground, the last thing he sensed was a needle jab into his side and something being injected inside him. That something knocked him out.

CHAPTER X

In The Shade of The Crow

It was mid-afternoon, and the Crow was parked in a quiet corner of the Reno Tahoe International Airport. Marx was outside it, standing in its shade while talking on his cellphone. He was busy cajoling Kristen back in New York City in a bid to try and stop her from resigning as his personal assistant.

'Listen to me, I simply can't have you just finish like this,' Marx said sharply. 'I realize you have fears, but you have a job to do and an obligation to me. It's just not acceptable.'

While Kristen replied, he kept an eye on Jack Day's van just some 100 feet away. It was parked beside a hangar. Inside it, Day counted the cash he was given for delivering Vacher and Irfan, who were now up in the Crow.

After a minute, Kristen finished what she had to say. None of it swayed Marx, but he acted otherwise to get what he wanted, so he softened his tone.

'Look, Kristen, I'm certainly not happy. I thought you

were made of sturdier stuff, but the best I can do is meet you halfway,' Marx said. 'Which means I want you to come to China with me, with Ivan and some of the team, for the three or so days of business,' he said. 'You won't be in New York in case that rumored earthquake does eventuate, and then when we fly back, I will take you to wherever you want in the U.S., to your family's home, and then you can finish up with no more qualms from me,' he said. 'That's not even a week, very generous considering I'm meant to have a month's notice.'

Kristen's ten-second reply to his offer was noncommittal.

'Fine, think about it some more, Kristen, and get back to me with a freaking proper answer. You have an hour to do so,' Marx said. He ended the call without a goodbye.

Marx looked up as he heard Day's van start and then watched it drive away. One of his mercenaries, positioned on the ground at the front of the aircraft, then alerted him that two other vehicles were approaching from the other side.

A van and an SUV.

It was Alfonso Lazcano's crew.

Inside the van were Quintus and Tina, both of whom were still out cold. They had black bags over their heads and their hands tied with heavy-duty cable ties. Despite some rough handling, they remained unconscious while they were transferred into the Crow.

Mad Man Raving

Quintus was unsure how long he and Tina had been airborne for when he became conscious. He first became aware when someone grabbed his legs and dragged him out from the plane's cargo hold and into the main passenger's cabin.

That someone then pulled the black hood off his head. It was Vacher, his face contorted with loathing. He roughly pushed Quintus into a sitting position on the floor and propped him up against a seat.

Quintus was still woozy and disoriented from the drugs. His hands were behind his back, restrained by the cable ties which bit into his wrists.

Vacher stepped back, and through bleary eyes, Quintus saw someone else, a seated man looking at him. He was dressed in a suit, drinking liquor from a tumbler, but due to his blurred vision, Quintus couldn't immediately make out the man's facial features.

'You've only got yourself to blame, you know,' said the man who, of course, was Marx.

'What the hell is going on?' Quintus asked with a slight slur.

'Speak only when told,' Vacher hissed.

'No, let my old friend have his say. He's earned it in a roundabout kind of way. What's more, he's a senior citizen, so we should show him due respect,' Marx mockingly said.

Quintus closed his eyes and quietly sighed. He didn't want to entertain any thoughts on who this person was or could be.

'It was only a matter of time, Quintus. I must say I'm

impressed by how you've managed to ramble around the world for so long and not get tired by it all,' Marx said.

'You've confused me with someone else,' Quintus said with his eyes still shut.

'Don't lie to me,' Marx shot back. 'You know full well that I'd find you sooner or later. True, the timing hasn't been at all convenient.'

Quintus then accepted who the gloating man was, but he didn't want to admit it openly. He opened his eyes, and, with more clarity, he studied Marx properly. It was unmistakable who Marx was — another Caucasian version of Meng.

Quintus sighed heavier this time. Nothing good came from meeting Meng's reincarnations in the past, yet he was not afraid. There was something fatalistic and even purposeful about it all, as odd as that might sound, and so he spoke.

'Do what you want with me or get whatever it is off your chest but just leave the girl out of it,' he said firmly.

'Leave the girl out of it? You and I both know that is not going to happen,' Marx said curtly.

'Touch her and —'

WHACK!

With a downward swing, Vacher struck Quintus hard across the face, leaving a welt on his cheek.

'No need for that yet, Vacher, in fact, you can leave now,' Marx ordered.

After giving Quintus a three-second death stare, Vacher did as he was told and went up front to join Irfan and the others.

'You'll have to excuse him; he's somewhat upset by what

happened at the diner with you kicking him around the place. His ego is somewhat fragile, but he doesn't know you two have a shared past and that there might be some animosity there,' Marx said. 'You do know who he was, don't you?'

'I don't care.'

'Oh, I doubt that. You will care. He was Andrei Vasiliev; remember him? That geriatric pyromaniac neighbor of yours back in Boise, Idaho.'

For a further five minutes, Marx described — with relish, I may add — what Vasiliev did on that awful day when Quintus lost his wife and daughter.

Quintus tried his best to hide it, but Marx's revelations hit him like a sledgehammer. Yet somehow, as Marx continued, he managed to remain poker-faced.

But as your narrator, I'll momentarily interject in what largely devolved into a long-winded monologue from Marx, something hard on the ears, so I'll filter much of what he said, mostly about their karmic ties, which included what occurred on White Dragon Mountain in 1966 when he was then the Red Guard known as The Hammer.

'I was tasked with neutralizing your overprotective master who was still, after all those years, skulking in that cave,' Marx said about the killing of Tai, as covered earlier in this tale. 'Admittedly, I didn't pull the trigger; I got someone else to do it, someone else still alive today, if only just, but nevertheless, the deed was done, and then you had no guardian angel, and Vasiliev was then meant to do you in stateside, but the moron killed your family instead.'

Marx then revealed to Quintus more about Vacher,

who, along with Irfan, was one of the three killed on the Reno train platform.

'You punched them and me back into oblivion,' he said. 'Do you remember?'

Quintus didn't reply, and so Marx promptly continued.

'They were both similarly involved with you being caged back in Ireland. Even further back to China.'

Marx told Quintus that Vacher and Irfan were, along with himself as Meng, the ones that he'd also killed on the mountain.

'It might sound like ancient history, but it all lives on till today; so it was you who got the ball rolling. Like I said, you've only got yourself to blame.'

Quintus closed his eyes, wanting to shut out Marx's words and the whiney sound of his voice.

'I don't want to hear to anymore,' Quintus said in unintended words.

'No, that's not how it works. But if it makes you feel any better, when I was that Red Guard, I died only a few days after your master was slain. Too much rice wine, and I slipped off a rickety riverboat just as we passed a giant Buddha statue carved into a stone cliff face. Comical, really,' Marx said. 'However, anyone who claims to drown is a painless way to die is kidding themselves.'

And then he continued, going on about how in the life before that, he was crushed to death in a Siberian mine by a boulder the size of a bus. He'd been a Japanese POW caught by the Soviets in 1945.

'I'd been with the Imperial Japanese Army's covert Unit 731 in northern China,' Marx bragged. 'In this unit, we conducted biological medical experiments on living people. Somewhat gruesome, but if you don't mind that type of work, it was rather gratifying,' he said. 'Not as gratifying though when compared to what I did as Meng or Entwistle, or that Red Guard or even mad crazy Chivington for that matter.'

Marx then gulped the last bit of liquor from the tumbler and poured himself a fresh round as he resumed talking.

'I guess I'm a bit like you, Quintus, with memories stretching back more than 2,000 years, but much of it, for me, was in the underworld where I made my deal. You know what that was?'

Quintus ignored the question and kept his eyes closed.

'You want to know the deal I made?' Marx asked again.

Quintus still didn't reply.

'You don't want the truth?!' Marx asked, this time borderline shouting.

Quintus maintained his silence.

'Well, I'm going to tell you anyhow!' Marx laughed. 'A big part of my deal was that I had my final revenge upon you,' he said. 'And for a while, it didn't look like it was going to happen, and I was beginning to think I'd been suckered in.'

Marx then spoke of how he now needed to be more of a pragmatist, as there was, he said, certainly more at stake if he failed to deliver on his part of the deal with the demon kings as opposed to the other way around.

After taking another quaff of his drink, he looked hard at Quintus.

How pathetic. Defeated. Spiritless, Marx thought.

'Difficult to believe you were once among the best that humanity had to offer,' Marx said. He then lent forward to emphasize what came next.

'Let me tell you something really juicy. Those three bashing murders you committed at the Reno railway station changed everything,' he said with hideous delight. 'The ramifications were immense. It allowed the demon kings to go ahead with their doomsday plot, prying open the door for what's now happening around the globe. The destruction of Venice, Rome, and soon New York City was all made possible because of your lack of self-restraint, your resentment, your anger, your filth.'

Quintus began to feel both dread and shame upon realizing what Marx was implying.

'The demon kings successfully argued that if you, a killer, were touted as an exemplar, then none deserve to exist, and nobody could really argue otherwise. They placed you on Hell's waiting list after Reno, and when I finally send you there, they'll put you, I guess, someplace among the wrathful and sullen,' he said.

Marx's cellphone rang, and he stopped talking. He checked the caller ID and chuckled in recognition.

'Oh, I love this.'

He took the call.

'So, Kristen, what's your answer?'

He privately listened to his PA's response which took some 15 seconds.

'Good, I'm glad you're staying on board for the few days as I requested,' he said.

Marx then put on the phone's speaker so that Quintus could hear her voice.

'And what else do you need to tell me?' he asked.

'The doctor you asked for, Shiro Ishii, is confirmed as per your earlier instructions,' Kristen said.

The sound of her voice took Quintus' attention. Its inflection was familiar.

'Excellent, you've made my day. How is my cousin?' Marx asked, referring to War.

'Still where he was, Mr. Marx, drawing away.'

'Good, I'll see you in the morning.'

After ending the call, Marx released a sigh of immense satisfaction.

'Quintus, believe it or not, that was your wife,' he sniggered. 'Those head demons sure have an absurd sense of humor sending her to me. They tricked her, of course, as she wanted to go elsewhere.'

Internally, Quintus tried rejecting what Marx said, but instinct told him it was true, and now a cold numbness overtook the cocktail of emotions that had been bubbling in his being. This woman Kristen once was Kaitlyn, and he could do nothing but listen to Marx explain why she was in his service.

'By having her on my staff, the idea was that I would have a greater chance at success in finding you; like fate — bit like you returning to Reno,' Marx said. 'What were you thinking anyway by getting married?'

Quintus didn't answer, nor did Marx expect him to.

'You're hardly marriage material Quintus, it was never

going to work out. Vasiliev, a.k.a. Vacher, did you a favor whether you care for it or not.'

And from there, Marx ranted on for a further hour, much of it about things that were not even related to Quintus, bits, and pieces about Marx's other lives and the reality of Hell. There was no one else on earth to who he could say such things and be taken seriously.

Around the 20-minute mark of Marx's tirade, Quintus disconnected from what was being said, allowing him to adjust his mental state. He wouldn't let the words of a madman affect him. A cool clarity replaced the numbness, offering him the means to mentally prepare himself to get himself out of this mess. He had just enough faith and hope left in himself that things would somehow reverse. He could not, would not give up.

As for Marx, his eventual hour-long monologue and continuous drinking had left him both exhausted and sozzled. The past few days had been a roller coaster ride, one that he expected would continue. With a slur, he ordered Quintus to be dumped back into the cargo hold and requested there be quiet on the plane. After taking some sleeping pills, he was promptly sucked into another dreamless sleep.

Consolation

As the sun came up over New York City, Kristen woke in her bed and did so alone. She sat up on its edge, somewhat confused yet comforted by the extraordinary dream she just had, a dream where she played a piano in a living room warmed by a lit fireplace.

The soulful, yearning music she played was interrupted by the joyful sound of a young child's laughter coming from elsewhere. It was not an unwelcome interruption. In the dream, she was glad of it, as if it was expected and familiar.

She left the living room and went to a part of the dream house that looked out over a suburban backyard where a girl of pre-school age talked with a man wearing mail armor and donning a bronze helmet with a traversing red crest on its top. He leaned on his shield as he spoke with the girl who held a stuffed teddy bear. The man was a Roman soldier, but Kristen saw he had a kind face. Then the girl and the ancient warrior noticed her, and they both waved and offered her smiles.

Then Kristen woke up.

A warm residue from the dream kept her company while she used the bathroom and afterward as she made breakfast in her small kitchen. It was when she turned on her television that she was reminded that the world outside had broken. Much of the undoing was occurring not so far from where she was. You see, the Big Apple was in a panic, according to the morning news.

'Roads out of New York City are choked with traffic while reports continue to come in of looting and acts of wanton anarchy across the city's five boroughs,' a news anchor said.

The broadcast was interrupted by the sound of an incoming text on her cellphone. It was from Marx; he was back in the city and was waiting for her downstairs in a parked limousine.

Stretched Limousine

Outside the apartment, Vacher stood beside Marx's stretched black Mercedes. In bemusement, he watched several looters smash the windows of a 7-11 further down the street.

Inside the limo, Marx, suffering a mild hangover, shared the back with Irfan and a 38-year-old scruffy Japanese doctor by the name of Shiro Ishii, who feigned being asleep.

Ishii was Marx's go-to man for any suspect medical needs, including providing medical support for his Black Crow security company.

Ishii was also a hopeless drug addict and, as such, was unreliable but easy to manipulate.

'Here she comes,' Irfan alerted Marx as Kristen exited her apartment building carrying luggage.

Given Marx now had Quintus, he had wondered if Kristen was still required, but he decided she was still useful in looking after War, at least until they got to China.

Vacher took her bag and opened a limousine door for her. The Frenchman was chagrined as Kristen ignored him as she stepped into the vehicle. She couldn't help it; Vacher's presence had always repulsed her, even more so than Marx and any of the others.

In the limo, she slid across the seat next to Ishii and opposite Marx. She nodded to her boss, trying to hide her anxiety while doing so.

'Kristen, we will take the doctor to the club, but before that, we will drop you at the office,' Marx said. 'I'd like you to continue looking after Ivan. I'll organize a car to take you both to the airport a bit later.'

After Vacher put Kristen's luggage into the limousine's trunk, he got in, and they drove off, avoiding the chaos further down the street as they went.

Inside The Devil's Pleasure Palace

After arriving in New York City, the night before, Marx had Quintus and Tina taken to his nightclub. There they were placed and locked up in the two shiny chrome cages dangling from the ceiling of the dance room.

Two of the club's bouncers, big burly guys with past convictions, were tasked with keeping an eye on them. Most of their time, though, was used watching the television they had set up in a corner of the room.

In her cage, Tina lay curled up in a fetal position. She no longer had her hands tied or a hood on her head. She had been unconscious since being kidnapped but eventually awoke around mid-morning. It took her several minutes to gain clarity and sit up. Upon realizing her situation, she began to fret, but the sight of Quintus standing in the neighboring cage gave her hope.

'Tina, save your strength,' he quietly said. 'An opportunity will come. We will get out of this, I promise you.'

His words helped restrain her fears and doubts.

'You feel okay?' he asked.

'Nauseated, I ache all over but could be worse,' she said.

Tina looked at the bouncers watching the TV, both had murky auras not dissimilar to the thugs at the Reno diner. One of them began laughing at the television.

'Oh yeah, I love this guy; he got the whole world

hooked no matter how crazy he may sound,' the bouncer said, referring to Chuck Goyette.

On the TV, three serious-faced breakfast show hosts were quizzing the cult leader.

'Mr. Goyette, can you describe how this nuclear war will start?' one of the program's hosts asked.

'Oh yes, I certainly can. About a week after the New York City earthquake, North Korean nuclear missiles will hit several major cities in the U.S. and in Japan,' Goyette said. 'So, there's a shrinking window of opportunity for the president to take pre-emptive action to lessen American losses.'

'Really?' asked a host.

'Really indeed. Tough decisions need to be made, so it shouldn't stop at North Korea, and I'm advising the president of the United States to strike China as well. The Chinese communists have an emerging first-strike capability, especially given their development in hypersonic weapons. Sooner or later, they'd be looking at using them or, at the least, giving them to the North Koreans.'

The other bouncer shook his head in disbelief.

'Man, someone should just nuke his sorry ass,' he said. 'That'd save the world.'

Another TV host questioned Goyette.

'Now, so the second horsemen of the Apocalypse, War, is he instigating all of this?'

'Yes, War, I guess you could say he is the puppet master in this regard,' Goyette replied.

From his cage, Quintus saw one of the bouncers read a text message on his cell.

'They're here. Kill the TV, and I'll let them in,' the bouncer told his colleague as he walked off.

The remaining bouncer turned off the television and then looked up at Quintus and Tina.

'Glad I ain't you two,' he said.

Tina stood up in the cage and tried appealing to the bouncer's better nature in the hope that he had some that she couldn't see.

'Let us go, please,' she said.

The bouncer only laughed.

'Girl, just save it! We took your hoods off and the cable ties. That's as good as it gets.'

Not long after that, his friend arrived with Marx, Ishii, Vacher, and Irfan following.

Tina didn't pay attention to anyone but Marx. She was so stunned by what she saw surrounding him that she nearly forgot to breathe. He didn't have an aura. Instead, he was surrounded by a thick fog of darkness full of demonic slithering forms. It even smelt like sulfur to her. The density of this darkness was so great she could hardly see when Marx gave the bouncers envelopes fat with cash.

'Thank you, gentlemen; if I were you, I'd get as far south as possible, that way, you may get to spend this money,' Marx told them as they left.

Marx then watched Ishii rummage through his small day pack, which doubled as a medical bag. He pulled out a blood-type test kit and began preparing it.

Marx then turned to his caged captives and smiled at Quintus.

'Well, Quintus, that must give you the warm and

fuzzies being back in a cage like that,' he said. 'It gives me warm fuzzies just seeing it.'

Quintus didn't reply, he just held Marx's gaze.

'Tediously predictable — always zero fun,' Marx said with distaste. 'But any way you two, the doctor needs some blood,' he said.

Tina voiced her opposition.

'I don't understand what —' she said before being cut off by Marx.

'Quiet! Don't freak out. Let's all go along to get along. The good doctor only needs a drop, that's all.'

Vacher and Irfan held a small ladder under Quintus' cage for Ishii to climb up and get some blood.

'Roll up your trouser leg Quintus so he can prick you,' Marx ordered. 'As I said, he only needs a drop of your blood.'

Quintus didn't move.

'Don't make it harder on yourself, you're not in the position to do otherwise. Unless you want the girl to suffer unnecessarily.'

Reluctantly, Quintus did as instructed, and Tina did the same not long after.

With samples taken, Ishii mixed the blood on test cards and got results.

'Both are O-negative. They're a match,' he said.

'Best news of the day so far. On your way then, good doctor,' Marx said as he threw a cash-filled envelope to Ishii, who, with it, scurried out of the nightclub.

Marx smirked.

'I once thought doctors were pillars of society,' he said as he turned to Quintus and Tina.

'And then I realized what a broad and largely incorrect generalization that was. Take China as an example, where some doctors are making a fortune from organ transplants,' Marx said.

'An organ recipient there pays top dollar for a second-hand liver or heart, which are dubiously sourced. It's a well-known secret that it is state-sanctioned, so it's usually very efficient, but I have an old friend who is sick in hospital. He's already had two liver transplants, but he is balking at a third because he refuses to kill any more prisoners of conscience,' he said.

'Given the country does not, in reality, have a functioning voluntary organ donation system, his odds of surviving are getting slimmer by the minute,' he said.

'Bad news for you, Quintus, is that he and his family have no qualms about his getting a body part from a low-life foreigner. As for you, young lady, we'll keep you in reserve.'

Marx turned to Vacher and Irfan.

'Put their hoods back on and tie their wrists for our flight to China,' he ordered.

The Boy Everyone Admired

Kai may have only been 12 years of age, but he had the bearing of someone older and wiser. He had an old soul, was what his nai nai (grandma) told others in their village situated close to the city of Leshan in southwest China's

Sichuan province. In fact, most of the villagers who knew Kai and his family regarded him with a sense of awe. He was not a typical boy, and he was certainly never naughty, they said. Even as a toddler.

Agreeing with that sentiment was his mother, not that she was with her son that much, but she traveled five hours from the mega-city Chongqing, where she worked, to check on him at least once a month. He was so capable and mature for his age that she often found herself deferring to him, not that the boy wanted that to happen. She was confident that he could soon take care of his grandparents if needed.

A large chunk of Kai's exceptionalism was due to some little-known Taoist methods passed on to him by his grandfather's brother. The relative gave Kai several Taoist manuscripts that were saved from the disaster of the Cultural Revolution. The boy, then only five years of age, read them ardently and repeatedly.

By his sixth birthday, Kai was able to meditate in a full lotus position for an hour, and it wasn't much longer before he developed some mystical abilities. He could recall past lives through dreams, and his celestial eye opened. What he read from the old manuscripts helped him to make sense of the deities, ghosts, and demons he began to see.

By the time he was nine, he was also mysteriously the equal of a black belt in Kung Fu. It appeared he was self-taught in that.

When it came to more mundane things, Kai spent time helping his grandparents or trekking the hills around their village.

Recently he informed his grandparents of his intention

to walk up a mountain someway further west of where they lived. This idea naturally freaked them out, especially given the government had made the area he spoke of out of bounds. Both grandparents thought they convinced him not to go until they woke up one morning to find him gone. An apologetic note was left on his bed for them.

'Dear nai nai and ye ye, I am visiting the mountain. Please do not worry, as I will safely return in three days. I am sorry for any concern this may cause you, but please do not be afraid. I shall see you soon enough.'

The mountain was just under 100 miles from his village, and it took him a three-hour-plus bus ride to get close to its base. Once on foot, armed with a walking stick that could double as a fighting pole and shouldering a small backpack full of food and bits of clothing, he headed up the mountain towards an area he'd seen in his dreams at least a dozen times over the past two years.

In these dreams, he saw a mystical place three-quarters of the way up the mountain, a place that felt familiar, like home. He presumed he'd been there before in another life. In his dreams, there was also a Westerner, a man with sandy hair and blue eyes. Additionally, he dreamt of a spring fountain in the rock wall and a mystical dragon guarding the area.

But as Kai walked up the mountain, he was unsure what he would find in reality. It wasn't until the last hour of daylight on day two of his trek that he reached his desired destination. As he approached, the first thing he saw was a group of white butterflies fluttering near the cliff's edge, which was the verge of a terrace that fronted the remains of the Taoist's sanctuary.

The area was more dilapidated than it was in his dreams, but when he walked onto the terrace, he did so with reverence. After 12 paces, he stopped at its center and observed the area. Two car-sized boulders covered half of the terrace's space. He rightly presumed they had recently tumbled down from further up the mountain. There was no longer a plum tree as per his dreams, and there was certainly no man from the West there either. Nevertheless, Kai knew it was the place of his dreams.

Kai made his way to the mountain wall where he dreamt the spring fountain had been, but he only found a small hole in the rock.

He put his hand inside it and found it to be dry and dusty. After pulling his hand out and dusting it off on a trouser leg, he moved towards what appeared to be a cave opening further along the terrace but stopped when he heard a loud clunk and felt a shudder that seemed to come from within the mountain itself. A second later, water began to flow into the rock hole he had just been investigating. The boy quickly returned to it. Initially, the water was muddy, but it quickly became crystal clear.

The biggest smile spread across his face. *This mountain is indeed alive*, he thought.

Kai retrieved a blue plastic cup from his bag and scooped out some water from the spring. He gulped it down. It was the sweetest water he'd ever tasted, and it made him feel good.

He pulled a canteen bottle from his bag, and as he

began to fill it with water, he felt the arrival of something behind him. He sensed it was large but unthreatening. He heard it shuffle closer to him and then felt its warm breath on the back of his neck. Kai turned and found himself face to face with the White Dragon of the mountain.

It was a glorious sight.

Both the boy and the mystical creature smiled at each other.

Flying To South-West China

Quintus and Tina were once again placed in the cargo hold of Marx's jet, this time for the 15 hours it takes to fly from New York City to the Chinese city of Chengdu. They sat on the floor with their hands zip-tied behind their backs and the black hoods over their heads.

Tina was distressed and confused by what was happening, but as long as Quintus was nearby, she was able to restrain her fears and sleep for half of the flight.

As for Quintus, he was trying to make the most of their predicament by keeping his mind clear, strong, and detached. In fact, he was buoyed by the news that they were going to China. He just somehow had to avoid getting himself, and Tina killed for their organs and then get himself to White Dragon Mountain as once predicted.

Marx's two minions took turns watching over them, and Irfan got the last leg of the trip. Towards the 15th hour, Vacher opened the door to pass on a message.

'We're landing in 10 minutes, make sure these two are awake and ready to move after landing,' he told Irfan.

'What time is it wherever we're going to?'

'Around 3.30 am, I was told.'

'You think the clubs will be open?'

'No time for partying. We gotta look after these two and make sure nothing happens to the Iranian.'

'You really think he's Iranian?' asked Irfan about War.

'It's only an educated guess. The Iranians and North Koreans are allies. So why not? Or is this about you?'

'What do you mean?'

'Is this a Muslim Sunni versus Shia thing?'

Irfan shrugged.

'Either way, get ready, we're landing soon,' Vacher said as he shut the door.

As the Frenchman returned to his seat in the middle of the cabin, he passed by Marx, who tugged at his arm, stopping him.

'Everything okay in there?' Marx asked.

'Yes, boss, everything is fine. They'll be ready to move out once we land.'

'Don't forget they do so only after Kristen and Ivan are off the jet and in vehicles driving away. Is Irfan clear on that?'

'Of course, Mr. Marx.'

'I certainly hope so,' said Marx, who nodded for Vacher to carry on.

Up at the very front of the cabin near the cockpit, Kristen was sitting next to War, who sketched on a drawing pad. She'd just woken up from several hours of sleep, which included another dream featuring the Roman soldier and the young girl. This time it was more serious, the soldier was holding up his shield, protecting the girl from something dark and sinister. Kristen didn't understand what it meant, but it added to her building sense of unease.

CHAPTER XI

Awaiting The Crow

Colonel Deng chain-smoked as he waited outside one of the six large hangars on Chengdu's Baishiyi military airbase. He was edgy, there was much at stake. It was true that if Marx's operation succeeded, Deng would be comfortably rich, but if it failed, he'd be dead or imprisoned for life. As backups, he had three escape plans if things didn't work out.

Deng's main concern was that the operation appeared rather ad hoc and overly reliant on bribery. Two days earlier, on behalf of Marx, he bribed the air base's commander to go on a holiday for a week.

In his absence, Deng was considered the base's ranking officer despite his being a logistics officer and not at all in any way or form previously connected to the airfield. It cost Marx $2 million in bribes for the air base commander, which Deng presumed would count for nothing if things really went awry.

Marx was paying Deng a larger sum of $4 million for his own role in securing control over both the security of the base and in the neighboring military hospital. Half of the amount had already been paid into an offshore account. With the money, Deng would retire to a life of ease outside of China, someplace where he couldn't be extradited from.

Deng considered the $4 million compensation enough for dealing with Marx and for being kept in the dark over what he was being a part of. The only thing he knew was that it involved supplying his sick uncle with a new liver and was related to Marx making inroads into North Korea. His cousin Lin told him it was a need-to-know-basis situation, and he had no need to know. Besides, it would be safer for him and everyone else if he was not fully acquainted with the details, he was told.

As he put out a cigarette, three military vehicles that were Chinese versions of the Humvee drove up with dimmed lights. They halted near him, close to one of the hangar's side doors. Deng approached the now parked lead vehicle, which Lin stepped out of.

'Hello cousin,' Lin said.

'Lin, how can you be sure Marx has a source of organs for your father?'

'He told me so. He has two matching specimens. Your hatred of Marx clouds your judgment.'

'You're taking a risk on his word,' Deng said. 'And they're late.'

'Yes, but they're about to arrive,' Lin said, looking back towards the start of the airstrip.

As if on cue, out of the early morning night sky, the Crow came into land.

Fate Awaits

Kristen was more than anxious as the Crow parked inside one of the hangars. Nervous beads of perspiration formed on her cheeks and neck. Her heart was beating furiously.

Through the window, she saw Chinese military personnel rushing about, and then she heard the hangar's large doors close behind. It all seemed very covert, especially as Marx told her halfway into the flight there was no need to go through customs or any form of immigration control once they got to China.

Every bone in her body now regretted coming on the flight. Things didn't seem right. It's an understatement to say that she would have much preferred to be back with her family in Texas.

Once the jet halted and its engines died down, one of the two pilots exited the cockpit to open the passenger's door, which became a set of stairs for passengers to ascend.

Kristen and War were closest to the door, but they balked at being the first to depart; they left that to Marx, who passed them and exited the jet to be met by Lin at the base of the stairs.

Marx and Lin limply shook hands.

'How's the general?' Marx asked, referring to Lin's father.

'Unfortunately, not getting any better.'

'Then we'll make sure he does. Where is Deng?'

'Outside.'

'Sulking?'

'Somewhat Mr. Marx, but I think he will be fine. Just a minor loss of face.'

'If he misbehaves further, Lin, your cousin, will lose much more. Is he able to fulfill his obligations?'

'Yes, he is.'

'I hope so, he didn't come cheap, and we can't afford any ineptitude,' Marx said as he turned to see Kristen and War descending the jet's stairs. 'The woman is my assistant, and that bearded fellow is who we need to get to North Korea,' he told Lin.

'The Iranian nuclear scientist?' Lin asked.

'Yes, that's him indeed.'

Just as Kristen and War joined them, Lin held out his hand for War to shake, but it was ignored.

'Oh, I hope you had a good flight,' Lin said, trying hard to hide his embarrassment.

'He's not one for awkward pleasantries,' Marx said. 'How about we just get them to where they're going to stay.'

Lin nodded.

'You'll be residing at the military hospital,' Lin said. 'It has comfortable accommodation. It's not far, just next to the airbase. Lieutenant Wu will take you both there,' Lin said as a Chinese officer with his aide stepped forward from behind him.

Marx indicated for Kristen to do as Lin requested.

'Take Ivan and get some rest. We will meet at midday local time. I have some minor matters that need addressing with the Chinese before then,' Marx said.

'What about the pilots?' Kristen asked.

'They're going to a hotel in the city,' he said. 'They're big boys. Don't worry about them. Now move along.'

The aide took Kristen's baggage, and the officer gestured for them to follow. After they exited the building, Lin turned to Marx and voiced his concerns.

'That nuclear scientist looks very young,' he said.

'Yes, he was a child genius, and now he'll help push forward North Korea's miniature nuke program,' Marx replied. 'And Pyongyang will pay you handsomely for it. Don't forget you're making 20 million dollars from it.'

It was all baloney, of course. Marx just had to get War near where the North Koreans had their nuclear-tipped long-range missiles. There War would say his incantation that would launch North Korea's missiles against Japan and the U.S. within a week.

Washington's response, of course, would be devastating. China and Russia, among others, would shortly thereafter get dragged into it.

By then, Marx planned to be in his well-stocked bunker in New Zealand, waiting out the nuclear war he helped orchestrate. It was the kind of conflict that'd kill off most of humanity.

But before then, many things had to fall into place. Marx looked at Lin and put his hand on his shoulder.

'Now, the important issue is that we must look after your father. We have two suitable donors on the plane, not just one,' Marx said.

'Good, very good, Mr. Marx. We need to get them to the hospital quickly, the surgical doctors and their team have been alerted,' Lin said. 'After the transplant operation, we can then fly you and your team to North Korea as you want, hopefully, the day after.'

'I need a solid confirmation on that as soon as possible,' Marx said.

'Yes, of course.'

'Vacher!' Marx yelled.

From inside the jet, Vacher acknowledged.

'Oui!'

'Bring them out, the surgeons are waiting.'

A minute later, Quintus and Tina — with black hoods over their heads — were escorted from the Crow by Marx's minions, who put them into one of the wannabe Humvees outside the hangar.

Soon enough, they drove off and passed through a security gate to enter the grounds of the neighboring military hospital. The vehicle parked near a nondescript iron door of the badly lit east side of a large hospital building. That's where Quintus and Tina were taken inside.

Truthfulness, Compassion, Forbearance

During her meditation, Luo Jia managed to still her mind to the point that it was as clear as the Lake of Five Flowers. There was no emotion, no fear, no concern — just a sense of clarity sustained by a foundation built on kindness and patience.

The remarkable thing was that the 35-year-old managed this despite being one of 12 women crammed into a dark and stuffy concrete cell with no window. None of them knew if it was day or night outside, but they each took turns lying down to sleep while others sat or stood to provide space to do that. Given they were all Falun Gong practitioners, many meditated or did their standing Tai Chi-like exercises.

Like the other women, Jia wore a drab blue prison tracksuit. Aged between 20 and 45, they were all good people trying to be the best versions of themselves, even in such hideous circumstances.

None of them deserved to be locked up. Jia was a schoolteacher before police caught her with a banner that read 'Truthfulness, Compassion, Forbearance is Good,' referring to the practice's three main principles.

Jia and 16 others had been sent to the cell from a nearby women's prison three days earlier. Over the course of the days that followed, five of them had been taken out and never returned. The remaining attempted not to dwell on their fate, but when they understood they were in a military hospital, they couldn't but fear the worst.

They were all aware that their fellow practitioners were targeted by the state for organ harvesting, it became widespread knowledge from 2006 onwards.

In the camps, each of them had already been forced to have medical checkups that focused on their vital 'commercial' organs. The details recorded presumably to match the needs of a cash-paying recipient. A prison guard told Jia five months earlier that local Chinese recipients preferred military hospitals for an organ transplant because it was cheaper than the civilian hospitals that targeted richer overseas clients, mainly from Japan, South Korea, and the Gulf states.

There was little surprise in this information, but Jia was shocked by how casually the guard mentioned it. It upset her that the land of her birth had become so amoral and evilly misled.

She tried not to think about such matters as she now meditated in the cell. She instead sought nothingness.

After meditating for close to an hour, Jia unfolded her legs, and as she waited for the tingly feeling in her feet to dissipate, she heard noises coming from beyond the door. People, presumably soldiers, had entered the area immediately outside the cell which they understood as part of the building's basement. Among the Chinese voices was a man with a heavy foreign brogue, which she correctly guessed belonged to an American.

'This one put him in here and prepare him,' the man said in his accented Mandarin. His voice was also harsh and unforgiving.

The sound of a male voice that followed was a stark contrast.

'Tina! Don't be afraid, I'll find you,' the voice said in English. Despite Jia being unable to understand what he said, she sensed the man's voice was full of hope and courage.

His gesture, however, sparked viciousness outside the cell. Jia heard men zap the English speaker's legs with electroshock batons before he was dragged off somewhere else as per orders of the man with the accented Mandarin.

'With the woman, put her in one of your holding cells. Just lock her away!' the man with the accent demanded.

Jia heard the guards drag someone close to their cell door.

On the other side of the door, the soldiers took the black hood off Tina's head and then the zip tie from around her wrists.

Another soldier hastily unlocked and opened the cell door, and two others then shoved Tina inside. The door was promptly shut and locked behind her.

Most people would have only seen darkness in that unlit cell. But she instead saw how it was immersed in bright, warm light.

The Baton

In a sparse room adjoining the basement, Vacher and Irfan threw Quintus onto a hospital gurney and used a pair of their stainless-steel cuffs to tie his already zip-tied wrists to it. Along with Marx and his henchmen, in the room, there were Lin, Deng, and three soldiers who had never seen Westerners up close before.

Marx pulled the black hood off Quintus' head and thrust the electroshock baton he was holding close to his face.

'Like how that stung?' he asked.

'How 'bout you just slither back to Hell,' Quintus replied.

'You'll be there before me, Roman.'

Marx zapped Quintus with the baton, this time to the

thigh. Quintus couldn't help but quiver as 900 volts coursed through his body. After what seemed like an eternity, the pain stopped. He opened his eyes and saw Marx admiring the torture device.

'I have substantial shares in the company that manufactures these handy-little things,' Marx said. 'They deliver a nasty shock. Non-lethal yet excruciating.'

Marx again jabbed Quintus with the baton, this time in the center of the chest. Lin stepped forward, alarmed.

'You will damage his organs!' he yelled.

'Don't fret, Lin, he can take it,' Marx replied as he continued zapping Quintus. 'In fact, it'll do him a world of good, and what's more, you'll find him to be more compliant.'

After half a minute of being shocked, Quintus was near senseless.

Marx halted the torment and was again in his foe's face.

'Now let me tell you, Quintus, how you shall die,' Marx said. 'The beginning of the process is simple enough. In a minute, you're going to get an electrocardiogram and an abdominal X-ray. The X-ray is first, right Lin?'

Lin nodded.

'Then, after a few other things, in five or six hours, you should be ready for the operating table. At that stage, you'll be injected with a paralyzing drug, so you'll be alive when the dissection begins, and you'll feel each and every scalpel slice as they carve their way to your liver,' Marx said. 'At some stage, you will die in the process.'

Quintus tried ignoring both Marx and the residue of pain he felt. Instead, he focused on maintaining the mindfulness needed if he was to take advantage of any opportunities to escape.

Meanwhile, Marx continued talking.

'Lin's father, an old friend of mine, will be the recipient of your liver. I'm not sure if they are going to bother with your other spare parts, but sometime later, the same will happen to that sweet young thing you befriended in Reno, and she will be killed as per demand.'

He paused and just stared at Quintus while savoring the moment.

'By the way, your wife is also here, so it's probably best we do something similar to her as well,' Marx said. 'After more than 2,000 years, this is how it ends for you. Everything you strove for, everything you went through, all for naught.'

Marx chuckled at the thought of Quintus' future.

'And then — Hell awaits Quintus, Hell awaits! You think now is bad, you just what till those demons get ahold of you.'

Marx chortled some more and then gestured to Lin, who took that as his cue to look at Deng, who in turn barked orders at two soldiers to take Quintus away.

'And your time in that Irish gibbet will seem like paradise!' Marx yelled as Quintus on the gurney was pushed out of the room.

The two soldiers rolled Quintus down a hallway towards an elevator that would take them higher up into the building proper. As they did so, Quintus focused on remembering where he was being moved from so he could retrace the journey and come back for Tina. That's what he hoped for anyway. There was no other way to think unless he accepted that he only had a few hours to live.

In the elevator with the soldiers, Quintus managed to watch the digital numbers on the button panel climb from B 1 up to level 2, where the elevator stopped and its doors opened.

They exited, and Quintus was taken down a corridor that turned right towards the X-ray room, where they were met by a yawning officer and an overweight radiology technician wearing a white gown and a facemask.

A Lifeline

Kristen stared at her unpacked bag sitting on the single bed that was the main feature of the no-frills single room situated on the building's fifth floor. She wasn't sure if she should open it and get out of her slim jeans and t-shirt and into her nightwear for sleeping. The uncertainty of her situation and its resulting unease was debilitating.

Upon hearing a soft-brushing noise behind her, she turned to see a folded piece of paper being slid under the door.

'Hello?' Kristen said to whoever was outside her door, but there was no reply.

She saw a shadow under the door move away. She presumed it was a Chinese staff member unable to understand English.

She went and picked up the paper and unfolded it. It was not at all what she expected. What she saw left her speechless. She sat on the edge of the bed and gazed at it for several minutes.

It was an ink drawing. Going by what she had seen in the boardroom in New York, she knew it was one of War's. It was an illustration of a Roman centurion with his shield raised, protecting a young girl who stood frightened behind him. The girl was dressed 1960s-style, and she was clutching a teddy bear. The soldier gave the impression he'd die before letting the girl meet any harm. He'd fight anything.

It was, of course, a scene straight from her most recent dream.

The spell was broken when somebody outside wrapped their knuckles softly on the door.

'Who's there?' she asked.

'Miss Kristen, it's me.'

She part opened the door to find War dressed as he was on the plane: cargo pants and his surplus jacket over a blue polo shirt.

'Ivan, you drew this, didn't you?' she asked, holding up the drawing for him to see.

'We must go,' he said.

'What do you mean?'

'You're in danger.'

'From what, from who?'

War looked back up at the hallway and then back to her.

'You must come with me,' he said.

Intuition told her that he was there to help. She grabbed her bag, and they left.

X-ray

The soldiers parked the gurney carrying Quintus just inside a radiology room. Quintus kept his mind clear as they talked with the officer and the radiology technician.

'For five minutes, the Westerner was blasted with an electroshock baton — there is no fight left in him,' a soldier said in Mandarin.

'He certainly looks somewhat frazzled,' laughed the bespectacled technician who next described what needed to be done.

The officer then ordered the soldiers to uncuff and untie Quintus so that they could take him from the gurney to the X-ray bed. Using a knife, a soldier cut the plastic zip tie from Quintus' wrists, and then the other soldier unlocked the handcuffs, making Quintus free of restraint.

His chance had arrived.

He sprang into action and sat up fast. He jabbed the nearest soldier under the armpit, paralyzing him. The officer tried to attack Quintus with a baton, but his intended target hit back with a well-targeted blow, and the officer flopped to the floor unconscious. The other guard met a similar fate.

The out-of-shape technician attempted to flee, but Quintus blocked the door with the gurney. The technician raised his hands as if surrendering.

'Don't hurt me. I'll give you money,' he said in English through his facemask.

'Where are we? What is this place?'

'This is 327 Military Hospital. Chengdu. South-west China.'

'Take off your jacket,' Quintus told the technician, who complied.

'Okay, now lift up your arm a little.'

The technician closed his eyes and did so. Quintus jabbed him, and the technician was paralyzed on the spot.

A minute later, Quintus left the X-ray room wearing the technician's coat, facemask, and a cap he found. As he walked the deserted corridor, he noticed the lights of the neighboring airfield through a window. He saw the shadowy shapes of six military helicopters on a concrete patch by the airstrip. He didn't have time to stop and see more, but he saw enough.

Quintus turned into the corridor where the elevator was. He kept his head down to hide his face from a wall-mounted CCTV camera. After reaching the elevator, he pressed the button and waited for the doors to open.

He hoped Tina was okay and wondered if what Marx said about the woman named Kristen was true. Was she somewhere in the hospital? And if so, was her life in danger? He didn't know and had no way of knowing. Marx could have just been playing mind games. Quintus had to act on what he knew was genuine.

The elevator bell rang. Its doors opened, and he stepped in and pressed the button for basement level one.

Visiting the General

Sickly General Zhou was startled when he sensed someone sitting in a bedside chair. It was dark in his hospital room, so he couldn't see who it was, nor did he have the strength to switch on a light.

'Who is there?' he feebly asked in Mandarin.

'Save your strength, general.'

'Aaron Marx, is that truly you?'

'Yes.'

The general sighed, and Marx wasn't sure it was a sign of disapproval or relief. Outside of that, it could have been just an indication of how near the older man was to death. It was some time before the general again spoke, and when he did, his voice seemed to come from a distant place.

'I have nightmares that I'm already in the underworld. Do you think such things exist?'

Marx couldn't help but chuckle. *Atheists are the biggest chumps*, he thought.

'Yes, well, Hell is certainly not for the fainthearted, and for some of us, dear comrade, it's inescapable,' Marx said. 'But try to rest and fret not. You won't be dying today — a new liver is being prepared for you as we speak.'

Interrupting Mahjong

Quintus watched the elevator's electronic floor numbers drop to B 1. Following a juddering stop, the elevator door opened, and he carefully exited.

After finding the corridor empty, he quietly made his

way toward where he thought the cells were. As he reached the corridor's corner, he could hear men casually talking.

He paused and peeked around the corner to see three guards playing Mahjong at a table opposite the cell doors. Above them was another CCTV camera covering the area.

Quintus ducked back and grabbed a fire extinguisher braced to the corridor's wall. With it in hand, he darted around the corner and threw it at the CCTV camera. A direct hit. The camera was smashed to smithereens.

Quintus then ran at the first guard who stood from the table and quickly immobilized him and did the same to another soldier reaching for a radio. The last remaining soldier swung a baton but missed. Quintus threw counterpunches, and that soldier crumpled to the floor.

Once he was sure the area was guard free, he took off the facemask and grabbed a set of keys hanging from a nail above the table, which he hoped were for the cell doors. Intuition told him Tina was behind the second door. One of the keys worked, and he unlocked the door. He opened it wide enough to let light into the cell. Inside it, he saw Tina sitting on the floor.

'Told you I'd be back,' he said quietly to her.

Tina smiled with relief, and he took her hand to help her to her feet. Around her, the Falun Gong practitioners either nodded or smiled at him as if what was occurring was all very matter-of-fact.

'Everyone out and fast before alarms start ringing,' he said.

'Quintus, what's happening?' Tina asked.

'These people must get out of here, or they'll be

butchered. It won't be easy to escape, but we have to try,' he said. 'The sun will be up soon, so we need to move quickly.'

Speaking in basic Mandarin, Tina repeated Quintus' concerns to the women as he began to free the occupants inside the other two cells. Inside them was a mixture of Tibetans, Uyghurs, several house Christians, and a democracy activist who spoke some English.

Soon enough, 30 bewildered prisoners, talking in hushed tones, were milling outside the cells. With anticipation, they watched Quintus approach a steel door that he guessed was the one that he and Tina were first brought in through. He saw another CCTV camera monitoring it.

SMASH!

The fire extinguisher was again put to good use in obliterating it.

He went to the door and tried the keys to open it. After two attempts, he found the right key and pushed the door open. It was still dark outside and, as far as he could tell, there were no guards on that side of the building.

Asleep on Duty

There were now two blank monitor screens in the hospital's main security room situated on the ground floor. But all 12 monitors in the room may as well have been turned off, as the soldier, a 20-year-old Kunming native named Wei Zexi, who was meant to be watching them, was asleep while sitting upright in his chair.

Over the past four months, sleeping on the job had become a habit for Wei, and he'd gotten away with it so far. Besides, his commanding junior officer was often off doing something similar somewhere else in the building. To both Wei and the officer, getting forty winks was the best use of their time.

Since his early teens, Wei had dreamed about joining a special forces unit, but he lacked the necessary fortitude and skills. Now he complained to his friends that he was only a glorified security guard. It was not even a military base. If he were a guard in the neighboring airfield, he wouldn't be falling asleep, Wei told himself. Nothing ever happened at the hospital in the early hours of the day, everyone knew it, and this was his justification for sleeping.

The hospital may have been run by the military, but it was a money-making machine for the higher-ups, especially the specialized doctors and local Communist Party officials. Along with expensive immunotherapy procedures, Wei knew the hospital made much of its money through organ transplants. Most of the staff knew how the organs were acquired, and he had seen via the monitors how the prisoners were pulled out of cells and then prepared. No one was allowed to talk about it, but they all understood those killed for their organs were enemies of the state, at least according to the higher-ups. He told himself it was none of his business and so there was no point losing sleep over it.

During the beginning of each shift, he usually set the alarm on his cellphone for 4.45 am so he would at least be awake for the final hour of his time on duty. After his phone alarm went off, on this morning we're focused on, he stood up from his chair and went to the bathroom to relieve himself and wash his face.

It was when Wei got back that he noticed two of the screens that should have been showing the basement were blank. He picked up the phone to make a call but paused when he saw on another screen, one that was working, two non-Chinese men in a hallway outside a room on the fifth floor. He didn't know who they were. One of them was making a call on his cellphone. Wei decided this was something he should report.

Vacher's Call

As Marx sat by General Zhou's bedside, he felt the phone in his pocket buzz. He pulled it out, checked the caller ID, and exited the room to take the call in the corridor.

'Vacher, anything wrong?'

'Sir, we can't find Ivan, and now we can't find Kristen,' Vacher said.

'What do you mean?'

'They are not in their rooms, and we have searched the whole floor. I've called her cellphone, but there's been no answer.'

'If you don't find them soon, I will hold you both personally responsible.'

Up on the fifth floor, Vacher looked at Irfan and raised his eyebrows, communicating that their boss had not taken the news well.

'Should we alert the Chinese? We could get Deng onto it. They can help search,' Vacher said just as four armed guards turned the corner and approached them. 'Oh, some Chinese have just shown up Mr. Marx,' he said.

Vacher was all smiles until one of the soldiers shouted orders that he could not understand. Both the tone and the manner were unfriendly, and that riled the Frenchman.

'Hey, relax. Everything is fine. We're your guests, for Hell's sake!' he said back at the soldier.

Another soldier attempted to take Vacher's phone, and a scuffle ensued, resulting in both foreigners being pinned to the floor.

CHAPTER XII

The Escape

History one day will recall when 30 prisoners of conscience escaped from 327 Military Hospital in Chengdu; how they managed to flee certain death and avoid being recaptured. Quite an achievement in an Orwellian state such as modern-day China.

It may not have been a prison but getting out of the hospital was still no easy feat. It was surrounded by CCTV cameras and a 12-foot-high fence topped with razor wire. Its exit and entry points were manned by guards. Beyond the hospital grounds was either the city's outskirts or the airfield.

Not that Quintus knew these details as he ventured out of the building. The others remained inside as he recced for the best avenue of escape.

Carrying the fire extinguisher, he went along the side of the building, which took him towards a hospital exit manned by two bored soldiers at a checkpoint. He made sure he was out of their eyesight when he knocked out two exterior video cameras with the extinguisher.

Satisfied there weren't any more cameras covering their intended escape route, he went back to the building door where the others waited. He told both Tina and the English-speaking democracy activist what he saw and then outlined a plan for them to relay to the others.

'I will take care of the guards, and once I give the signal, everyone has to rush out the gate and get into the city, split up, and do what they can to not get caught from there on,' Quintus whispered to them.

Just after Tina and the activist told the others the plan, Quintus pulled her aside and spoke to her softly.

'I will stick out like a sore thumb here. Tina, you'll have better luck without me if you go into the city and get to the nearest U.S. consulate,' he said.

'What are you going to do?' she asked him.

'I'm going back to the airfield to steal a helicopter.'

'What? Why?'

'It's the best idea I've got right now. It's hard to explain.'

'The security there would be ten times worse than here.'

'Maybe. Probably.'

'If you do get a helicopter, where are you going?'

'It sounds weird, but I need to go to a mountain.'

'Then I want to come with you. I'm okay with weird. I like mountains.'

'No, it will be more dangerous.'

'I can handle that. Weird, dangerous, no problems. It's been an ongoing theme for the past few days!'

For the next two minutes, they debated in hushed tones over what Tina should do. Quintus was right to a point about her chances without him, but behind that — the idea of them splitting and her being alone amid all the danger made him feel uneasy; made them both feel uneasy.

Despite the darkness, he noted tears brimming in her eyes, and he now knew he had no choice.

'Okay, alright, we're sticking together. Let's not worry about the consulate for the time being,' Quintus said. 'Once we're over there and stealing military hardware — you just need to do what I ask of you, okay Tina? Your life may depend on it,' he added.

Tina nodded, and as she wiped away a tear that fell down her left cheek, he patted her on the shoulder. 'After the mountain, we'll get stateside, somehow,' he said.

Quintus next told the activist to inform the others it was time to go, and soon he led them up the side of the building. Upon reaching the corner, they stopped in the shadows. The exit and its checkpoint were just ahead. Quintus indicated to Tina and the others to remain while he went forward. At a crouching run, he snuck up on the checkpoint where one guard was now asleep, and the other was barely awake in a booth.

He had little trouble knocking them both out.

But as he prepared to wave the escapees through, a 4WD military vehicle approached from within the hospital grounds. He signaled to Tina and the others to stay put, and he hid behind the booth just as the vehicle pulled up at the checkpoint's boom gate. The driver inside the 4WD looked around for the guards until his door was yanked open, and he was pulled out by Quintus and given a paralyzing jab.

Quintus half expected alarm bells to start ringing, but none did. The only sound was the 4WD's idling engine. He dragged the paralyzed soldier into the booth and lay him next to the already stunned pair. After taking a flashlight from one of the unconscious soldiers, he checked once more to see if anything was coming their way or if he had been seen, and it seemed all good on both accounts.

He waved to the escapees at the corner, and they knew what to do. As fast as they could, they ran from the corner and through the exit, and into the surrounding neighborhood. Through the fence, Tina saw the Falun Gong women make their way down streets, each of them glowing with kindness, lighting up their surroundings. Then she saw Quintus waving for her to carefully join him, and she did while remaining unaware that they were being watched.

At the corner edge of another building, War and Kristen had just witnessed what occurred. Kristen, by now, was in a state of disbelief close to shock. Her current situation was one she never expected to find herself in; she was fleeing some military hospital in China with an odd man who could draw her dreams and who now warned her that her life was in danger.

On top of that, she just saw someone, the spitting image of the dreamy Roman soldier, take out three Chinese soldiers and then direct a whole bunch of people to flee the hospital. Then that same man and a young Asian woman ran in another direction, into the shadows and out of sight.

Again, and not for the last time, Kristen wished she was back with her family in Texas.

A minute after the man and the young woman disappeared, War told her what their next move would be.

'See that vehicle?' he whispered, pointing at the idling 4WD at the hospital's exit.

She nodded.

'That's ours,' he said.

Berating Soldiers at 5.10 AM

As Marx exited the elevator onto the fifth floor, he shouted into his cellphone at Deng, who was elsewhere in the building.

'I simply don't care if you just went to bed, Deng, my men are having issues with security on the fifth floor, this indicates you have not done your job ensuring we're to be treated as expected!' Marx yelled. 'Get here now and sort this mess out,' he said before ending the call.

He turned a corner to find Vacher and Irfan pinned to the floor by the Chinese soldiers, who now numbered around seven. Some of the soldiers looked at the well-dressed Westerner with bewilderment until he started berating them in Mandarin.

'What is this? These men are guests of General Zhou!' he yelled.

Marx managed to spook some of the guards, but the most senior of them — a non-commissioned officer — wasn't so easily swayed, and a noisy argument began. Marx wouldn't back down, and neither would the soldier.

The Fence

Keeping to the shadows, Quintus and Tina ran along the side of the largest building on the northern part of the hospital facility. To their left, the fence line eventually became shared with the airfield, and at that point, they stopped. As she caught her breath, Tina noticed Quintus' attention was fixed on both the fence and the area beyond it.

'So, what now?' she asked.

'The helicopter we need is in there,' he said, nodding at the airfield. He gauged the height of the fence and then looked at Tina, who he guessed weighed around 110 pounds. *That's manageable*, he thought.

'How are we going to get through the fence?' she asked.

'By hopping over.'

'What?! How?'

'I'll piggyback you.'

Tina had to question if she heard right.

'Sorry, you'll what?'

'Trust me,' Quintus said as he crouched for her to get onto his back.

'Audentes fortuna iuvat,' he said quietly.

'What does that mean?'

'Fortune favors the bold, it's Latin.'

She still hesitated, so he gave her a subtle reminder.

'C'mon, a deal's a deal.'

And with that, she smirked her way through any anxiety and hopped onto his back. He then stood up straight with her holding on.

'Don't let go or yell as we fly over. Everything is going to be fine,' he said.

Fly? she thought.

'Holding tight?' he checked.

'Yeah, holding tight.'

With Tina securely on his back, Quintus ran a short distance and then jumped and rose in the air, and much to her astonishment, they levitated over the fence, clearing its razor wire by a good two feet. They landed gently on the other side on the grass with the hospital behind them.

'Stay onboard,' he told her. 'It's about a quarter of a mile to those choppers I saw. It'll be speedier if I keep carrying you.'

Before Tina could respond, Quintus began running toward where he thought the helicopters were. True to his word, he could run fast, as fast as an Olympic sprinter, in fact, despite still carrying her. It wasn't long till the shapes of a half-dozen parked choppers emerged ahead of them out of the darkness.

At the sight of them, Quintus sighed in relief. They were Harbin Z-9s, variants of a French model that he'd flown and done mechanics on years before. He knew them like the back of his hand.

The Call

Back inside the hospital, the heated dispute between Marx and the non-commissioned officer was interrupted by Marx's ringing cellphone. He held up his hand to pause the argument and fished his phone out of his pocket. After glancing at the caller's ID, he answered it aggressively.

'Lin, what do you want now?'

For the next several seconds, the Chinese guards, and even Vacher and Irfan on the floor, watched Marx turn beetroot red as he listened to what Lin had to say.

'You have to be kidding me. He did what?!' Marx finally yelled, spit flying from his mouth. 'How did he escape? Of course, your father's operation can't proceed, especially if the others have also somehow managed to get free!'

As Marx continued ranting on the phone, Deng arrived on the scene, and he quickly pulled rank on the soldiers who had pinned Vacher and Irfan to the floor. The soldiers freed Marx's henchmen, who got back onto their feet. Meanwhile, Marx ended his call with Lin and glared at Deng.

'Now Deng, you have to really earn what I'm paying you for,' he said.

How to Steal a Chopper

It took Quintus and Tina less than a minute to run from the fence to the concrete square where six Harbin Z-9 helicopters were parked between the runway and a hangar. After reaching the first camouflage-painted chopper, Quintus let Tina off his back.

'Why aren't you out of breath?' she asked.

'Shhhhhhh,' Quintus replied with his finger raised to his lips. 'We aren't out of the woods yet.'

From one of his trouser pockets, he pulled out the torch

stolen earlier from one of the paralyzed soldiers and shone its light into the helicopter's cockpit.

'Will it get us out of here?' she asked him in a hushed tone.

'Hope so. With full axillary tanks, it should fly around 500 miles, enough to get us where we need to go,' he said just as quietly.

'The mountain?'

'Yeah, and then after that, perhaps, all things going well, as far as the southern border and hopefully into Thailand,' Quintus said.

'Thailand, oh, I like the sound of that,' Tina said.

'Yeah, just thought of it; thought you'd like it. Now standard military protocol is to have helicopters on standby, ready to fly with a full tank. If so, then we are in luck.'

'Don't you need some keys?' she asked.

'No keys required.'

He opened the cockpit door and gestured for her to get in.

'Quickly in you go.'

Quintus carefully shone the light to help Tina climb into the cockpit and take a seat. After she did so, it wasn't long before he was in the seat next to her. He put on a pair of headphones he found and then pointed at another set hanging to her left.

'It'll get noisy. Put them on so we can talk via intercom,' he said and then briefly told her how they worked. Then he gestured outside, which was becoming lighter as an unseen sun rose in the east.

'Now Tina, while I get this thing ready to lift, I need you to keep your eyes open for any security guards,' he said.

As Tina played lookout, Quintus began running through his mental checklist; he first checked the foot pedals, then the cyclic and collective-pitch levers. After that, he checked the circuit breakers were in and then tested if the master alternator was on, etc. As fast as he could, he went through all the procedures needed for lifting the chopper into the air. Eventually — for what seemed an eternity to Tina — Quintus pressed the starter button. The engine began to whine, and soon the rotor blades above them began to spin slowly. It was about then that Tina saw the shape of a vehicle driving their way.

'There's a vehicle coming,' she said.

Damn, Quintus thought. *We're still over a minute away from liftoff.* ·

'What are we going to do, Quintus?' Tina said.

'We'll be in the air soon enough.'

Quintus looked in the direction of the approaching vehicle. It was a 4WD, like the one from the hospital. He saw its headlights flashing on and off. His past World War II training told him the flashes were Morse code; the message was S.O.S.

Forty feet from the chopper the 4WD abruptly stopped. Two people exited it, and despite the darkness, Quintus realized they weren't soldiers and that the person hopping out from the passenger's side was a woman. He slid open a window and waved to them with the torch, indicating for them to approach.

Quintus next flicked a switch that turned on four

exterior lights on the chopper's lower fuselage. It was enough to help the two get to the Z-9's slide door, and as they got there, Quintus realized something about the woman — it had to be Kristen, the woman who Marx had told him about. He instantly saw how she appeared like Kaitlyn. Her strong jawline. Her eyes. Even her ears.

War slid the door back for her to enter, and a gush of sentiment hit Quintus as she got in. He quickly suppressed his feelings. Other matters needed doing, importantly getting the Z-9 in the air before airfield security personnel were upon them.

'Tina, ask our new friends to buckle up,' he said.

With a smile, Tina told War and Kristen to be seated and to put on their belts. As she next indicated to them to put on headphones, she saw how Kristen's glowing aura indicated she was a good person, but she couldn't figure out the bearded man who had neither an aura nor a shroud of darkness. Just nothing. She had never witnessed anything like it before, only the dead had no aura. She did not understand what it meant but, given the circumstances, she had not time to ponder it.

'Okay folks, it's time to go,' Quintus said.

The sound of his calm voice returned Tina's thoughts to more immediate matters, and she resumed looking out for security personnel. It wasn't long till she spotted the shapes of several armed soldiers running towards them from buildings.

'Men with guns over there, coming our way,' she said, pointing.

'Hope everyone is buckled up,' Quintus said. 'Time to get this whirlybird airborne.'

The engine's RPMs hit 2,500. The rotor acceleration was complete. He rolled the throttle, and the Z-9 rose in the air.

BLAM! BLAM! BLAM!

Three 7.62mm bullets fired from ground level hit the helicopter as it reached a height of 30 feet. One round punched through the cabin floor's not-so-protective plating, missing Quintus' left foot by mere inches before smashing into parts of the control panel, specifically the satellite navigation system.

'Ignore that, folks, we will be out of range soon,' he said coolly in another bid to soothe any frayed nerves.

Quintus managed to keep the chopper on course and increased its speed. After leaving the airfield and the hospital behind, he steered around the city's edges till he spotted the weaving imprint of a river that shimmered with the first hints of daybreak. He banked the Z-9 towards the river and once he was over it, he kept the chopper low to avoid radar.

When Quintus realized the Z-9's satellite navigation system was knocked out, he knew he had little choice but to fly south via 'human survey.' He was thankful daylight was emerging, allowing him to see better. He figured if he followed the river southwards, it would take him near where he needed to go.

Back in Canada, contemplating a return to China one day, he had studied Google Maps of the area around White Dragon Mountain. He recalled where Chengdu was in relation to the mountain and understood that the waterway he was flying over was most probably the Min River which eventually passed through Leshan, a city famous for a giant Buddha statue that overlooked the river. The 233-foot-high figure was carved out of an orange-rock cliff face. It was unmissable. For Quintus, the Tang Dynasty creation was important because it overlooked a junction where the Dadu River joined the Min. Once he saw it, he knew he had to turn and go up Dadu River, which would take him in the direction of White Dragon Mountain.

But first, they had to get there, and he now had two more people to take care of. The added responsibilities weighed on him and even had him questioning if he should go to the mountain at all and instead attempt to fly them directly to Thailand or even Myanmar. His train of thought was broken when Kristen spoke over the intercom.

'Okay, excuse me, pilot, my name is Kristen,' she said. 'Thank you so much for helping us.'

Her voice even sounds like Kaitlyn's, Quintus thought.

'Not a problem. Despite our current circumstances, it's nice to meet you, Kirsten. I'm Quintus, and my copilot here is Tina,' he said. Tina turned around and gave her a smile and a hello wave which was returned.

'Lovely to meet you both, and this is Ivan,' Kristen said, gesturing towards War. 'Can you tell us —'

Kristen was interrupted by Tina, who pointed westwards at the early morning sky.

'Sorry, but jets!' she said. 'Over there!'

Quintus turned his head to see two military aircraft a half-mile away flying parallel with them above a mountain range. They were CAC FC-1 Xiaolongs, single-engine lightweight combat aircraft. He watched their maneuvering, and after several minutes it became apparent they were tracking them. There was no way they'd make it flying to the border. It made his decision easier. They'd go to the mountain.

The Man Who Wanted to be Elsewhere

An agitated Colonel Deng was trying to act like he was in command of the half-dozen personnel inside the airfield's control tower dealing with the theft of one of their helicopters. But more than one of them was giving him a sideways glance. They'd earlier been told Deng was in charge while their commanding officer was away on holiday, but they quickly realized he didn't know what he was doing. To them, the whole thing appeared dubious and certainly not within regulations.

Deng himself also had little faith in his role, and he began to fear for his future. That sense of dread grew as he watched, via a pair of binoculars, the figures of Marx, Vacher, and Irfan board one of two helicopters already carrying 10 soldiers between them. The plan now was that Marx would take the two helicopters to intercept the stolen Z-9 somewhere near Leshan and somehow force it to land.

The two Xiaolong jets had earlier reported the stolen Z-9 was following the Min River in a downriver direction.

But as the choppers rose and headed south, Deng only had one thing on his mind — how he was going to get out of this mess. As mentioned earlier, he had three plans to fall back on. Deng now recognized he had to take the most drastic choice, which would require a three-and-a-half-hour drive to the U.S. consulate in Chongqing, where he would attempt to defect sometime early afternoon. Deng assumed he could offer the Americans plenty of things they should be interested in, be it Marx's relationship with members of the Chinese Communist Party or the true scale of forced organ harvesting in the country's hospitals.

His greatest concern was that, despite what he'd have to offer them, the Americans would still deny him asylum and turn him over to his own government. Indeed, Deng had found Americans to be unfathomable people.

A day earlier, one of his colleagues told him that the Americans now believed the world was coming to an end and that their population was losing the plot, rioting in the streets, and giving their money away to some cult leader. How they ever managed to become a superpower was beyond him.

Center of Attention

Chuck Goyette wouldn't have expected anything less but a sold-out event at the National Press Club in Washington D.C., and on that evening, that's what he got. Eager media representatives and curious club members were seated around tables while photographers and TV crews hovered on the fringes. As he answered questions from behind a podium, they hung off his every word. A reporter towards the back raised a hand to ask a question, and Goyette nodded for him to go ahead.

'Frank Flick from KW wire service,' the reporter said,

introducing himself. 'There have been calls made for the arrests of those individuals you have named as Famine, Death, and War. How do you respond to such statements?'

Goyette chuckled for a bit before answering.

'Ha, ha, ha, yes, well, look, history has come to the point where what some people say or even do matters very little. The one I have named as Famine is doing his thing Down Under, and Death is on the job, of course, and there's very little you can do to stop her,' Goyette said. 'I can tell you; she is recently arrived in the United States and is well prepared for what she needs to do.'

Despite a murmur of unease from the audience, he continued.

'Then there's War, who's currently in the Far East. He's overseeing the nuclear Armageddon, but that's all I'll say about that. Don't ask me anymore about War or the conflict to come because I won't go there tonight,' he said.

Goyette then felt his on-mute cellphone vibrate in his trouser pocket, but he ignored it, just as he did to several other calls or text messages he had received over the past ten minutes. Instead, he focused on the next reporter's question.

'Can the end of the world, as we know it, be averted?' the reporter asked.

'Well, that truly is the million-dollar question, yet it's something I'm unable to answer,' Goyette said. 'But I can tell you that I will surely discuss such matters with the president later tonight when I see him at the White House.'

Waiting to Intercept

The helicopter that Marx and his henchmen were in had landed on the riverbank opposite the giant Buddha statue at Leshan. Nearby the other helicopter, full of Chinese soldiers, was parked and waiting as well. The engines of both aircraft were left running as they prepared to lift off the ground at a moment's notice.

Seated beside the lead chopper's pilot, Marx was again trying to call Goyette. He desperately needed to speak with the cult leader about how War had gone off-script. As he waited in vain for Goyette to pick up the call, he looked over at the scene of his last death. It was an odd twist of fate that he was now opposite where he had drowned in 1966 — when he was The Hammer — in waters just below the Buddha statue. Now tourist boats puttered about where he had once tumbled off a ferry he and other Red Guards had confiscated.

For Marx, such memories, at the very least, were mere distractions from the predicament he now found himself in, one that could cost him the very throne he had bargained for. He now feared mission failure could be upon him. He knew if he couldn't play his agreed-upon role by getting War to North Korea, then he would share the fate of every other condemned soul sent to Hell, a prospect that terrified him. If he didn't get War back, all was lost — at least from his perspective.

Having finally accepted that Goyette wasn't going to answer his calls or text messages, he pocketed his phone and began kicking the paneling in front of him out of frustration. His venting attracted the attention of Vacher and Irfan, who were behind him in the cabin with three PLA soldiers.

Since they had been in China, Marx's mental state had worried both of his henchmen. They were already familiar with their boss' volatility but now, as they waited in the chopper, they suspected he was on the verge of having a complete breakdown. Their concerns began in earnest after he went into mind-boggling fits of rage at both the hospital and then the airfield in Chengdu. The nastiest explosion occurred when Marx watched the CCTV of War and Kristen leaving the hospital area in the stolen vehicle and then joining the other fugitives in the stolen helicopter that they were now chasing.

During their pursuit flight, Vacher also couldn't help but notice Marx muttering to himself like a madman while sending text messages or trying to make unrequited calls. But as they sat there on the riverbank waiting for their quarry, Vacher actually felt sympathy for his boss. He leaned forward and tapped him on the shoulder.

'Hey, Mr. Marx, no need to worry, sir. We will squash these rats,' Vacher said but got no reply or recognition. Indeed, Vacher was confident that their target had little hope of getting out of China, and he believed they were already one step ahead of them. Given the two pursuing helicopters flew 75 miles in a straight-line overland from Chengdu, they were now ahead of Quintus, who was flying low, following the river's twists and curves.

They'd only been sitting on the riverbank for five

minutes when the military jets radioed them to say the stolen helicopter was only minutes away.

Giant Buddha

Quintus flew the helicopter some 70 feet above the brown waters of the Min River, now edged on both sides by the beginnings of Leshan city. He glanced at Tina to see how she was holding up. She saw him looking at her.

'Everything okay?' she asked.

He nodded and returned to looking ahead at a bridge and adjusted the chopper's height to comfortably get over it. After flying over the bridge, they passed the confluence of the Dadu and Min rivers to their right, while on their left was the giant Buddha cut into the cliff. Seeing the statue, Quintus banked the helicopter sharply, maneuvering it back towards Dadu River.

'Hold on, we need to make a turn,' he told his three passengers.

As they swung around, he noticed two military choppers — both Z-9s — taking off from the riverbank opposite the statue.

'You see those two helicopters?' Tina asked him.

'Yes, sure did.'

'You think they're after us too?'

'I suspect so,' he said. 'Those two jets still somewhere around Tina?'

'I can't see them; I got a feeling they've gone elsewhere,' she said, looking about. 'I think we might have only helicopters to contend with.'

She was correct. Running low on fuel, the jets had turned back to their base.

Tina hoped she didn't sound alarmed as she spoke, but she was. The lead helicopter following them was cloaked in a dark mist.

With the pursuing helicopters a quarter of a mile behind them, Quintus brought the Z-9 up to a higher altitude of around 2,000 feet. He now aimed to fly in a straight line in what he thought was the direction of White Dragon Mountain.

Behind him, Kristen was taking videos with her smartphone. It could be useful evidence to prove what was happening to them if they survived, she supposed. After a minute of that, she put away her phone and spoke into the intercom.

'Anyone able to tell me our destination?'

'A mountain,' Tina replied.

'Okay, if it helps as another option, I was Googling before, and there's a U.S. consulate in Chongqing, which is kind of near here, or is the closest one to where we are, where ever that is,' Kristen said. 'I don't mean to be rude, but why are we going to a mountain?' she asked.

Before Quintus could answer, War spoke for what was the first time during the flight.

'Because it was foretold,' he said in a deep soft tone that rose hairs on the back of necks.

By most people's standards, it was an odd thing to say. The remark left them all speechless until Tina decided to break the silence with some humor.

'Well, prophecies seem to be all the rage now,' she said, making Kristen smile.

'Let's hope it's not one from that guy Goyette,' Kristen said.

'No, it's a much older prophecy,' Ivan slowly said, again raising hairs on the back of necks.

Quintus now figured that War knew way more than he should, but it was not the time to ask any more questions, as White Dragon Mountain was coming into view through the dull haze 12 miles in front of them.

'Well folks, prophecy or not, there's the mountain straight ahead,' Quintus told his passengers.

'What are we going to find there?' Tina asked.

'To be honest, I'm not 100 percent sure,' Quintus replied. 'Let's call it a leap of faith.'

CHAPTER XIII

A Boy and The Dragon

Chinese dragons rarely reveal themselves to people, but the White Dragon made an exception for Kai, who was different. A fact recognized by the universe. In an earlier life, the boy and the dragon had been long-time friends. Kai, of course, was once Tai, and the bond with the dragon was not broken until 1966 when the Red Guards led by The Hammer desecrated the sanctuary and killed the ancient Taoist.

As the Red Guards dragged Tai out of the cave, the White Dragon was fighting the seven-headed Red Dragon in the sky above the mountain. While the fight was brutal, it went unseen by human eyes. The White Dragon lost that battle, and afterward, it sought shelter in a cave for a decade to recover from its wounds. It wasn't until the 1976 death of Chairman Mao Zedong that it emerged from the cave to resume guarding the mountain, hoping that his old friend would one day return.

But when that day arrived, the mythical creature was unsure if the boy was able to recall their connection. Nevertheless, it didn't matter, the dragon witnessed the joy on the boy's face when they first met, and it could see into his heart, seeing rare goodness within it.

After he arrived at the sanctuary, Kai stayed overnight and slept beside the dragon whose long, fury body kept him warm as the temperatures dropped. At daybreak, the boy woke and had himself some of the spring water. The dragon somehow knew that Kai had to leave the mountain to return to his grandparents.

As Kai packed his things and prepared to say farewell, he and the mystical creature heard the approaching drone of a helicopter. They both moved closer to the edge of the terrace and saw the distant black dot of a helicopter coming their way. Further back, two more dots followed.

The sight of them filled both Kai and the White Dragon with trepidation. The dragon especially could perceive other things that Kai was not able to. It roared fiercely and shook its head. After taking some steps back, it then ran forward and jumped off the ledge.

Kai watched as the dragon flew in the direction of the helicopters. Halfway across the stretch of air that separated the mountain from the coming aircraft, the dragon vanished from sight, slipping into a parallel dimension to fight an old foe.

The Landing

From inside the chopper, Quintus could see how the sanctuary had aged and how the fallen boulders half-covered what was the terrace. He then noticed someone standing on the terrace.

Tina saw him as well.

'There's a kid down there!' she said.

Tina didn't add what else she saw about the boy who, in her eyes, glowed like the morning sun. His aura was as great if not greater than what she saw in Quintus.

'Well, as long as he moves a bit, we won't squash him because that's exactly where we're landing,' Quintus said.

'There's not much room,' Tina remarked.

'It's tight but doable. When we land, you need to get out ASAP. Everyone clear about that?'

He heard three affirmatives, and then he sent the helicopter into a sharp descent. At the final moment, he worked the stick and pedals to level the Z-9, and he then swung it around, and it came in laterally towards the terrace.

As expected, Kai moved clear, and he stopped just out front of the cave opening. The boy ignored the wind from the chopper's rotors and enjoyed the spectacle of watching it land on the terrace. It was a near-perfect touchdown.

Inside the chopper, Quintus killed the engine

'Okay, time to get out,' he said.

Kristen, Tina, and War exited. The two women made their way towards Kai some 40 feet away while War strolled over and sat on the smooth rock that'd been sat on a million times before. Quintus soon followed.

The Text Messages

From the front of the helicopter, Marx could see the stolen Z-9 parked on the sanctuary's terrace. Its rotor blades were slowing to a halt. He saw people nearby and counted five of them. One appeared to be a youth. The fact that Quintus had reached the sanctuary further unnerved him, but he reminded himself he needed to focus on retrieving War. Nothing else at this stage mattered.

Marx turned to his Chinese pilot and ordered him to land on the terrace.

'There is no room to land,' the pilot replied in Mandarin.

'If those fools can do it, you can too.'

'With that helicopter already parked on it, there is simply not enough space.'

'If you can't land, just get us as close as you can so me and my team can get out onto the mountain,' Marx said sternly. The pilot still looked unconvinced. 'Unless you want to spend the rest of your life in prison, you'd better do as ordered!' Marx shouted. 'Find a way to make it happen!'

Now more fearful of the crazed foreigner than a dangerous landing, the pilot dropped the helicopter's nose towards the terrace.

Marx looked back at Vacher and Irfan with the PLA soldiers in the cabin. Both men were prepping their FN SCAR assault rifles they retrieved from the Crow before boarding the chopper.

'You two, remember we just need Ivan alive, the others I now no longer care about,' Marx said. 'Just don't screw this up. Everything is riding on it.'

His minions nodded but still had no appreciation of the seriousness of the affair. Their job, they thought, was simple, get War.

Marx felt a buzz in his pocket. It was a text message. *This better be Chuck Goyette finally replying*, he thought. By the time he'd pulled out his cellphone, two further messages had been received, but he soon discovered none of them were from Goyette. They were all from Lin, and for Marx, each one was a horror story.

- The first text read: 'My father (General Zhou) just died of cardiac arrest.'

- The second text read: 'We've lost control of the situation at the airfield/the hospital. Deng has fled, wants to defect.'

- The third text read: 'You're now on your own. Leave China while you can. Do not contact me anymore.'

As you'd expect, Marx immediately wanted to vent, but as the chopper descended towards the terrace, he managed to bury his fury. He reminded himself that he had to remain composed and motivated to complete his mission. The mess back at the airfield and the hospital had to wait.

Just Run

A bewildered Kai was glad to discover at least one of the people from the helicopter spoke some passable Mandarin. She was the only Asian among them, and she introduced herself as Tina. The young woman said she was an American who had escaped from some bad people, of which he had no doubt.

He was bemused by the bearded man who sat on the rock and pulled out a pencil and a small pad from his coat pocket and began sketching.

How odd, the boy thought, given the circumstances. More curious than afraid, he went and looked at what the man was drawing. To his surprise, he saw it was the beginning of a sketch of the White Dragon fighting the seven-headed Red Dragon in mid-air.

'You can see?' Kai asked War.

'Yes,' replied War in perfect Mandarin. 'They're fighting just beyond those approaching helicopters.'

'Who is winning?' Kai asked.

'It's too early to tell at the moment.'

'The White Dragon is sure to win,' the boy said.

They were interrupted by Quintus, whose sole concern was that the helicopters were dangerously getting closer.

'Everyone needs to get going,' Quintus said, looking at Kristen and Tina.

'There should still be a path that runs along that ridge,' he said, pointing past the cave entrance. He then looked at Kai with War.

'Who's the kid? What's he doing here?'

'He said he's here to help,' Tina replied.

'Take him with you; you all gotta get off this mountain. These guys are going to play rough,' he said.

'What're you planning to do?' Kristen asked him.

'Soon, one or both of those helicopters will try and

land. I'll hang back and hold them off, and then, with any luck, I'll catch up with you,' Quintus said.

He noted the hesitation in Kristen's eyes.

'But if I don't catch up with you, get yourself and Tina to that U.S. diplomatic mission in Chongqing that you mentioned,' Quintus said. 'But you must go now. Take them,' he said, referring to War and Kai. 'There are no other options at this stage.'

Kristen nodded and called out to War.

'Ivan come on; we have to go.'

War, still drawing, shook his head for no.

There was no time to argue his answer. The Z-9s were getting nearer. Their engines were ominously beating like war drums.

Quintus and Kristen looked at each other.

'Take Tina and the boy, I'll look after him,' Quintus said, referring to War.

Kai shouldered his rucksack and threw Quintus his walking pole, and indicated that it could be used as a fighting stick.

'Thanks, now you all best get moving,' Quintus said. The boy gave him the thumbs up. 'I'll see you all soon,' Quintus added as they finally turned to leave in the direction of the mountain path. As they left, Quintus turned back to War on his rock.

'Why don't you go?' Quintus asked him.

'I should ask you the same thing,' War replied. 'You've done what you had to do.'

'Do what exactly?'

'You fulfilled the prophecy; you came back to White

Dragon Mountain at the right time. Despite everything, you did not give up. That is all you had to do,' War said. 'Your master would be proud.'

'Who are you?'

'There's no time for chit-chat,' War replied as the closest helicopter approached to land at the sanctuary. Marx was now visible in the front of the chopper.

'This man will surely kill you. He and his sycophants hate you with all their being,' War warned.

'I've dealt with them before,' Quintus said. He then looked in the direction where Kristen, Tina, and Kai had fled towards. 'If you're an immortal — can you protect them?'

'I cannot alter their fate at this point. Neither can you. You should leave.'

'No, that's something I can't do.'

'Then finally, you will die, and a respectable death is a fine thing. But then again, you've faced greater odds and survived, so I have faith in you, Quintus.'

No more could be said between the two as the noise of the first helicopter — now less than 100 feet away — began drowning them out.

The Chinese pilot adjusted his approach so the Z-9 would also land laterally on the remaining space on the terrace. Behind them, the other pursuing chopper peeled off to fly in the same direction in which Kristen, Tina, and Kai had just run off towards.

As Marx's helicopter got nearer, one of its side doors slid open, and Quintus saw Vacher and Irfan inside it, armed to the teeth. He held their gaze for a second and then dropped the fighting stick, which rattled on hitting the stony ground. He looked at War and offered a parting nod as he swiftly retreated into the cave.

War went back to his drawing while ignoring the helicopter that landed in front of him. Despite the small space available and the proximity of the cliff wall, the pilot managed to successfully put the chopper down. The first to exit was Vacher, followed by Irfan, both with weapons ready. Moving in a crouching run, they bypassed War on his rock and went to the cave where Quintus was last seen going inside. They stopped at its entrance and awaited orders from their boss, who was exiting the Z-9. The three PLA soldiers did likewise but were somewhat confused by what was going on and why they were there.

Somehow Marx managed to maintain his composure as he walked the 18 steps from the chopper to War on the rock. Upon reaching War, he coughed to herald his presence, old-school style. War ignored the gesture and kept sketching. After the sound of the Z-9's engine finally died down, Marx spoke.

'It's been an appalling morning Ivan, but despite it all, I'm ready to overlook everything,' Marx said. 'You and I have obligations, ones that are larger than both of us. You know what they are and what it means, so let's not mess about; please get on my helicopter.'

War looked up at Marx for a second, but then he returned to his sketching.

'Don't do that, don't ignore me! I don't know where all this treachery is coming from, but I'm not having a bar of it,' Marx sneered.

War just ignored Marx and kept sketching.

To avoid having a complete meltdown, Marx left War and went over to Vacher and Irfan by the cave's entrance.

'Where is he?' Marx asked about Quintus.

'Inside the cave, somewhere,' Vacher said.

Marx shoved Vacher aside so that he could be next to the cave's entrance.

'Quintus! Have you found your grandmaster's bones in there?' Marx yelled into the cave.

There was, of course, no reply.

'Actually, no, you wouldn't; that's because we dragged his filthy flea-ridden carcass out of there and shot him dead. Then we flung his body over the ledge. Odd thing is, the young revolutionary who pulled the trigger was my recently expired comrade who needed your liver. Funny how things eventuate, isn't it?'

Again, no reply.

'Quintus, there's nowhere for you to run to!' Marx shouted. 'I don't know why you bothered to return. The magic disappeared from this place a long time ago, and now it's just a tomb, your tomb.'

Marx looked to his men.

'Do you have any grenades?'

Vacher and Irfan shook their heads for no. Marx looked behind at the three PLA soldiers and asked them the same question in Mandarin. He got a similar response.

Realizing they'd soon be ordered to enter the cave, Vacher and Irfan fitted small flashlights to the ends of their assault rifles.

'Okay then, you two, get in there,' Marx ordered.

Irfan turned on his flashlight and entered the cave. Vacher followed, then Marx. Quickly they discovered it was empty, with no sign of Quintus.

His frustration rising, Marx began shrieking a litany of swear words until he was interrupted by Vacher, who found a hole in the top left corner of the cave.

'That's the only place he could've gone, but where it leads to is anyone's guess,' Vacher said, shining his flashlight into the hole.

The Climb

The hole in the cave led into a meandering shaft that went up some 500 feet and down a further 1,000 feet. Back when Quintus was a student of the Way, he had climbed up and down the shaft multiple times, perhaps to prepare him for this very moment.

On this occasion, Quintus was venturing upwards, and due to his levitation abilities, he was making decent progress. He held the stolen flashlight in his mouth so that he could illuminate the way ahead.

By the time he heard Marx and his team entering the cave, he was only 20 feet away from the exit he was looking for. Then he heard an eruption of distant gunfire. It sounded as if it was perhaps a quarter of a mile outside. He tried not to think the worst, but he did. Kristen? Tina? The boy?

The unseen men back in the cave also heard the shooting, and it sent them into fits of laughter.

'You hear that, Quintus, old man?' Marx bellowed.

'That's the magnificent, glorious sound of those you love being shot to shreds!'

Pinned Down

The airborne Z-9 had located Kristen, Tina, and Kai on the trail along the side of the mountain — they were hiding behind some boulders, huddling together. As the Z-9 got closer, their cover lessened, and once it was at a certain height, they were exposed, becoming easy targets. At this point, the chopper hovered only 80 feet away, and the PLA soldiers inside it began to fire their weapons from open doors.

It should have been a turkey shoot, but it wasn't.

Kristen, Tina, and Kai may have kept low, but that didn't save them. The barrage of bullets was intense. They should have been torn apart, but not one round got close. Kai looked up and saw the reason why they were still alive. Invisible to everyone else but him, the White Dragon was lying above the boulders, protecting them with his bullet-proof body. As rounds bounced off him, the White Dragon looked at the boy and smiled. As for the Red Dragon, it was nowhere to be seen, and Kai knew in his gut that they'd be safe from evil from here on in.

A Quivering Heap

The sound of gunfire propelled Quintus to ascend the shaft even faster. He disregarded the pain as bare knuckles hit stone and skin was lost. Upon reaching the fissure he was looking for, he squeezed through it and found himself on a tiny ledge overlooking the two helicopters parked on the terrace. After spitting out the flashlight, he saw three soldiers below him and the pilot getting out of the chopper. He also saw War still on his rock, drawing away as if nothing was amiss, but he couldn't see Marx or his thugs, so he assumed they remained in the cave.

Once he had the basics figured out, he didn't wait any further. Prompt action, he decided, was the only hope of saving Kristen, Tina, and Kai, and so he stepped off the ledge. He dropped 60 feet to the terrace at speed, but at the final moment, his fall slowed, and he landed softly between Kai's fighting stick and the somewhat surprised pilot.

Quintus quickly picked up the fighting stick and used it. After some well-targeted prods, the pilot dropped into a quivering heap.

In response, the three soldiers lifted their weapons, but Quintus moved behind a helicopter and out of their aim. Two of the soldiers began yelling at each other to go around the chopper while the third began talking into his two-way radio.

From his rock, War looked up from his drawing to watch Quintus make his way around the bad guy's Z-9 to flank one of the soldiers, who he, in short order, jabbed into a temporary standstill.

The other two soldiers, including the one with the radio, were next. Neither of them had a chance. They were promptly paralyzed as well.

As Quintus dealt with the last of them, he noted the distant sound of gunfire had ceased, but there was little time for him to reflect on it as Irfan and Vacher burst from the cave with weapons aimed. Both were eager to shoot Quintus down, but that required a greenlight from Marx walking behind them.

'Sir, can we take him out?' Vacher asked, nearly begging.

Before Marx answered, War dropped his sketch pad to the ground and stood from his rock. He took five steps to his left, putting himself in between both parties. He gestured to Marx and his minions to stop.

'There's no need to shoot anyone; I'll go with you on the condition that you leave the Roman alone,' War said in his slow manner.

As much as Marx desperately wanted Quintus dead, he had to restrain himself for the sake of War's offer. Getting War to North Korea was still his priority. Everything else was secondary. Even ancient revenge wasn't a consideration at this stage.

'Don't shoot,' he begrudgingly told his men.

'Feel free to change your mind at any time, sir,' said Vacher, who kept his rifle aimed, ready to fire.

As he stared down both barrels, Quintus felt calm, clear, and focused, ready for what might happen next.

'Well, this is an unexpected twist,' Marx said, looking at War. 'You think you're going to take charge now, do you?' he added.

'No, but my terms are simple yet non-negotiable. I will go with you now, but leave him here unharmed,' War said, pointing at Quintus.

'And call off the other helicopter from hunting down the others,' Quintus added.

Marx snorted in disgust, his madness bubbling to the surface.

'That's pointless. They're already dead. Couldn't you hear the shooting?' said Marx, looking hard at Quintus. 'You were too late back in Boise, Idaho, and you're too late again today.'

Quintus didn't offer a reaction. There's no point arguing with a madman, and besides, he had not given up hope.

Marx returned his gaze to War.

'Why are doing this? You were sent to help me! The demon kings won't show you any leniency,' Marx told War.

'Your masters are nothing. Even cockroaches have more potential,' War replied. 'Order your men to lower their weapons. This is your last chance.'

Marx laughed bitterly.

'Really?! When the demon kings learn of your attitude, let alone your treachery, you'll be as damned as this fool,' he said, pointing at Quintus.

Nearby, Vacher and Irfan shared looks of disquiet over their boss' seemingly unhinged ramblings, which continued until the sound of the other Z-9 grew louder, its engine's clamor reverberating through the valley.

'Hear that, Quintus? Here they come, they can tell you how many pieces your loved ones are now in,' Marx gloated.

They all turned to see the Z-9 flying alongside the mountain coming their way. Once the chopper reached the sanctuary, it stopped and hovered some 200 feet away. Its soldiers could be seen at open cabin doors. Irfan waved at them until he realized they were pointing rifles their way.

BLAM! BLAM! BLAM!

Given that Irfan and Vacher were armed, they were designated first targets. A bullet hit Irfan. He was dead before hitting the ground. Vacher was shot twice in the torso. He fell, wincing in pain.

Luckily for Quintus, he wasn't in any line of fire, but War was in the open, yet he appeared immune to both the bullets and the chaos. He just stood there calmly looking at the chopper, staring at the shooters. Daring them to try and destroy him.

As bullets whizzed around, Marx dived for cover behind a large slab of rock. It was there behind stone that he finally grasped how his plans had completely come to naught. Everything was lost.

Marx correctly guessed someone up the PLA chain of command wanted to clean up what transpired back at both the hospital and the airfield, and getting rid of any foreigners involved was part of that.

There was no coming back from this now. Only a deluded optimist would think he could still get War to North Korea and kickstart a nuclear Armageddon. He had failed the demon kings, and this filled him with a rising sense of terror. Instead of his being seated on a throne alongside them, his future was one of suffering beyond description. He would be plunged to Hell's lowest level — the ninth ring of the thirteenth circle — a punishment reserved for the worst of the worst. As he hid behind the rock, this realization soaked into every bone, every sinew, and each cell. It wasn't long before he was moaning like a wounded, cornered animal.

Meanwhile, Vacher was making the most of his final

moments on earth. Despite his wounds, he managed to get to his feet. The Frenchman certainly had serious character flaws but giving up wasn't one of them. In the last 15 seconds of his life, he picked up his FN SCAR and blindly fired it at the helicopter. He managed to empty his 20-round magazine, and at least one bullet smashed the tail rotor.

If a helicopter has an Achilles' heel, the tail rotor is it, and the Z-9 went into a spin. From where he stood, Quintus could see the soldiers holding on as they swung back and forth inside the helicopter. With a busted tail rotor, there was very little the pilot could do to stop the aircraft's downward spiral. It dropped out of Quintus' sight, and nor did he care to watch it smashing on the ground in the valley below.

While this occurred, War retrieved his sketch pad from the ground and reseated himself on the rock, where he resumed drawing.

Both he and Quintus did their utmost to take no notice of Marx's uncontrollable sobbing behind them.

Quintus went to check the bodies of Vacher and Irfan. It was quickly evident that both henchmen were dead. Near the cliff's edge, he ignored any urge to look down at the wreckage of the helicopter. Instead, he looked in the direction where Kristen, Tina, and Kai had earlier fled to.

Running Back

After they stopped being shot at, Kristen was the first out from behind the boulders. Instead of fleeing further down the mountain, she headed in the same way that the PLA helicopter had flown off towards. She wasn't sure where her unthinking boldness came from, but it pushed her forward. It wasn't long before Kai and Tina were both following her.

Kristen looked back and offered Kai and Tina a brave smile.

'You both okay?' she asked.

Tina and Kai nodded.

'Let's go see if we can help Quintus,' Kristen said.

Kai guessed what was asked and offered her a big thumbs up. Ahead of them, he saw the White Dragon flying in the same direction, keeping them safe from unseen threats.

Then gunfire was heard.

'Oh no,' Kristen said.

The sound of violence did not slow them down, and they kept running in the same direction. The shooting was followed by the sound of a helicopter crash heard just before they reached a mountain bend that provided a view of where they wanted to be. After stopping at the bend, they caught their breath and saw the crashed helicopter smoldering at the base of the mountain.

It was Tina who first saw Quintus standing at the sanctuary ledge, glowing like a mini sun. Through the mass of light, she was also able to see War sitting on the rock.

'They're okay!' she exclaimed.

Then she saw something dark emerge from behind them, a running figure surrounded by dense swirling murky mist.

Moans of a Madman

Screeching and hollering like a lunatic, Marx rushed from the rock slab he was hiding behind and ran to one of the paralyzed Chinese soldiers. Quintus and War both turned to see him grab the soldier's dropped assault rifle from the ground.

Marx quickly switched off the weapon's safety and swung it around at his intended targets, only to find Quintus with Kai's fighting stick upfront in his face. A split second later, Quintus knocked the gun out of his hands.

'No!' Marx screamed. Next, Quintus whacked him twice in the guts and once on the head; blows that flattened Marx but didn't paralyze him. On the ground, Marx was winded, withering, and gasping like a fish out of water.

With one hand Quintus picked up the assault rifle and threw it over the cliff ledge. He returned his attention to Marx, who managed to sit himself up while still struggling to catch his breath.

'I'd say that's game over,' Quintus told him.

Despite struggling to catch his breath, Marx started screaming at War, seated 30 feet away on the rock, still drawing.

'Why?' Marx yelled. 'War, just tell me why, you Judas!'

War ignored Marx. Kept sketching, further incensing the fund manager.

'You petulant son of a bitch, you signed up for this!' Marx screamed.

War put aside his pencil and closed his sketchbook and then looked at Marx, who got to his feet. They held each other's gaze for several seconds until War threw his sketch-book toward Marx. It landed a few feet in front of him and skidded the rest of the way stopping by his right foot. Marx picked it up.

'You want answers? Open the book,' War said.

Marx did so, but he was somewhat hesitant, if not nervous. He quickly flicked through about three-quarters of the sketchbook that was full of images, mostly associated with this tale. Quintus as a Roman Centurion. Master Tai with White Mountain Dragon. The gibbet in Ireland. Quintus with his family in Boise, Idaho. The incident in the Reno diner. Quintus escaping the hospital with Tina. A woman who looked like Kristen hugging a man and so on and so forth. It all infuriated Marx. He closed the book, having not looked at it all but seen enough.

'Answers? There are no answers here. What are you? Some Quintus fanboy!?' Marx yelled.

War just smiled.

'The answer is on the last page if you dare,' War said.

'Just tell me instead,' Marx insisted.

'Maybe remind me again what the question was,' War said.

'No, don't do this to me! I'm returning empty-handed. Do you know what that means?' Marx screamed.

'Yes, I do. If you want to truly grasp your future, see the last page,' War said with some mercifulness.

Marx noted War's tone. The fund manager didn't want to contemplate what was to come for him. He didn't reopen the book. Instead, he threw it back at War and shifted his attention to Quintus, who was looking at him.

'And you, what are you staring at? You ruined every-thing!' Marx yelled.

Quintus felt near nothing as Marx screamed at him. No rage. No hatred. Nothing like he experienced in Reno, 1871.

If he felt anything, it was a fleeting pity that promptly disappeared when Marx sprung at him with a scream. It caught Quintus somewhat off guard, and Marx managed to grab him for several seconds until Quintus spun his way out of trouble, and they uncoupled. Still, with the stick in hand, Quintus used it to jab down hard on one of Marx's feet which knocked the fight out of him. Marx howled in pain.

Quintus followed through and jabbed Marx with the stick under an armpit, followed by another well-aimed poke just above his left hip.

Marx was now left frozen on the spot. All he could do was breathe, drool, and sweat. Locked in, he impotently cursed and internally raged to nobody but himself.

'You talk too much,' Quintus said quietly to Marx's incapacitated figure as he walked away.

Quintus then saw Kristen, Tina, and Kai at the distant bend, and he was nearly overwhelmed that they were alive, and apparently, from what he could make out, unhurt.

War picked up his sketchbook from the ground where Marx had thrown it and resat on the rock. He observed how relieved Quintus appeared while waving to the trio, who soon enough resumed running towards the sanctuary. War thought it may take them five or so minutes to reach where they were.

For a moment, he thought about telling Quintus some

heavenly secrets; that Tina was once his daughter Abby and that Kristen was not only his past wife Kaitlyn but also, further back, the young Irish woman called Alba. However, he decided against it. Humans, even someone like the man in front of him, are best left ignorant about such matters.

But some things, War knew, needed to be said.

'I'm delighted how this has finished for you,' he told Quintus, who looked over at him. 'I have to admit I'm surprised you're still alive. Your master indeed trained you well.'

'He taught me here for centuries,' Quintus said.

'He did,' War said.

'How do you know?'

'Not important.'

War opened his sketchbook and ripped out a page from it.

'This was the last page,' he said.

'What was drawn on it?' Quintus asked.

'His not-so-distant future,' War said, gesturing at Marx's immobile figure. 'Too horrifying, too dark to contemplate. Be glad you are not him.'

War scrunched up the page and threw it aside. He then placed the sketchbook on a nearby rock.

'Give the book to the boy, he will cherish this day, and the images will remind him of what happened here,' War said. 'One day, when China is free, you two will reunite. You will need to teach him what he once taught you.'

Quintus nodded as if what War said made sense which in an otherworldly kind of way it did.

War sighed deeply and looked at his hands as if they were foreign to him.

'It's the first time I've been among humans. It's been interesting having a human form. Your mode of thinking is difficult to master. It's erratic yet constrained. Man was indeed made to suffer.'

He then looked at Quintus.

'You know this more than most Quintus, but one must center oneself to stay on track. Stay with your practice, stay true to the Way. Maintain your courage and resolve,' War said. 'All this drama is now over, it's been reset, but human-kind still needs to get its act together. You're free of your responsibility Quintus but see if you can help them change for the better. Help them to return to a path of tradition.'

War paused for effect and closed his eyes.

'Time is short.'

Quintus wanted to ask War a ton of questions, but he understood there wasn't time to do so. He could only watch as the being on the rock sat up straight and breathed in deeply.

War put his hands on his knees and smiled. A gust of wind engulfed the sanctuary area, and he then just vanished into thin air.

Left alone, it finally hit Quintus that the moment he'd been trained for had come and gone, and it did so in a very fast and tidy manner. Humanity was, as far as he was concerned, apparently no longer in peril. Any words would understate how he felt at that moment. The point of all his wandering and waiting over the centuries had occurred, lifting a huge weight from his shoulders. The future no longer owned him nor mankind.

Ignoring Marx's nearby paralyzed figure, he went and sat on the well-worn rock that War had been on and waited for the others to arrive.

This sense of relief stayed with him as he flew the stolen helicopter with Tina and Kristen from China southwards to Thailand.

That's a Wrap

Despite being asked nearly three hours' worth of Apocalypse-type questions Chuck Goyette wasn't tired. In fact, he thrived on all the media attention thrown at him. Under the glare of the National Press Club's stage lights, he hadn't even raised a sweat.

It was around 8 pm that Valeri Chambers, the club's president, gestured to Goyette to wind up his talk. It irked him a bit, he could have gabbed on from behind the podium for an additional hour.

She came up beside him from left stage.

'Thank you, Mr. Goyette, you have given us much to reflect on,' Chambers said.

She then addressed the audience.

'Unfortunately, that's all the time we have tonight. Our guest has to visit the White House, where he will have a one-on-one discussion with the president,' she said. 'So, on behalf of everyone here at the club, I'd like to thank you, Mr. Goyette, for taking the time to share with us your thoughts and insights, no matter how unsettling they may be.'

As the clapping began, Goyette began to blush in embarrassment. It wasn't because of the applause. It was due to his picking up on what had occurred on the other side of the globe. War had just vanished, and now everything had changed.

Still, behind the podium, he sheepishly raised his hand and interrupted the ovation. After the clapping died down, he spoke.

'I beg your pardon, madam president, there's one more thing,' Goyette said. 'Actually, it's somewhat a big thing which may get a mixed reception as it negates much of what I've just said tonight. You see, the end of the world is a complicated and volatile thing.'

Goyette paused for 10 seconds to ensure he had everyone's full attention, and once he felt that was the case, he continued.

'You see, it's like this, in the past couple of centuries or so, there have been earlier attempts by several other Four Horsemen types to bring about humankind's demise. Why there always had to be four of them, I don't know, but I do know on each occasion, at least one of them found a reason for not completing their mission,' he said.

'One of whom?' someone yelled.

'One of the earlier Four Horsemen kind of characters,' Goyette repeated.

'Why would they do that?' yelled another.

'Usually, it's a case of one of them finding compelling evidence that you lot deserve another chance,' Goyette said.

'But are you the false messiah?' a reporter yelled.

'No, I'm more of a trickster really, but that's certainly not important as what I'm trying to say is that doomsday, once again, has been called off,' Goyette said, now somewhat deflated.

There was a collective gasp from everyone in the club.

'Never before has it come as close, so consider yourselves lucky,' Goyette said. 'Now, as per my end-of-the-world guarantee, the paying members of my temple will, of course, have their money returned. This will be overseen by my team, who I cannot praise highly enough,' he said, looking at his stunned staff seated around a table to the side of the platform.

The press began yelling more questions that Goyette ignored.

'As for me, I will humbly leave you to your own devices. Lastly, I can only advise mankind to avoid complacency because one day your time will certainly come, be it in the form of A.I. or pollution, something will kill you off, so do not forsake decency.'

He stepped away from the podium and gave the dumbfounded club president one last look.

'It's been a blast, my dear,' he told her.

And with that, he too simply vanished and did so in full view of everyone in the club and anyone watching the globally broadcasted event.

For the other two, called Death and Famine, everything now was similarly different. They may not have been at the press club or watching TV, but they, like Goyette, sensed what had transpired in China.

Death, not that long off her flight from Rome, was in New York City's Times Square preparing to begin her mantra when she instead disappeared as per War and Goyette.

The incantation-mumbling Famine did likewise in outback Australia. Just as he crossed a small bridge over a dry gully, he disappeared, and as he did so, he gave a world-weary sigh of relief.

The Tree Line

With his fighting pole back in his possession, Kai moved nimbly along a limestone ridge. As he ran, he could hear the sloshing of spring water in his canteen and feel War's sketchbook jostling around in his backpack. He was now a couple of miles away from where he said goodbye to the three friendly foreigners who had flown off in a helicopter destined for Thailand.

Upon approaching a line of pine trees, the boy slowed his pace and eventually came to a stop. He knew that once he was among the trees, he'd be in cover and out of sight for anyone above.

Before he disappeared into it, he looked back up at the mountain. He could just make out the sanctuary and the figure of the bad man who was stuck to the spot. The boy's attention was then taken by movement further along and at the top of the mountain's peak — it was the White Dragon. He doubted his mystical friend could hear from so far away but nevertheless, he shouted his farewells because it felt like the correct thing to do. He knew they'd meet again. Once things settled down, he would return.

Then something down in the valley caught his attention.

It was the Red Dragon. It was grounded, injured, and crawling in a pitiful manner. Its bat-like wings were ripped, and at least two of its seven heads appeared lifeless. Those heads still alive screamed in rage at the Heavens. The monster began to flap its damaged wings, and after a minute, it managed to lurch itself into the air. As it cumbersomely fled the valley, it cried furiously at anything good. The awful sounds reverberated through the valley, forcing Kai to cover his ears.

Once the dragon was out of sight, Kai pulled his hands from his ears. He could no longer hear the beast's screams, but instead, he heard the buzz of helicopters. It wasn't long until he saw five more Z-9s flying at speed toward White Dragon Mountain. Each was filled with PLA soldiers wanting the chance to kill meddling foreigners. Kai took this as his cue to disappear into the trees and continue his journey back to his grandparents.

Protruding Ears

Marx still couldn't move as this new group of Z-9s arrived. The Quintus-inflicted paralysis still had him fixed to the spot. Given the lack of space on the sanctuary's terrace, only one of the five choppers could land, and from it, six soldiers alighted. It wasn't long before a couple of them were guarding him while others searched the area. He wanted to tear them apart, especially the one dousing the lifeless bodies of Vacher and Irfan with fuel.

But of course, Marx couldn't, so impotent was his situation.

Once the soldier finished drenching the bodies with fuel a commanding officer approached and handed the soldier a box of matches. Marx's attention quickly went from the soldier lighting up the cadavers to the fresh-faced officer, a young man with protruding ears. As the officer approached him, Marx realized who he was many lifetimes ago — the young soldier Meng killed in the one-sided swordfight.

Marx broke out into a sweat and pissed his pants, two indications the paralysis was lessening, not that it mattered at this point. When the officer reached Marx, he promptly unholstered his pistol and put it to the foreigner's forehead, and didn't hesitate to pull the trigger.

BANG!

Hell's Pit

Marx's ghost was dragged down to the netherworld where the 13 Demon Kings of the Pit waited. When his senses returned, he found himself lying naked in the center of a pentacle carved into the stone floor of a steaming-hot dark chamber. It was quiet until 13 voices screamed in unison from somewhere in front of him.

'We provided you with everything Marx, yet you failed us. All you had to do was join the dots. A 4-year-old could have carried it out!'

Marx was about to yell excuses, but it wasn't going to

happen. A metal muzzle instantly clamped onto his mouth, gagging him.

'We're not listening to your pathetic pleas or explanations,' said the voices which Marx now saw belonged to a line of shadowy demons seated on rocky thrones hewn from the chamber's wall.

'You currently feel no pain only because we want you listening with undivided attention,' the demons said. 'Do we have your attention?'

Marx could only nod, and the demons proceeded.

'Soon you will suffer and do so in the full knowledge that your rival, the Roman, is no longer among those to be cast here!' they yelled.

'When he killed you in 1871, our venture seemed assured, but you spoiled it to the extent that your mistakes brought a God into our affairs to perform divine intervention.'

Indeed, not long before Marx was killed, a divine being visited the netherworld and informed the demons that Quintus was no longer theirs. Due to his good works, his name had been fading in the netherworld's ether for some time, so it did not take much effort. You could even say it was a mere formality. The final decision by the Heavens to clear his name came after he freed the prisoners — the Falun Gong practitioners and others — from the military hospital.

So, it was now Marx's fault, the demons claimed, that Quintus succeeded.

'You helped him fulfill a half-baked, half-forgotten prophecy, you placed him in a position to again prove his bravery and kindness!' they screamed. 'Ultimately, it was you who aided and abetted him.'

A muted Marx could only shake his head in protest.

'You should have crushed the Roman when you first had the chance! If you had, you would be sitting up here with us judging him where you now are,' they said. 'Instead, you returned him to China. What were you thinking?'

Marx, of course, could not reply.

'You made us fools in front of our master, and the Red Dragon has been mortally wounded. For such misdeeds, you must pay.'

The demons had now finished what they wanted to say, and the only thing Marx could do was dread what would come next. First, the metal gag disappeared from his mouth, and then he was sucked through the floor into Hell's lowest level for an eternity of inexpressible woe.

CHAPTER XIV

House by the Lake

Kristen had heard enough Idaho talk-back for one day, so she switched off the old radio on the kitchen bench. Be it local or nationwide, most American media were still pre-occupied with how the world nearly came to an end two months earlier.

From a trouser pocket, she pulled out her iPhone and placed it next to the radio, away from the area she was going to make bread. It wasn't long before she was listening to her Dean Martin collection from it and kneading dough at the same time. The combination of bread making, Dean Martin, and the view from the kitchen out onto the expanse of Lake Pend Oreille made it easier for her not to think about what occurred in Asia.

Not that the experience scarred her.

She felt fortunate to survive what they went through, a feeling somewhat soured by the over-the-top interest in their adventure, first by U.S. consular officials in Thailand and then by the FBI and CIA when they got stateside. Quintus, Tina, and Kristen had nothing to hide. They told the truth, and Kristen had video from her phone to show the officials some of what occurred in China.

There were still others who wanted to know what they went through. A team of Canadian researchers wanted to speak with Quintus about organ harvesting in the Chinese military hospital while an FBI agent in charge of dismantling Marx's financial empire sought to interview Kristen. She was due to speak via phone with that agent in the days to come.

For the past three weeks, she had been staying at the lakeside holiday house, recharging her batteries, figuring out what she would next do with her life, but that was pretty much looking like it would be a shared decision. As she kneaded the bread and looked out the window, she could see Quintus repairing the property's small jetty that jutted out into the lake.

For reduced rent, the elderly landlord agreed to let Quintus fix the jetty and do some small renovations to the house. 'You two young'uns can stay as long as you like,' the landlord said after seeing the quality of Quintus' work.

Their time together at the lake had so far further cemented what began not long after they arrived in Thailand from China via helicopter. Kristen had never felt so comfortable in anyone else's presence as she had with Quintus.

Yet she had never met anybody like him, in this life at least. This man and his ways amazed her. He was rugged yet kindhearted. He was incredibly capable yet humble to the extreme. He was unconventional yet traditional, especially when it came to romance. They both had separate bedrooms in the holiday home. 'If we got married, that would change,' he told her.

'Well, hurry up and ask,' she replied good-naturedly. 'I'm not getting any younger.'

The Dilemma

Wearing only shorts, Quintus waded into the cool water and made his way to the side of the jetty walkway to fasten replacement planks of wood. Using a hammer, he began thumping in the nails. Whilst he worked, his thoughts returned to what he'd been mulling over the past few weeks, about if he should tell Kristen who he was and about their shared past life.

As he did back in the 1960s, he played out scenarios in his mind on how he could at least tell Kristen without freaking her out.

He again told himself it was impossible. The truth was too fantastical for her to consider.

Several days later, however, Quintus couldn't hold it back. He began to carefully tell her everything, something that would take decades to complete.

Closure

I hope my telling has done justice to this story and the people in it. There is only so much I can share, and I'm, of course, limited because of who I am. Nevertheless, even explaining what occurred in such a rudimentary manner wouldn't have been possible if I, your narrator, the one referred to as Ivan but mostly as War, hadn't walked among you as I did, albeit only for a month or two.

The demon kings chose me initially because of my role in creating armies, and they saw something in me that gave them the impression I was willing or at least worth taking a chance on. After centuries of me helping you tear each other apart, it was only natural that I became despondent about you all and my role in that. It was this whiff of hopelessness that drew the demon kings to me, thinking they could use it to have me become part of their nefarious plot.

Such creatures as the demon kings are unable to leave the netherworld, and they required others to fulfill their plans; hence why they needed me, the three others, low-level spirits, and the likes of Marx to do their dirty work.

It was their master Satan who allowed them to have their shot at destroying humanity, despite him having separate plans himself for the very same endeavor. The Great Deceiver initially didn't think the 13 could actually pull it off, but when Rome was demolished, he thought they might actually have a chance.

But you see, some all-knowing divine beings were one step ahead of the demon kings, and they approached me earlier, telling me of the demon kings' scheme. It was probably more out of respect for such divine beings than my love of humanity that I then agreed to their request to subvert the demons' goals.

Actually, it was touch and go there for a while. That's how the universe is, and the continuation of humanity often dangles on the edge of a knife. Because of the principle of free will, there was always the risk that I could have instead gone along with what the demons had envisaged.

Thankfully for you, through the likes of Quintus, Kristen, Tina, Kai, and others, I realized that there is hope for you. Indeed, after my time in your realm, I remain buoyed by such faith that there are those of you worth saving, worth the effort, worth risking everything for. You're more special than you could ever fathom.

Acknowledgments

Many thanks to Teresa Sutakanat, Kate Burke, and Craig Skehan for offering editorial advice and spotting typos. A big shout out also to Cameron Burke for his suggestions and support in the creation of Book of Bravery. Many thanks to Don Mark Noceda for his illustrations.

About the Author

Australian-born James Burke is a family man who has worked in the media for much of his professional life. He has a university degree in modern history. This is his first book.